STANDING ROOM ONLY

STANDING ROOM ONLY

ONLY

Eva Rice

FLAME
Hodder & Stoughton

Copyright © 2000 by Eva Rice

First published in Great Britain in 2000 by Hodder and Stoughton
A division of Hodder Headline

The right of Eva Rice to be identified as the Author of the Work has been
asserted by her in accordance with the Copyright, Designs and Patents Act 1988.

10 9 8 7 6 5 4 3 2 1

A CIP catalogue record for this title is available from the British Library.

ISBN 0 340 76684 0

Typeset by Palimpsest Book Production Limited,
Polmont, Stirlingshire
Printed and bound in Great Britain by
Mackays of Chatham plc, Chatham, Kent

Hodder and Stoughton
A division of Hodder Headline
338 Euston Road
London NW1 3BH

For Quentin, Dodger, Tom, Martin and Strooz,
without whom . . .

ACKNOWLEDGEMENTS

Bouquets to . . . Mum, Dad, Donald, Luigi Bonomi, Alex Armitage, Kate Weinberg, Alex Rice, Rachel Connolly, Alice Norman, the Camden Falcon and all those record companies.

Special thanks to . . . Kirsty Fowkes, my editor, and all at Hodder & Stoughton.

Lyrics from 'The Humbling of a Good Man', 'Watercolour Serenade' and 'Boxer' reproduced by kind permission of User.

Lyrics from 'Supposed to be a Gas' reproduced by kind permission of the Regular Fries (copyright control).

Lyrics from 'High Flying Adored' reproduced by kind permission of Evita Music Ltd.

The Flesh Failures (Let The Sunshine In)
Words and music by Gerome Ragni, James Rado and Galt McDermot
© 1968 United Artists Music Inc/EMI United Partnership Ltd, USA
Worldwide print rights controlled by Warner Bros Inc, USA/IMP Ltd.
Reproduced by kind permission of International Music Publications Ltd.

'I'm up to my knees in unfulfilled dreams
Self-obsession's a lonely profession'

                    User – 'The Humbling of a Good Man'

Chapter One

'*Manchester, England, England, across the Atlantic Sea, and I am a genius, genius . . .*'

Emma has this thing for musicals. She's always singing bits from *Hair*, and that afternoon I remember her repeating one line over and over again. It's crazy what you remember when you put your mind to it. Everything is out of focus until the day I met Felix. Then, slowly, it becomes clear, like a Polaroid taking form, colour and shape. It's as if the finger of destiny slipped from *pause* in a moment of carelessness and pressed *play*.

If I close my eyes I can feel the morning. I was dreaming I was standing in some place I thought I knew, and this loud fire alarm was going off. I tried to move, but couldn't. The sound became strangely familiar, edging persistently into my consciousness and dragging me away from sleep. My arm shot out and picked up the phone by my bed.

'Hello, hello?' I croaked, jolted awake emergency-operator style.

'Lydia? It's Ben.'

'What time is it?'

'Eight-thirty. Listen, I'm sorry to ring so early but I need to know if you're definitely coming to the party.'

'What? Is it now?' I propped myself up in bed.

'No, no, no, no!' Ben laughed the laugh of one who had already woken up and had several sensible conversations that morning. 'Course not. It's tonight. I just wanted to catch you early to remind you to get up here. Most people are arriving at about eight. I told Emma to get the train from Euston at quarter to five – it arrives seven-thirty, so you'll have time to grab a taxi down to Wilmslow Road.'

The chat was far too official.

'Ben, *Ben*! I've only just woken up, let me sort everything out. Don't worry, Emma'll be there—'

'Don't be silly!' he exclaimed too loudly. 'I want to see you too!'

'And as your friend I can promise you that my sister will be there. Get on with organising your night. We'll see you later.'

Capital Radio floated chirpily up the stairs accompanied by the smell of frying bacon. '*Another scorching hot day in London, that was Don Henley with "Boys of Summer",*' said Chris Tarrant. There didn't seem to be enough summer songs, I thought. Either that or they always played the same ones.

As soon as I replaced the receiver Emma called up to me.

'Who was that?'

'Ben – checking about the party,' I shouted.

'What did he want to know?'

'Just comfirming that he's going to have the pleasure of your company!'

'Why?'

'He must still really like you!'

'Oooh! What shall I do?'

'Look, will you come up here to have this conversation?' I barked. 'I'm making myself dizzy with all this shouting. Actually, I'm awake now, I'll come down.'

The day that I met Felix was unusually hot. The August sun had drugged London. Nobody wanted to work during the week, and nobody wanted to move during the weekends. I didn't want to get on the train to Manchester. I only agreed to go to the party to keep Emma company. And even that was with extreme bad grace. I pulled on a T-shirt and a pair of pink shorts and wandered downstairs to the kitchen. Emma was stuffing her face with a large bacon sandwich while dialling the Talking Clock.

'You know I really don't want to go to Manchester,' I said. 'If I hadn't promised Ben we'd be there, I certainly wouldn't be going.' I flicked on the TV. Emma slammed down the phone.

'I don't want to hear this,' she said. 'You're always moaning about how boring everyone's become since you left college. What could be better than throwing yourself back into student life for a night?'

I shuddered. 'I'll feel like I'm reversing down a road that I hoped I'd never see again,' I said, opening the fridge. 'It's so *hot*! What happened to good old crap British summers?'

3

Eva Rice

'Greenhouse effect, or whatever,' dismissed Emma airily.
'Honestly, there's no pleasing some people.'

'What are we supposed to wear tonight?' I asked.

'Well I'm going in my glittering Versace frock,' she said
sarcastically. 'Just wear anything!'

'I'd rather wear nothing in this weather.'

'Look, I don't care what you wear or don't wear, but
you're coming and that's final. Now, what am I going to do
about Ben?'

On cue, Mimi walked in and added her contribution to the
debate. Mimi is our mum. Emma and I have always called her
by her first name.

'Ben's a lovely boy,' she said. 'Good-looking, too.' She began
to unload the dishwasher.

'Oh *please!*' cried Emma. 'He blow-dries his hair and wears
Gucci loafers!'

'I don't see why that should count against his character,' said
Mimi in surprise. 'In fact, it shows that he knows how to look
after himself.'

Emma giggled.

'I still don't want to go, loafers or no loafers,' I said.

Emma shook her head. 'You know what your problem is? You
don't get out enough. You're twenty-three not forty-two.'

'Listen, Ben Lawson's party in Manchester is not going to
change my personal course of history.'

'It won't if you don't let it,' observed Emma darkly.

I was living at home the summer I met Felix, which was proving
to be increasingly difficult after three years of existing on no
money and a diet of music, spaghetti bolognese and late nights.

4

All through my life I seemed to have drifted from one thing to the next with a vague, flighty humour that had become my trademark. I attended the school at which my dad taught, then went on to study archaeology at university because I had never been able to let go of a childhood fixation on dinosaurs. The year that I left college I had moved back to London and in with my parents and sister in Shepherd's Bush.

On my return I applied for a job in a museum that specialised in showing children how the earth had existed before man. I got the job, much to the amusement of Mimi and Dad, who found it deeply ironic that I should be spending my days surrounded by seven-year-olds when I still seemed like such a child myself. After nearly two years in the job, I still didn't feel reliable.

Mimi, or Miranda Taylor as she was in the sixties, used to be the backing singer for a pop star called Papa Jones. His biggest hit was the corniest love song known to man called 'If Only Love Was Easy'. My dad, an English teacher, fell in love with her in Spain where Papa Jones was touring at the end of the decade.

When they got married and moved to England, Mimi's grand plans for a solo career vanished.

The day that I met Felix, Emma and I took the tube to Euston. Emma was excited, because she's the kind of girl who gets excited about parties, and because she was looking forward to talking to her friends about Ben.

'It's OK for you,' I said to her as we waited for the platform number to be announced. 'You're always in a good mood and always look pretty and everyone loves you.'

'And you're always in a bad mood, always look like shit and

5

everyone hates you,' said Emma, sitting down on her squashy overnight bag.

'I didn't mean it like that,' I protested.

'Look, you're not going home now so you may as well make up your mind to have a good time.'

'OK, *OK*! But these student parties are always the same. I shouldn't be going to them at my age.'

'Come on, Grandma,' said Emma briskly. 'The platform's up.'

So we boarded the train. Emma flicked through *Marie Claire* and I stared moodily out of the window like you're supposed to do on trains. Every time we entered a tunnel I caught a glimpse of my reflection. I've got the kind of looks that people bill as 'unusual' because I don't really fit into any category. I'm no English rose – my features are not refined enough – and although I'm tall, I lack the curves and self-confidence to be described as sexy. With long, mousy hair tied back in a messy pony tail, pale blue eyes and the sudden unexpected swoop of a straight nose that turned up at the end, a pointed chin and a big mouth, at best, I would have said that I was 'interesting'. I was always being told that I had a faraway look about me, like I was permanently dreaming of being somewhere else. That look was certainly inherited from Mimi, who was drugged on nostalgia most of the time. But while she dreamed of the past, I dreamed of what might be.

The boy sitting opposite us peeled off his sweat-shirt and glanced over at Emma.

Emma is a prettier version of me. It's as if someone set out to make us identical, but lost concentration halfway through. Maybe I just don't care enough. Emma had spent all morning working on her outfit for the party, washing her hair and applying make-up. I had spent the morning on the phone to my best friend, Frankie, until Mimi had come in to my room to remind me that I was paying my own phone bills and was I aware that Frankie was in New York?

Well of course I was aware. Frankie, who was the model for the Butterfly underwear campaign, was never around any more. I missed her. But it meant that I had no time to wash my hair, no time to arrange some delicately cool outfit.

There were still two hours of the journey to go. I rummaged around in Emma's bag and found her make-up bag. I pulled out a stick of foundation and a pot of glitter.

'Can I borrow this?' I asked her.

'Sure,' she said in surprise. 'It won't bite.'

I lurched through the carriage looking for a mirror.

'So did you see Alex and co this week?' Emma asked me an hour later as we tucked in to sandwiches and a bottle of red wine.

I nodded. 'That's the problem with my life,' I said between mouthfuls of a rather mangy BLT. 'I've got friends who aren't my friends.'

'For once, I agree with you. Alex is the most self-centered, boring girl I've ever met, and for some reason she's the controlling figure of that bunch you're always with – you know, Lisa and Laura and Rachel – I don't know why you put up with her.'

'Neither do I. The scary thing is that I don't know how to stop it. Frankie's away, and now Jeremy and Ned have gone to Mexico for a year I feel completely abandoned.'

'Oh, my heart bleeds for you,' said Emma dramatically. 'You know, it's up to you to do something about all this.'

'When you're working five days a week, there's not much

7

chance to meet new people,' I said defensively. 'Something that you will discover when you get a job. If you ever get a job.'

'Give me a chance. I've only just finished my degree,' cried Emma. 'But you can be sure that I won't be hanging around in All Bar One and the Rat and Parrot every night. They're just Ikea with booze. You've got to go to different places, do different things – stuff that you wouldn't imagine yourself doing.' Emma was warming to her *carpe diem* theme. 'You know, sometimes you've got to jump off the edge and not care where you land.'

'Yeah, yeah,' I smiled at my gorgeous sister who was shaking her head with an expression of earnest conviction. 'Live out your own perfect weekend.'

'Exactly.'

'Anyway,' I changed the subject as we pulled into Stoke-on-Trent, 'do you really like Ben?'

'Not *really*,' considered Emma. 'I mean, the only reason I have to fancy him is that he's good-looking, funny and very sweet.' We both burst out laughing.

'Just not good enough, then,' I said.

Manchester, like London, was shrouded in tropical August heat, and the city had an Italian feel to it, with the smell of food and motorbike fumes. I stopped for a can of Coke before we set off again, and drank it all down in a few gulps, the icy fizz making my newly mascara'd eyes water. Emma's make-up had given the evening a kick. I wore boot-cut Diesel jeans, a long pale blue jacket with a Blur T-shirt underneath and red open-toed heeled shoes.

We got into a taxi and swept off through the muggy evening. As the cab pulled up outside the house huge drops of summer rain suddenly began to fall from a fast blackening sky, soaking us in seconds as we paid the driver. As the front door of number 8, Wilmslow Road closed behind us like some cheap horror movie, a crash of thunder sent us scampering into the house, screeching and sliding on the steps in our heels.

'Ugh! Students!' I exclaimed theatrically, tripping over the telephone wire to reach Ben, who was bending into the fridge in the kitchen and accompanying Jarvis Cocker on 'Common People'.

'Emma! Lydia! You made it. I'm wrecked already,' he announced, pouring an absurdly strong vodka-based cocktail into a Peter Rabbit mug. Through the strains of Pulp and the tubes of Pringles I felt a creeping annoyance. Why the hell was I here? It was going to be a long night. Staring out of the window at the rain frantically covering the streets outside, I saw people hurrying past the door, soaked and delighted to be cooled down after sultry afternoons in their offices spent dreaming of the sea.

I picked up a handful of peanuts and a glass of warm Pimms and headed out of the kitchen and into the noise. Someone passed me a spliff on the way through. I dragged on it deeply. I hadn't smoked a spliff for ages.

Aglow with alcohol and slightly paranoid from strong grass, I felt trapped inside tacky banality, like I was acting out a part that everyone who reached twenty-three had to perform. I was light-headed but cramped by the trappings of my generation, and there they were, all around me. Girls in five-inch cork-soled platform shoes danced with admirable co-ordination in their hipsters and baby blue halter-necks. There were too many blondes in the room for them all to be natural, and for every stripy head of highlights there were the accessories – glittery tiaras, sequinned hair slides in cute shapes, butterflies, feathers, flowers. That poignant summer smell of Clarins fake tan and CK One mixed happily with cigarette smoke and spliff. The boys slouched self-consciously in T-shirts slightly too small and combat trousers slightly too big. Scruffy but fashionably correct trainers filled the room.

Every available surface was cluttered with evidence of the twenty-somethings in the late-nineties: the worn copies of *High Fidelity* and *The Beach*, the well-thumbed edition of *Loaded* magazine with Denise Van Outen on the cover, the final warning electricity bill, the mobile phone, the reproachful A4 pads with only a few pages used for lecture notes, the Sony PlayStation, the empty Dominoes Pizza boxes, *The Simpsons* and *Friends* videos, the safety net of Massive Attack, Pulp and Garbage CDs. Like Ben, the furnishings couldn't make up their minds whether to be modern, post-modern or nostalgic, and a sense of confused identity prevailed over the spiritualist's Indian drapes on the wall, the purist's white table in the centre of the room, and the Monet prints lining the walls in peculiar alliance with the Naked '98 calendar free with *Sky* magazine.

I sat on the floor by the window watching the rain. No one in the room meant anything to me – no one in the room made any sense to me. They were foreigners, grating, uncomfortable. Yet it was ridiculous to imagine that I was anything more than any of them. In fact, I deduced, I was probably considerably less. I hated that feeling – the scary selfishness of youth blindly letting me believe that I had been *chosen* somehow, that great things would come my way and that I would make an impact. Yet the fact remained that I had done nothing at all to make this happen. In the back of my mind I felt that if it didn't happen *now* then it never would. Who could blame any of these people, I thought.

All of them under twenty-four, all of them under pressure, all of them hoping. All of them drinking and smoking and making a noise. There we all were, trudging through the nineties, being told what to do and how to feel by everyone but ourselves. And whose fault was that?

In that instant, I decided that this was going to change. How insignificant I seemed, how *silly* my lifestyle. The words from the stereo screamed out at me with relentless relevance: '*Every day begins and ends the same.*' But it was no use letting other people express what I felt. *I* needed to feel, to do, to cast off impotent sameness.

And that was the incredible thing. I didn't know it then, but I was just minutes away from the changes, from the scariest and most humbling thing that any girl can do. I was just minutes away from meeting an extraordinary boy.

I stood up and moved towards the door, swaying slightly, suddenly desperate for quiet. Use of the stairs was blocked by several chairs, which I navigated my way around, the walls spinning. I needed to find a bed, to lie down. At last – a door. I opened it and banged it behind me before attempting to focus my eyes on the room within. It was a bathroom. In the centre stood a huge bath resting on golden lion's paws. Irrationally I noticed the hundreds of shampoo bottles, soaps and hair sprays that littered every surface – boys were just as vain as girls in certain cases – this must be Ben's bathroom.

Sitting on the floor, cross-legged and more than a little jolted by my sudden appearance, sat Felix. I almost giggled at first, it was such an astonishing sight. He was smoking a spliff with a guitar resting on his knees. His fingernails were coated in sludge-coloured nail varnish and his long streaky hair was scrunched into an elastic band to form a tiny pineapple on top of his head, allowing me to stare straight into his eyes. Even in my dizzy state I could see that he was wearing eye-liner, which gave the swampy greeness of his eyes frightening definition.

But what a face! His nose was crooked, his skin pale and half in shadow from the indigo storm still raging outside. His mouth was huge and opened in surprise at seeing a strange girl in the bathroom beside him. In that instant, he reminded me of an angelic nymph who had been out on the town with a group of naughty goblins – he was Puck with a terrible hangover. He was so beautiful that I shivered and heard a ringing in my ears. *'He's the one!'* yelled a voice inside my head, jumping up and down and pointing. *'For Christ's sake! He's the one!'*

I passed out.

Isn't that incredible? I met the boy of my dreams and I did the right thing and full-on fainted.

Chapter Two

I woke up at 5 a.m. in a huge bed. I was actually in the bed, properly under the duvet, still wearing my Blur T-shirt and knickers. Silently, I congratulated myself on investing in a pair of yellow and blue striped knickers from Calvin Klein. I fancied that I looked not dissimilar to Kate Moss in her early shoots – all tousled bed hair, pale legs and dull eyes. A visit to the adjoining bathroom confirmed the pale legs and dull eyes, but nothing more. The mirror also revealed an almost luminous whiteness to my skin. I sloshed some cold water on to my face and padded back to the other room, only to find an uncommonly good-looking boy lounging on the bed right next to where I had been. He didn't even look up as I re-emerged from the bathroom. He was reading a book called *Pop Quiz*.

'Duet between Aztec Camera and Mick Jones of the Clash. What was it?'

My mind boggled.

He looked up. 'Do you want to ask the audience or phone a friend?' he mocked. It was the boy I had seen playing the guitar in the bathroom last night. The situation was becoming more and more surreal.

'"Good Morning Britain",' I blurted. 'And could you pass me my trousers, please?'

'Certainly.'

My Diesel jeans flew across the room and hit me in the chest. In great haste, I stepped into them. He flicked to the back of the book to check my answer.

'One hundred per cent correct,' he said in surprise. 'Very good. Do you like the Clash then?'

'They were a great band,' I mumbled.

'Well, they *meant* it, didn't they?' said the boy. He looked at me expectantly.

I coughed. 'Look, I don't want to be funny, but how did I get in here and what were we doing in the same bed? The last thing I remember about last night is the bathroom, and as I recall, you were there . . .' I tailed off.

'Correct. You don't need to know anything else. Don't worry, I didn't do anything. I'm far too vain to try and get girls into bed when they're too drunk to care. It's a real self-confidence killer for all involved.'

'Oh.'

'Your sister came looking for you and I told her I would make sure you were OK. I kind of like the idea of girls passing out in front of me, and you were wearing a Blur T-shirt which was enough for me to deduce that you're reasonably clever with an over-developed sense of irony, unless of course you like Damon for his cute smile and nothing else. What's your name?'

I opened my mouth to respond.

'No, wait, wait! I've been guessing, what does it start with?' he demanded, standing up to reveal long legs and painted toes. He wore nothing but a pair of Homer Simpson boxer shorts. Maybe he swung both ways, I thought. Damned 'anything goes' nineties.

'L.'

'You're Lydia,' he said simply.

'You knew already, you didn't guess!'

'Actually, Ben told me about you. You're the girl who didn't want to come to the party. He said I'd like you, and I can see why.'

It was strange, because he spoke so unselfconsciously, almost as if he was reading from a script. I began to laugh.

'I'm Felix,' he said. 'Nice to meet you.' He shook my hand. 'Now, let's get up and get out of here. I am not letting you hang around Ben and his crew today. Far too dangerous after what happened last night.'

Felix (now that I knew his name, no one could appear more cat-like) pounced on his shorts and toothbrush. It was a bizarre scenario indeed, I thought, as he cleaned his teeth and organised his guitar.

'Let's go,' he said, then suddenly uncertain, 'That is, if you want to come with me? I'll drive you back to London.' His eyes were on my face, properly on my face like boys' eyes should be when they look at you. He was tall, at least six-foot-three, and I felt tiny beside him. 'I'd prefer the journey with you to being on my own.'

Suddenly my brain was working with previously untapped

15

mathematical accuracy. Manchester to London on a hot Sunday in August would take at least three and a half hours, possibly four allowing for the inevitable stops along the way. That would give me enough time to find out about Felix. Emma could find her own way home, I decided.

Leaving Wilmslow Road wasn't as easy as I had hoped. It was mid-day by the time Felix and I ventured out of our room (I liked the sound of that already), and people were surfacing from the wings like characters from a Broadway musical. Cries of 'Hey Felix! Hey *Lydia*?' could be heard chorusing from every mouth, the question mark audible at the unlikeliness of what they assumed was last night's coupling. Let them believe it, I thought gaily, half tempted to slide down the bannisters with a whoop of delight.

Clearly, Felix and I had left the party before things got messy. Most of the guests seemed to have collapsed mid-conversation and were reawakening only to relight spliffs from the ashtrays beside them. Some masochist even had the decks going again. The girls had given a little more thought to how uncomfortable a night like this could end up and had crashed out in Ben's parents' bedroom in sleeping bags. I strolled in to tell Emma that I was off and found her cleaning her teeth with Colgate and her finger. She couldn't express her excitement fast enough. I noticed that the remaining six girls in the room were listening to her with ill-concealed amazement.

'I spoke to Felix last night and he made it quite clear that he wanted to look after you and no one else. You know he is the most good-looking boy in the world *ever*.' She made him sound like a dodgy compilation album, I thought, grinning inanely in agreement.

'How do you know him? When have you met him before? And why is he here?' I demanded.

'He's in that band I was telling you about, with Ben's cousin Justin.' I had vague recollections of Emma disappearing off to Camden to see some band a few weeks ago and returning with a lot of smug 'They're going to be *huge*' type prophecies. I hadn't given it any thought.

'You know, I went to see them play and they were literally incredible – the best band I've ever seen.' Even allowing for Emma's penchant for exaggeration, I could believe every word. 'Listen, do you know who his mum is?' she questioned, her voice thick with rhetorical conspiracy.

'No, who?' I felt like I was running through the script of an episode of *EastEnders*. One of the streaked blondes cut in at this point, unable to contain herself any longer.

'Carolyn Stewart!' she cried.

'The actress?' I asked stupidly.

'Of course!'

If it *had* been an *EastEnders* script, the episode would have ended on my look of amazed stupor, before the crashing of the drums and rolling of the credits. On cue, Emma and I were interrupted by Felix at the door.

'Lydia, are you coming? Let's get out of here before we get roped into the clearing up.' One of the streaked blondes giggled.

'Lyds, it's OK, I'm going to a concert at the Apollo tonight. I'll be back home tomorrow afternoon,' said Emma coolly. 'Drive safely,' she added crisply to Felix's departing back.

I guess at that stage I had the same impression of her as everyone else, but it's hard to remember exactly what that was now. It's impossible to imagine that there was a time when I would open a magazine with Carolyn Stewart's face on the front with the same detached interest with which I would read about any other famous woman. It's so odd to think that I ever saw her as just another celebrity.

From the second that I connected her with Felix, she became real. The fact that she was real to Felix — his *mother*, the woman he so longed to impress — lifted her off the cover of *Vogue* and into actuality where her touch was extraordinary. When Emma first told me about her I wasn't really surprised. It was quite possible to reconcile him with this woman, despite the fact that I had met him in Ben Lawson's bathroom. Felix had a spark about him, a dark, bewitching glamour that I had never seen in anyone before. I remember reading that Carolyn had a reputation for hanging out with the younger crowd in New York — the Leonardo DiCaprio set — like a godmother with serious attitude. Felix's *mum*.

We left Manchester in blistering sunshine, but after the rain of the previous night it was less claustrophobic. Felix paused on the way out of the door to check his face in the hall mirror.

'I'm not vain,' he said quickly. 'I'm just concerned about my hair.' He gave a self-deprecating laugh.

I followed him and his guitar out of the house and felt like a thousand years had passed between last night and this morning. 'Beautiful day,' I murmured.

'Thanks,' he said obscurely. 'My car's just round the corner.' He took my bag from me and slung it over his shoulder to join his guitar. 'It's in a bit of a mess but I wasn't planning on having any passengers this morning.' He stopped beside a classic-looking old

Jaguar and started fiddling around for his keys. It was the oldest trick in the book, standing beside the coolest car on the road and pretending it was yours, but I knew immediately that this really was Felix's car.

What else? He wasn't one of the clapped-out VW Golf crew, with their overflowing ashtrays and selection of wires hanging out like intestine where the radio had been stolen. Nor was he a nippy little Nissan Micra or Ford Ka. Felix was pure Jaguar – high maintenance and oozing style.

'I managed to persuade Mum –' (there was the first mention of her, though Carolyn Stewart as 'Mum' was paradoxical enough to make me want to laugh out loud) – 'that buying a third-hand Jag 240 was a better idea than a new Peugeot 305,' he said, as if reading my thoughts. 'It's beautiful, isn't it? When I first got it I just drove around for days wanting it to tell me its story. It was made in 1969. Imagine that? The car smelt of memories that I didn't even have.'

I looked at Felix to see if he was trying to be funny but his face was totally straight. I tried to imagine Carolyn Stewart arguing with her son over the purchase of a car. It was difficult, but just as I was wondering whether Emma could have been joking and perhaps the whole Carolyn thing was a wind-up, Felix asked, 'You know who my mum is, don't you?'

It caught me offguard, him coming out with it like that. But then I guessed it was something that you wanted to tell people sooner rather than later. You could hardly keep it under your hat for a later date, then say, ultra-casual, 'Oh yeah, my mum's an actress, you may have heard of her.'

'Yes, I do know who she is – Carolyn Stewart.' I giggled and turned to look at Felix, still half expecting him to roar with laughter and ask me where the hell I had got that idea from. He was biting the nail varnish on his right thumb. He looked up.

'It's strange,' he said slowly. 'It's a real curved ball, isn't it? She doesn't look like she could really be anyone's mother.'

'I understand what you're saying,' I said. 'My sister told me about your mum this morning and my first reaction was "So what? Why are you telling me this, as if it's relevant".' I was quite pleased with this, although it was a lie, which wasn't ideal having only known Felix for a matter of hours. He was one step ahead of me.

'Well, the thing is, it *is* relevant. It changes a lot of things and I've always lived with that. But thanks for being so sweet about it.' Anyone would think we were discussing the fact that he only had one arm and that my consolation was falling on deaf, resigned ears.

'It must be fun having a famous mum. Especially someone who everyone thinks is so great,' I said genuinely.

'It's great and it's not so great,' sighed Felix. Just for a second a shadow seemed to fall across his face. He swivelled round to fumble on the back seat for his shades. Calvin Klein, I noticed.

'Tell me about *your* mum,' he said.

'My mum's, er, actually, she used to be a singer,' I volunteered. 'She was a backing singer in the sixties for a band called Papa Jones and the Swingers.'

'Papa Jones?' repeated Felix.

'You won't have heard of them. They weren't that big but . . .'

'Papa Jones as in "If Only Love Was Easy"?' he asked.

'Yes! Mimi sang on that track!' I squeaked excitedly.

'Mimi?'

'Yes – I call Mum by her name, it was easier to say when I was little,' I explained routinely.

'Holy shit, Lydia, that's incredible!' said Felix in apparent awe. 'About her singing on that track, I mean.' For the second time in as many minutes I glanced at him to see if he was being funny. But I realised then that there was no room for sarcasm in Felix's repertoire. It didn't matter to him that his mum was on the cover of this month's *Vanity Fair*. My mum had sung on a hit record. He was impressed.

We drove out of Manchester and on to the M6 to the sound of The Beatles' *Rubber Soul*. Felix gave me a full and unedited rundown on who had been present at each recording, why each song was so important and why it was vital for anyone in a band today to understand the music that inspired the people who inspire them.

'You've got to look back with music as well as forward, all the time,' he explained, lighting another cigarette and shaking his head. 'The Stones were into R and B, blues, country, folk music. You've got to go back before you can possibly go forward. Influence is everything in music. Do you know what I mean?'

'Of course – like Blur and The Kinks,' I replied.

There was also no time for awkward silences in the opening part of the journey thanks to Felix's mobile ringing constantly. Every time it rang, he glanced at the face of the phone to see who it was, then pressed 'busy'. Busy talking to me about The Beatles, I thought. How cool.

Felix had the kind of voice that reminded me of phoning boys aged thirteen and hearing their ice-cold, scary older brother on the other end of the line. He drove with nonchalant abstraction, as if being in the car were merely circumstantial to what was really

21

important – which was what was being said in the car. There was no talk of the best route into London or of how long the journey was going to take. He wore a pair of frayed denim shorts, a faded grey T-shirt with *Loser* on the front (which you could only possibly wear if you were the polar opposite), and no shoes.

'Why the nail varnish?' I inquired when Felix paused for breath at the end of the tape and started rustling around for another.

'I play the guitar,' he answered, opening the glove compartment to reveal a half-eaten packet of Salt 'n' Lineker crisps, several Cadbury's Picnic wrappers, at least three empty fag packets and a dozen cassettes.

'Why does that mean you have to paint your nails?' I asked, feeling stupid.

'My nails get fucked and horrible so I paint them. Anyway, it looks nicer. I'm using this colour called Garbage at the moment, from a company called Urban Decay. You know, it sounds really American and sad, but painting my nails helps me to relax, too.' He looked across at me, the virtual stranger in the Blur T-shirt, and laughed. 'Girls are lucky, getting away with wearing make-up. I wear a bit on stage for the simple reason that it makes me look better. I'm coming across as a real jerk, aren't I?'

'No, not at all. I've always thought it unfair that boys don't get to wear make-up. Or dresses and skirts, because they're so much cooler in the summer.' I was the one gibbering on now. I glanced at myself in the wing mirror, sleepy eyes, hair matted. I had always held fast to the theory that late nights only made you look more intriguing, but I couldn't help feeling that it was a shame that Felix had to see me looking so awful.

'Look for the tape with *Moja demos* written on it,' he said. I shuffled around in the glove compartment. 'That's my band –

Moja?' he explained to me in a questioning tone which implied that he was looking for a gasp of recognition. 'We recorded it last week. It's not mixed or mastered, but you'll get the general idea.'

'Right,' I said, not having the first clue what mixing was, let alone its mysterious companion, mastering.

I took in Felix's collection of tapes, which seemed to feature everything from Chopin to the Prodigy. *Music for the Jilted Generation indeed*, I thought. I couldn't imagine for a second that Felix had ever come close to being jilted. I found the tape he wanted and shoved it into the car stereo. The song was shameless pop as far as I could make out, sung by a girl who sounded curiously like a cross between Debbie Harry and Baby Spice. Felix's guitar playing was, to the best of my knowledge, brilliant, but then the harsh reality was that I didn't have a clue. It was summer music, driving music with spiky, unexpected words. I guess it must have had the desired effect, however, because I had the first Moja tune I ever heard firmly stuck in my head for three days afterwards. My God, I thought, never underestimate the power of a three-minute pop tune.

'How many people in the band?' I asked.

'Four.'

'Who writes the songs?'

'I do. All of them.'

'Wow. That's amazing, I mean, that's really cool. You're very, um, well, talented.'

'I know I am. Well, compared to most of the stuff we're up against. If you compared me to the true greats, I'm nothing. But my band are pretty amazing. Our lead singer, she exudes *everything*.'

'Everything?'

'Everything you need. Too much of everything, actually – she's a superstar. You know when you look at someone and they look famous already?'

'You do too,' I remarked with perfect truth.

'Not in the same way,' said Felix. 'And I'm not even sure that that is a compliment, but I'll take it as one.'

'Are you with a record company? I mean, do you have a recording contract or whatever?'

'Not at the moment,' he said slowly. 'But we *nearly* do.'

I wondered what this meant, and asked myself whether I liked the music simply because it was Felix playing.

'It sounds really good – very commercial. I like the words,' I offered.

'It's all right, not perfect yet, and we had to sample the drums as Nicky was away on holiday, the slacker,' said Felix dismissively. 'Do you sing?' he asked.

I took a deep breath. Maybe this was the ultimate test for Felix. Maybe he had to have a girl who could sing. But I couldn't possibly lie about that – I would be found out within seconds.

'No,' I said bravely.

'Thank God,' said Felix. 'Singers do my head in.'

'So who is she?' I asked. 'Your exuding-everything singer?'

'She's called Amber Metivier. She's a very old friend of mine.'

There was a pause. Suddenly I didn't want to know anything more about Amber.

The car ground to a halt in a jam of traffic. Felix's phone rang again. This time he answered it. Only hearing one half of the conversation was enough for me at that point. I tried to busy myself with a packet of Hula Hoops I had found under the seat, but they were so stale that I had to spit them out as carefully as possible without Felix noticing. His voice on the phone rose several decibels so it was impossible for me to pretend that I couldn't hear what he was saying.

'Amber? Yes, I went to Ben's party last night. I'm on my way back now . . . No, I'm with a girl I met last night . . .'

I could hear the squawk down the receiver and Felix looked at me, raising his eyes to heaven.

'Lydia er . . .' He looked over to me. 'What's your sur-name?'

'Lewis,' I squeaked.

'Lydia Lewis,' Felix repeated into the phone. 'Her mum sang backing on "If Only Love Was Easy" . . . Oh shut up. Where the hell were you last night anyway . . . have you got the new bass amp for Justin? . . . No, I'll see you at the soundcheck. Hello? hello? Thank you, fucking Vodafone,' said Felix, chucking the phone on to the back seat. 'No reception,' he explained to me. As if I couldn't figure it out for myself.

Two minutes later the phone rang again. 'Amber? No, we just got cut off . . . She might come to the gig, I haven't asked her . . . Chill out . . . No, she doesn't sing . . . Well, if you're late for the soundcheck you're out . . . No, nothing happened . . . OK – no, wait! wait! Amber – record *The Simpsons* for me!' Felix chucked the phone away again and grinned at me. 'The girl's a nut case,' he explained as the traffic freed up and we gathered speed again. 'Totally paranoid. And I don't see why she has the right to give me such a hard time.'

He didn't explain what he meant, but after the conversation that had just taken place, I rather hoped that I was the cause of the paranoia. Wow, nothing had even happened between us and I was being treated with satisfactory hostility by this mysterious singer. I had never been the kind of person who induced worry and jealousy in other girls, although the idea was not without appeal. But then, I had never had a boyfriend long enough to worry about them running off with another girl either. Felix cut into my thoughts as we pulled off the motorway for petrol.

'Amber goes out with Justin, our bassist,' he said. 'They're actually the best combination of all time though they don't know it themselves.'

'Oh. Right.'

'What were you doing at the party then?' Felix changed the subject. 'How do you know Ben?'

'My sister was at college with him in Manchester,' I explained. 'He really likes Emma so I said I'd come along with her last night. Well, as you know, I didn't want to go to the party at all.'

'I'm a friend of Ben's from last week,' said Felix. 'He's also Justin's cousin. Justin couldn't make the party last night so I went in his place. And I'm *very* glad about it, too,' he said, shooting me a glance that made my stomach turn to jelly, 'or we would never have met and I wouldn't have had the pleasure of your company on this fine summer's day.'

'When are your band playing again?' I asked. Even if nothing progressed beyond this car journey, at least I could go and see him perform.

'Tuesday night,' he said. 'You should come along. It's this great little venue in Camden – the Lemon?' he said questioningly.

'Oh, yeah, I think I've heard of it,' I lied.

'I mean, it's not exactly Wembley Stadium, but it's got a good vibe about it. We play there the whole time. They kind of love us at the moment because we always get a big crowd and they spend loads of money at the bar.'

'I'm sure they love you because your music is so great,' I suggested.

'No, no, no. I doubt they give a fuck about that,' said Felix dismissively. 'Anyway, come along, bring whoever and see what you think.'

'I would love to,' I said.

Chapter Three

Felix pulled off the motorway at Thame, exit eight of the M40. He said he knew a good place to eat.

'There's no point in doing a long drive unless you can break it up somewhere you'd never normally go,' he said. 'Now, where the hell are we?' He shuffled forward on the leather seat and slowed the Jaguar down. We appeared to be following signs to a place called 'Le Manoir'.

'I came here with Mum when she was last over,' said Felix, turning into a beautifully kept driveway. I had a sneaky feeling that I had seen the place on TV. Felix confirmed my suspicions.

'Mum knows the guy who owns it, Raymond Blanc. I wonder if we can get some kind of snack here?'

He parked the car and led me into the cool interior of the hotel restaurant. His presence was so electric and his demeanour so charming that even in his frayed shorts and scruffy

T-shirt we were welcomed. He spoke to the pretty reception-ist.

'Good afternoon. My mother is a great friend of Monsieur Blanc, I was wondering if he was around? I was driving past the hotel with my girlfriend and I thought I might drop in and say hello. I'm sorry to inconvenience you with my lack of booking.'

The pretty French girl smiled at Felix. 'One moment, please Monsieur,' she said. She picked up the phone and held a rapid discussion in French. I hardly dared to breathe. Felix had called me his girlfriend. What was going on? It was like the best dream that I had ever had. I was convinced that at any moment a fire alarm would start ringing and I would wake up at home. But there was Felix, so real and so relaxed, leafing through a pamphlet of local attractions on the desk. And anyway, I decided, even my vivid imagination could not have stretched my dream boy to being Carolyn Stewart's son.

'I'm just going to the bathroom,' I whispered. In front of the mirror I delved into my bag and found a lumpy old mascara, then stained my lips a darker red with a lipstick of Emma's that had found its way into my possession. Glitter would be going too far, I thought. My eyes were now wide and excited, despite little sleep, which gave my face an unfamiliar glow.

When I returned Felix was smiling. 'It's all cool,' he said. 'We can sit outside and have sandwiches and stuff in the sun. Mum's friend's not here but I think they believe me.' We were led on to a beautiful terrace and sat down under a large parasol, half in the shade. 'I've ordered you a glass of champagne. I'm having boring old lemonade but we can pretend I'm getting drunk too.'

On cue, the drinks arrived, the champagne so chilled and

sparkling that it stung the roof of my mouth. Felix demolished his lemonade in one gulp and asked the waiter for another.

'This is my perfect afternoon,' I said. 'Sitting in the sun drinking champagne with –' I paused – 'my gorgeous boyfriend.' I smiled at Felix almost mockingly. He had called the first shot, and I could always say that I was just playing along if he roared with laughter. It was up to him now.

'Isn't it just the best?' he sighed. 'When England's like this, who needs anywhere else?'

I was nonplussed. Should I ask him what he had meant earlier or just shut up and enjoy the ride?

He was studying the menu. 'What sandwiches shall we order? I'm starving. Smoked salmon? Chicken? Tuna mayonnaise?'

'Oh, I'll eat anything, I mean, you order anything you feel like.'

'Well, what do *you* want?' he asked. He seemed genuinely concerned.

Food was the last thing on my mind, but the more we had to eat, the longer we would stay, and the more time we could be together. 'Do they have prawn, do you think?' I asked.

'Let's find out,' said Felix. 'Ooh! And there's *mousse au chocolat* for later on.'

It was all just too much.

'Are you always like this?' I asked five minutes later when Felix had placed our order, including another drink for me.

'Like what?' He pulled his shades over his eyes and leaned back on his chair so that his face was exposed to the sun. His slightly uneven nose gave his profile a chaotic impression.

'I mean, do you spend a lot of time helping drunken girls

31

into bed at parties and looking after them the next day in your Jaguar?'

Felix looked surprised. 'Not at all. You're actually the first girl I've seen into the Jag. At parties I just can't be bothered. There are far too many other things to be getting on with.'

'Like what?' I asked. A glamorous couple were drinking cocktails on the next table. They looked over at us with interest, probably trying to work out what film they had seen Felix in.

'Last night was the first party I've been to in about a year when I didn't play guitar with the band,' said Felix. 'I guess I started suffering withdrawal symptoms halfway through the night and had to go and play on my own. You know, if the music's good at a party, I don't really bother about anything else. I sound like a poncy git, don't I?' he added as an afterthought.

'No, it's just that I— nothing.' I wanted to tell him that I never ever wanted the day to end. Good sense prevailed. 'What's it like?' I asked. 'Being in a band?'

'It's like family. You can't escape it. It drives you crazy, but you can't walk out on it. It's certainly the most intense relationship I've ever had.' I wondered if he was referring specifically to Amber. 'And I mean that in *every* way. It's not like a normal friendship where you don't call someone for months then pick up where you left off. It's there all the time, whether we're loving or hating each other.'

'It sounds terrifying. Do you love them all at the moment?'

'I loved them last time we were all together. It's like smoking spliff – mostly it's great but sometimes it completely fucks you up.' He laughed. 'My God, I can see them putting that in bold type when I get interviewed in Q magazine!' He looked over to me again. 'You are such a beautiful girl. You've got the most luscious mouth I've ever seen.'

My heart was thumping so loudly that I was surprised he didn't hear it and ask if he could sample it for his next recording. He spoke as if what he was saying was factual evidence that required no further comment, especially not from me. Our lunch arrived.

'This is some snack,' I conceded as the waiters fussed around us with pristine napkins and fresh black pepper.

'Beats Little Chef,' said Felix, devouring a sandwich in one mouthful.

'So what are you doing tomorrow?' I asked him. 'What does Monday morning mean to you?' I was intrigued to know how Felix spent his time. Maybe he drifted from one expensive restaurant to the next with a different girl in tow every time.

'Is it Monday tomorrow?' he asked. 'I suppose I'll do a bit of work on a couple of new songs, then I might go to Denmark Street and look for a new guitar, then I'll probably go out for some food with my little brother.'

'Sounds like a pretty great Monday,' I said.

'*Every day is like Monday*,' sang Felix with a grin. 'What will you be doing? Do you have a job or anything?' He spoke as if having a job was the equivalent of some rare tropical disease.

We hadn't discussed work yet, which was a miracle. Usually the 'what do you do?' question was the first thing that anyone asked. What else was there to talk about, after all?

'I'll be going to work,' I admitted.

'Where do you work?'

'South Kensington. In a museum.' I waited for the usual

response: '*Really?*' followed by a frown and a swift change of subject.

Felix raised one eyebrow and looked suspicious. 'What do you specialise in?' he asked.

'Dinosaurs. I take school-children on a tour that shows how life on earth existed before man.'

'How extraordinarily unlikely,' said Felix. 'You know your stuff then?'

'Well, yeah. I mean, you get asked every question imaginable by seven-year-olds.'

'What do you get asked the most?'

'*Where's the loo?*' I confessed with a weak smile. 'Then *When can we see the Tyrannosaurus Rex?*'

'Do you like what you do?' he asked.

'Not really,' I said. 'I thought it would be great and I was really looking forward to having a job – genuinely I was. But the routine really frightens me. I just get scared that this is it, you know?' I bit my bottom lip. I hadn't confessed this to anyone, not even Emma. 'I just feel that I'm too young to be doing what I'm doing every day.'

'I guess it's not surprising that you feel like that when you're working with fossils and relics from another age.' He flicked a wasp off his lemonade glass. 'No doubt you walk around in a daze all day having every problem put into perspective by the dinosaurs.'

'Kind of, yeah.' I grinned at him.

'Well, I think it's very important to put things in perspective,' said Felix. 'I get so insanely obsessed by the band and we haven't even made it.'

'I'd love to be obsessed,' I said dreamily. 'But I couldn't deal with being in a band. The stress involved must be far more exhausting than what I have to deal with.'

'Why?'

'It just sounds like the most impossible thing to be trying to do.'

'Yes, but we know it'll work out in the end,' said Felix. 'It's almost like we have to go through all of this to justify the end result. Amber's freaking out again? I just think – it's another test, get through it. The others are all broke again? I just think how great it'll be when they can pay me back. We're in limbo. We're just waiting. Every single hour of every day, just waiting.' He looked thoughtful. 'Sad isn't it? You know, it gets to the stage where you have so much to prove that you kind of forget why you're doing it in the first place.'

'What, pressure from fans and stuff?' I asked.

Felix snorted. He had a great indignant snort. 'If only,' he said dryly. 'It's more the pressure from people who know that we've been doing this for three years. The people who are now earning shitloads in some bank somewhere who ask you, "How's the, er, band coming along?", and then the other classic line, "When can we see you on *Top Of The Pops*?" The problem with people who don't understand the music business is that they can't appreciate how hard it is. They just think we must be doing something very wrong because they haven't seen us at the Brit Awards yet. You can hear the pity in their voices. Either that or they just assume you're bumming around doing nothing with your life and using the band as a convenient excuse not to get a job, which, incidentally, is exactly what I *am* doing at the moment.' He smiled. 'Don't tell anyone.'

'But you said you'll be writing new songs tomorrow.'

'Yes, but it's hard to see that as work. I just have to do it because I really can't do anything else. And I can do it whenever I want. If I want to sleep until one in the afternoon, I can. If I want to write until four in the morning, I can.'

'So how much does it get you down – not having the record deal, not being on *Top Of The Pops*.'

'I used to think that I wanted the fame part of it so much. But really the best part for me is writing and recording the song. Once that's done I kind of lose interest.'

'Oh come *on*,' I protested. 'What about the fame and the touring and the *girls*?'

'I'm really bad at all that,' muttered Felix. 'Amber wants all that attention thing. But to do what I want to do, which is to be her guitarist and the bloke who writes the songs, you've got to deal with all the other shit, the press and stuff.' He shivered. 'They scare the hell out of me. And meanwhile we have to show all those guys who never thought we'd make it. Either that or I could arrange for our drummer to go and punch their lights out.'

'Aren't you talking about the people who show up to your gigs?'

Felix snorted again and showed some long-overdue rock 'n' roll attitude. 'Probably,' he said. 'But I still want to punch them.' Then he reconsidered. 'Well, maybe that's going a bit far. I could just give them a really bad Chinese burn. Anyway, even if the public love us, the industry and the press will hate us.'

'Why should they?' I asked indignantly. 'Your songs are great – you play your own instruments and all that.'

'All they'll care about is the fact that we had too much to start with,' said Felix. 'We're just a bunch of toffs compared to everyone else in a band.'

'What's wrong with that?'

'Everything. The prejudice is just incredible. Jesus, Lydia, I shouldn't be sitting here sipping champagne in the sun at one of the country's most élite hotels if I really want to make it.'

'Whyever not?'

'This is the kind of thing you do after you've won your first Brit Award. Or at least after you've signed a deal. But the thing is, I've tried and tried to be economical and live like a proper struggling musician, and I just don't really see the point. And none of the others in the band have any money, so I'm really like a permanent cash-point for them. Maybe that's my subconscious justification for not having a proper job and all that—' He stopped suddenly. 'I don't know.'

'Where does your money come from?'

'Mum. She's never around, so my brother and I have the house to ourselves. She stacks up our accounts with ludicrous cheques every three months. I think she must have lost all comprehension of how much most twenty-three-year-olds live on. I haven't seen her since last Christmas. She phones us a bit and she's always wanting to know what's happening with the band. She likes the idea of us making it . . .' Felix must have decided that he had said too much all of a sudden as he changed the subject and asked me about Mimi and her days as a backing singer.

Felix had eaten most of the sandwiches and then two plates of chocolate mousse, but I didn't mind. After two and a half glasses of champagne I was floating on air. *I was driving past the hotel with my girlfriend* were the only words that I would ever need to hear again.

Felix was a match for my mercurial, meandering conversational style, and our chatter sauntered from one subject to the next with the easy swagger of true soul mates. That afternoon was so sweet and smooth it was like licking golden syrup off a spoon. I had no idea what he was going to say next, but I somehow knew that whatever it was, it would be right.

At about four o'clock Felix asked the waiter for the bill. He hardly glanced at the total.

'Can I give you some money?' I asked feebly, as he emptied the back pocket of his shorts.

'Don't be so silly,' he said, 'I've got enough here.' He extracted several crumpled notes from the mess of receipts, sweet wrappers, Rizla papers and guitar picks. 'I guess we should *frappez la route.*'

'Huh?'

'Hit the road.' The afternoon sun had dusted a few freckles on the end of his nose. His blond-streaked hair was still pulled back off his face.

'I don't want to go,' I bleated.

'Neither do I,' said Felix. 'Let's see if we can distract ourselves further on the last hour of our journey.'

We made our way back to the car. The pretty receptionist stopped Felix on the way out.

'May I pass on your greetings to Monsieur Blanc?' she asked.

'Oh yes, please tell him that Felix stopped by. Actually, you might want to mention my mum,' he said.

'And she is?'

'Carolyn Stewart?' said Felix, with an absurdly unnecessary question mark in his voice.

The girl's eyes widened and she gulped. She gave a little

gasping laugh. 'Certainly,' she said, regaining her cool. 'I'll pass that on.'

'Thanks,' said Felix.

We had only been going again for ten minutes when I spotted our next distraction.

'There's a sign for a fun fair!' I squeaked. 'We have to go! Please!'

Felix looked at me quizzically for a second and narrowed his eyes. 'Let's do it,' he said. He jacked up the volume on the stereo and Moja's music filled the car. Even though I had only heard the songs for the first time that day, on second hearing they were even better. Felix wound down the windows and sang along very loudly.

'I love this song!' I shouted.

'WHAT?' yelled Felix. The warm summer breeze blew my loose hair all over my face and a clump stuck to my lip-balmed mouth.

'I SAID, I LOVE THIS SONG!'

Felix laughed out loud, then leaned across to me and kissed the top of my head.

He put his arm around me as we scampered into the fairground. The lights, the pulsating music, the summer crowds and the big wheel created the perfect back-drop to the perfect pop-video. The garish confusion of colour and noise was a curious contrast to the grandiose exclusivity of Le Manoir. Felix was equally at ease in both scenarios. He grabbed my hand.

'Let's do the Ghost Train,' he said.

'Oh no,' I mumbled. I had a childhood paranoia of that kind of thing.

But Felix was shoving me into the little carriage.

'Two please, mate,' he said to the bloke in charge of the ride. As soon as the money changed hands the car jerked into action and through the creaking doors.

'Felix, I know it sounds pathetic but I hate these things!' I whimpered.

He slung his arm around my shoulders. 'Don't be frightened, sweetheart,' he said. 'I look far scarier than any of these guys first thing in the morning.'

I shut my eyes and shuffled as close to him as I could. There was something about the way he smelled that was just so right. The little car bashed through another door.

'That guy looks like our old manager – hey, Lydia, open your eyes,' giggled Felix.

I peeked out and saw a man dressed in a white sheet splattered with red paint ricocheting off a wall.

'Very convincing,' said Felix. 'And I thought *The Shining* was spooky.'

Felix won me a stuffed skunk by throwing hoops over a plastic duck. To celebrate this victory he bought us both a large stick of candy-floss. The sweet buds of pink sugar melted in my mouth as I followed him through the raucous crowds to the big wheel. Mums and dads with small children, teenagers with attitude, and starry-eyed young lovers made up the extras on my film set. We walked fast, keeping in step with the changing rhythms that pumped out of each ride. Felix's stride was so graceful and sexy he almost appeared to be dancing. He moved like a star, with a self-possessed elegance that was recognisable after spending no more than a few hours in his company. Certainly his pretty eyes and his coolly sultry demeanour set him apart from the crowd; but more than that, it was the fluidity of his manner that made him different. I was enchanted.

We reached London as the sun set over Notting Hill Gate. The M40 had crawled into Shepherd's Bush, crammed with people driving back into town after the weekend, still in bikinis and sun hats, noses reddened and hair bleached, windows down and radios blasting. Even so late in the day, London shimmered with heat and Tarmac burned under the Westway. Felix and I talked non-stop, pausing only to adjust the radio to the Top 40 as the countdown to Number One began.

'I mean, Mick Jagger and Keith Richard really lived it,' he was saying. 'They lived the image. It wasn't image – it was them. That's rock 'n' roll. Not putting on your leather trousers for *Smash Hits*, then going back to the hotel room to sip herbal tea while watching *Honey I Shrunk The Kids* and reading *The Road Less Travelled*.'

I was startled by the directness of Felix's criticism and the specifics of the viewing and reading material that he considered so dreadful.

'But you bought *Smash Hits* today,' I said, pulling it out of the bag as if it were an exhibit in a libel case.

'I like to keep up with what the nation's under-fourteens are into. It's just research,' he said defensively, and lit another cigarette.

When we pulled up outside my house, Felix leapt out of the car and to my absolute horror started waving at Mimi, who had optimum vision of my arrival from the kitchen window. She waved back, cautious and completely thrown. Anyone would think I'd just arrived in a spaceship, I thought. A few seconds later she opened the front door.

'Can I come in and dump Lydia's stuff for her?' Felix was asking.

It took her a few seconds to respond, so engrossed was she in Felix's appearance and his car. Fair enough, I reasoned, the boy was staggeringly pretty and I had never arrived home with anyone who had ever addressed Mimi with such obtuse politeness. She pulled herself together.

'Of course you must come in – I've just opened a bottle of wine,' she said, swirling around in her scarlet A-line mini-skirt and heading back into the house.

'Lydia told me you sang with Papa Jones in the sixties,' he said. 'What an amazing band. It must have been an incredible time.'

Mimi looked startled for a second. 'It was,' she said, a little harshly, in that voice she always used when she talked about the past. She had that slightly sorrowful, faraway look in her eyes, and for one horrific moment I thought she was going to start pouring out her regrets to Felix, whose relaxed, gentle admiration appeared to have unleashed some desire to reveal secrets. But Felix was already on the move again.

'I must go,' he said. 'Lydia, will you come out to the car with me?'

'Sure.'

Once safely outside he leaned against the bonnet of the Jag. Whenever he stood still, which was not often, I longed to touch his face.

'So . . . will you come to the gig?' he asked.

'Of course. I can't wait, I really can't wait. Look at me, I'm completely overexcited about it already,' I said. 'Will you make me a copy of the demo?'

'Sure, sure,' said Felix. 'Look, I have to go.' He seemed distracted suddenly and I felt like Cinderella realising that she had overstayed her time at the ball.

'Give me your number,' he said, 'but I'm telling you now that I'm not going to use it until after the gig.'

He pulled out his mobile and I punched the digits into the phone.

'What's wrong – are you scared that I might blank you?' I mocked. 'You think that I might avoid your calls?' I laughed out loud, it was so absurd.

'Exactly,' he said. There was a strange thundercloud look on his face.

I took a deep breath. 'I just want to tell you that you're the most beautiful boy I've ever seen,' I said. 'And you might as well know it,' I added quickly. There was something about Felix that made me want to tell him exactly what I was feeling, however deeply uncool it was. Make things happen, I thought. Seize the . . . evening.

'*That's good to hear, but unimportant,*' sang Felix softly. Then, when I looked confused, 'That's a line from *Evita*. You seen it?'

'No, I, er, my sister loves musicals,' I said.

'You're so sweet,' he said. 'I think you're very beautiful, too.' He managed to say it objectively, as if I was a painting that he had been admiring.

'I had the best day ever,' I said. 'Just the best day.' He smiled, the cloud vanished, and I felt that unfamiliar butterfly feeling surging around my stomach. Never before had anything hit me so physically.

I sat outside on the doorstep long after Felix and his Jaguar had purred off into the distance. He had said I was beautiful, and for the first time in my life I felt as though I believed it. I watched the stars come out, realising with a pang that this was happiness – this was what happiness amounted to. How fragile it was, but how perfect. I felt the earth spinning for me alone, singing in perfect harmony with the vanishing sun and the eerily climbing milky moon. Happiness was my warm feet on the hard steps and my nose still a little burnt from the sun. Happiness was recalling the smell of the Jaguar, and the way my stomach had flipped upside down when he smiled at me. Happiness came down to something as obvious but elusive as this; knowing that I was going to see him again soon, and knowing that nothing could ever change the fact that Felix had spent practically the whole day, nearly twenty-four hours, with me. Happiness was anticipation. It didn't matter to me that night that the way Mimi of all people had reacted to Felix made it clear that there were girls all over the country who would be falling over themselves for the boy.

When I eventually moved inside she was flipping through the *Daily Mail* with a resigned expression.

'Well, I don't know what's going on between you two,' she said in the kind of voice that implied that she had already formed her own extremely accurate idea of what was going on, 'but I can't believe he was interested in you in that terrible T-shirt.'

'I had my perfect day,' I said. I was still dazed. 'My perfect day.'

And the T-shirt was what had brought us together. He liked Blur. I lay awake for three hours that night listening to *Modern Life Is Rubbish*. At the moment, for once, modern life was proving to be quite good.

Chapter Four

Tuesday night, the Lemon club, Camden. I wore new boot-cut hipsters from Kensington Market and a tight T-shirt with The Verve on the front. I wore silver Nike Airs and painted my nails with glitter. Basically, I wore the kind of distant coolness that can only be achieved through real effort, and is therefore easily exposed as entirely *un*cool. Inside I was a wreck. Shaking with hope and anticipation I paid my three pounds on the door of the club – if you could call it that.

All my experience of clubbing in Manchester could not have prepared me for the Lemon. The walls were slimy with damp and grease and sweat. And the stage where I assumed the band would be playing was no more than a raised platform of creaking, rotting wood that looked like a death-trap for a drum kit let alone any human life-form. Thank God I was with Emma, who had assumed total control as she had seen the band play before. She consulted the flyer she had been given on the door.

'It says that they're on at eight-thirty, but that means nine o'clock,' she said with authority. 'They're probably backstage. Come on, let's go and say hello,' she said, striding towards an area marked *Bands Only*.

'No! Wait! We can't just interrupt them before they go on,' I whimpered, terrified that Felix would see me and think I was being far too keen by saying hello like a groupie, or worse still blank me completely. I stalled again as Emma tried to drag me behind the stage, where I could dimly make out a couple of guitars and a microphone stand.

Calling the area 'backstage' was optimistic to say the least; all I could see was a room not big enough to sit down in, with walls covered in graffiti, presumably as a result of bands who had hung out there over the years, churning through cigarette after cigarette and discussing the order of songs for that night. 'Hung Like Horses will piss on U2' was scrawled in black marker pen by one hopeful musician. 'The Lemon is a shite hole – suck it and see' someone else had volunteered, with a good deal more accuracy. I suppressed an appalling desire to giggle. This was serious – it was Felix and his band about to stun the crowds; it was the raw reality of life on the road.

And there was Felix. His beauty, especially in such dire surroundings, seemed to light up the whole area.

'Have you noticed that only the shit bands who never make it write on the walls?' he was saying to the boy beside him. Emma gasped and grabbed me by the hand. He wore a long coat in deep blue velvet and a pair of exquisitely cut snakeskin trousers. Anyone else would have looked like a Bon Jovi roadie, I thought in amazement, but Felix was born to prance around in tight trousers and – Holy cow – stiletto boots?! He came straight over to us and kissed me on the forehead with theatrical panache.

'Lydia, my angel, you made it!' he announced as if I had flown in from Australia that day. 'Listen, get a place in the front and I'll see you when we finish. Come on, Justin, for God's sake, we're on in ten minutes.' Stepping out from behind Felix, like an accomplice in a crime, came a tall, dark-haired boy swigging from a bottle of Becks. Although the lighting in the Lemon was far from revealing – it was so dark that the only real light seemed to be coming from Emma's fluorescent footwear – I could sense his confidence, his rock star chic and his *Just Visiting This Planet* poise. His eyes were so dark that they seemed to cast shadows over his deathly pale skin, giving him the mysterious allure of a creature of the night. He was at once the vampire and the victim.

'You're the latest, are you?' he drawled, raising his eyebrows without smiling.

'I – um – I dunno,' I replied lamely.

'A word of advice – tell Felix you could hear him properly over the noise of the band,' went on Justin. 'He freaked out in the soundcheck and said that his guitar wasn't loud enough. All you need to do to get him into bed tonight is tell him he was substantially louder than the rest of us. Even *Amber*,' he added. He spoke slowly and lazily, which added to his intimidating demeanour.

'Oh. Right,' I said.

I was slightly irritated that he just assumed that I knew who Amber was, even at this early stage. I hadn't met her yet, but she was clearly the kind of girl who was worthy of a metaphorical drum roll whenever she was introduced to someone new. Now

47

Justin was arguing with a skinny bloke with dreadlocks and a fag. I noticed how his public-school drawl morphed into an inoffensively noncommittal 'mate'-punctuated accent as he spoke to him.

'. . . No, mate, all I was saying was that last time we played we headlined, and we thought we would be headline tonight.' He pushed his hair from his milky forehead.

'Yeah, well, it's been a busy week for us, what with Crack playing here last night. Someone had overlooked a double-booking of you lot and Dirtbox.' Skinny Bloke stubbed out his fag and pulled a new pack from his pocket.

'Fucking hell! Were Crack playing here last night?' Justin asked incredulously.

'Yeah, we kept the bar open and Brett Anderson's cousin who's in this great band – Tarnish, you know them? – came up on stage and duetted with Dex Alive on their new single.'

'Why the *hell* didn't I know about this, mate?' asked Justin, with all the anguish of one hearing that he'd missed out on the Stones playing an acoustic set in his local pub.

'They were booked very last minute. That's why we were all confused about tonight.'

'Oh, *mate*, that's all right, if I had known that Crack were here I wouldn't have asked. Talk about coming back down to earth with us lot!' It was difficult to tell if Justin was taking the piss, but I decided that rather worryingly, he wasn't.

'I'll make sure the levels are better than they were in the soundcheck. You lot are sounding good – have you been gigging a lot recently?'

'Yeah, mate, every week at the moment. You know, just trying to keep it real. We've got Dizzymusic and Element coming tonight, but to be honest, mate, I'm just so *not* into signing to a major. We're really hoping to get some indie labels down next time.'

'Yeah, the majors are all fucked at the moment anyway.'

'Completely. The whole industry's fucked.'

'Fucked.'

'Completely.' Justin turned back to Emma and me. 'What do you think?' he asked. His dark eyes glittered dangerously. There had been infinite kindness in Felix's expression when he had questioned me about the Clash that fateful morning, but there was something harsh and frightening in Justin's. Even though I had only just met him, I could tell that it was a test.

'I agree with you,' Emma said boldly. 'You need to be really careful at the moment. Don't you think, Lyds?' She nudged me in the ribs. I suspected that all I was required to do was agree with them all.

'I really don't know what you're all on about, actually,' I confessed. 'Surely great music is always great music? I mean, I don't care what record label any of my favourite bands are signed to. I don't see how it can be that hard to get someone to believe in you.' I smiled at Justin. I had meant to sound encouraging. After all, I had heard the band on tape and had been genuinely impressed. But Justin had no intention of letting me get away with my remark.

'If it's so easy,' he said lightly, smiling at me nastily, 'why don't you get out there and get us a deal?' He turned and loped off to the stage, where he began fiddling with wires and amplifiers.

'Why did you say that?' hissed Emma.

'Well, he took it the wrong way. Why is he so touchy anyway?' I felt relieved that I had confessed ignorance, but surprised at Justin's bitter response. I didn't even *know* the guy. I wondered what Felix would have thought. I wondered how they could be such good friends.

Emma and I ordered drinks from the bar. Five minutes later there was a screech from a microphone and I turned towards the stage. Felix and Justin stood either side of an infuriatingly beautiful girl dressed in a sparkling white halter-neck top, a turquoise tasselled mini-skirt, and pink, high-heeled sandals. A jewel glittered at her naval and red roses burst out from her long, dark hair, which under the stage lights looked almost blue-black. I was incensed that anyone on the planet could carry off such an outfit – and make it look as wonderful as she did. She had fluked the genetic lottery numbers to combine perfect green eyes with a large, pouting mouth. Every single head in the Lemon swivelled towards her, as if drawn by the improbability of such a sight in such a place. The sound engineers and miserably derelict regulars were startled out of their previous apathy. Clearly used to greasy, sweaty boys with delusions of becoming Liam Gallagher or Richard Ashcroft as soon as they set foot on stage, they fell silent as Amber introduced the first song. Her voice was low and full of magical Eastern promise, like a Narnian Turkish Delight.

'This is called "Heavy Traffic", and we wrote it in a little house, far away from here, on the very edge of the planet,' she said.

'Near Inverness,' offered Justin into his microphone, to giggling from Felix and the drummer. There was a screech of feedback from Justin's amp as they began the song and I could see Amber turning to him and shouting to start again. I began to think that perhaps they were completely useless and all hype due to the fact that the entire band looked so staggering, when suddenly it all came together and they were off.

It was impossible to dislike Amber's performance. She was

everything that everyone in the audience could possibly have wanted her to be, and although I was encouraged by the fact that her voice was not that great, it was so full of character and expression that she charmed me into feeling that I was witnessing an early act from a great star. She told a story through every word of every song, her tiny frame seemingly encapsulated by the moment. The other members of Moja seemed to move with her, sympathise with her, love her. And how could I blame them? (I assured myself that I would have to find a way, and quickly, or there would be no hope at all for Felix and me.) I had never spoken to her before, but I realised how good she was at what she was doing, because she made me feel as if I knew her. She sung every word as if she was thinking it and feeling it for the first time. I wanted to know her. I wanted to get to know her.

Meanwhile, Felix was bouncing up and down one minute, then standing as still as a rock the next, gazing theatrically (I hoped) at Amber, then laughing out loud with Justin. I noticed a cluster of girls standing in front of Emma and I who were screaming his name and singing along to everything. I nudged Emma. 'Are they friends or punters?' I asked.

'They were here last time. They're too young to be friends. They can't be more than fourteen. It's the Moja fan club – or should I say, Felix's fan club,' she replied.

'My God – genuine *fans*!' I gasped.

'Watch out, you've got competition!' said Emma as a plump girl with a Moja T-shirt threw herself on to the stage, baying in delight at having broken through the nonexistent security line. Her removal took rather longer than expected as she had a fair amount of weight behind her which bounced off the speakers and drum kit as she flailed, squawking around the stage, chased by the club's owner who had lumbered up from the back of the room and was clearly enjoying his impromptu moment of glory.

'Security! Security!' yelled Justin in a faux American accent, fearing for the safety of his equipment in the presence of overexcited youth. I was dumbstruck. Not only was Felix the most magnetic character I had ever come across, but his band were inspired, funny and well-rehearsed. I had to be part of this. How could those long, dull evenings in the Rat and Parrot or All Bar One compare to this?

'Well, what do you think? Isn't it just *brilliant*? Don't you wish that you were doing something like this?' Emma was shrieking to be heard above the next song. I told her to shut up. I wanted to listen – and anyway, she was preaching to the converted.

The band took a break for five minutes because Felix had broken three guitar strings. Emma vanished to buy cigarettes from across the road rather than ripped off by the vending machine. I smiled at the skinny bloke who Justin had been talking to before the gig.

'All right?' he said, smiling back. 'You seen them before?'

'No, never,' I said. 'First time. Never seen them before.' It was as if I needed to say the words to convince myself that this was the case. I could not believe that Moja had played all over London, maybe even all over the country for all I knew, and that I had not been a part of it. What the hell had I been doing?

'They're a great band.' Skinny Bloke inhaled deeply on his cigarette. 'I'm Martin.'

'Hello Martin. Lydia. I'm a, er, a friend of Felix, he's the, er—'

'Yeah, I know Felix,' said Martin with a burst of laughter. 'Justin's a nice bloke, too. Can be a bit of a paranoid git,' he spat out the word git, then let out a loud cackle, 'but he's good company.'

'What about the girl?' I found myself asking.

'Great tits. Need I say more?'

'It doesn't give a *totally* accurate character reference.'

'She's a fucking superstar, I can tell you that much. Moves like a young Kate Bush, looks like a young Liz Taylor.' Martin looked smug at his assessment.

'Do you think they'll get a record deal soon?'

Martin looked thoughtful. 'It's actually not a question of *talent* – We know that they piss all over every other band around at the moment. It's more a question of finding the right person for the job. You'd be amazed at how many A and R men have walked through that door –' my gaze followed his pointing finger – 'who have seen Moja play and have just not *got* it.'

'What do you mean, not got it?'

'Exactly. How can you not think that they are the greatest band to come out of London in the last five years? But you know the industry is full of idiots.'

'Do they have a manager?'

'They did have one but something went wrong, I think. They're very disillusioned, and you can't afford to be in this business. God knows, I used to be bitter as hell, now I just don't give a fuck.' Martin sighed. 'It's no place for the old, either.'

'You're not old!'

'Ah, but I am. I'm over thirty, so I'm old. Listen, I'm a dinosaur compared with you people – Felix, Justin, yourself.' Even being associated with Felix and Moja in this tenuous context made me excited. Get a grip, I thought.

'Which record label do you think they should, er, sign to?'

53

I asked, changing the subject quickly. I wasn't in the mood to discuss youth and wisdom.

'I told Justin tonight to try for this bloke at Conspiracy Records,' said Martin. 'They're a good label. About the only label not in real trouble at the moment. They need Moja as much as Moja needs them. That's the important thing. I mean, that guy over there, the one who's just walked in wearing the green T-shirt, talking on his mobile.' Martin waved a fag towards the bar. 'He's a twat. Works at Element Records, thick as a fucking post. Signed an act last year who sold ten thousand copies of their first album then got dropped. Artists have no time to develop any longer. So he goes and signs that new boy band, you know . . .'

'A-OK?' I suggested.

'No, you know, that other one.'

'Guyz Rize?'

'No, NO! The other one!'

'HotBoy Five?'

'Yeah, HotBoy Five, that's it. And you can bet he won't stick around to see Moja finish the set.' Martin grimaced. 'Makes me so damn mad.'

'Me too,' I agreed wholeheartedly as Emma returned with her cigarettes.

'Being chatted up?' she asked me in a low voice.

'No, this bloke's been telling me all about trying to get a record deal. Sounds like hell on earth. It just seems so unfair, all those crappy boy bands having deals rather than people with genuine talent.'

Emma shrugged. 'I guess it's like everything in life – if you want something bad enough then you stick around till you get it.'

'It's just not fair though. Someone has to do something.'

The band had moved back on to the stage.

'One, two, three!' yelled the drummer, and they took off again.

Chapter Five

Felix found me sitting on my own by the entrance to the Lemon, watching the crowd filing out into the night. I was trying to decipher who might be from a record company, but like undercover cops I presumed they concealed their identity. Felix looked radiant – mascara smudged and his hair standing on end. Emma had left me alone, determined that I should not be hindered by her presence, but I was desperate for reassurance now, and suddenly overcome.

'You were so, so brilliant, you should be so pleased with yourself,' I said uselessly as he opened the door for me.

'Did you really think so?'

'God, yes!'

'Justin's amp stopped working halfway through the set and the feedback from Amber's mike was awful.' He looked tired, suddenly. Then, just as quickly, he snapped out of it and was making plans.

'Listen, the band are coming back to my mum's place – she's not there, don't worry – and I'd love you to come along too,' he said.

My heart lurched. 'I'd love to,' I croaked, losing my voice at that crucial moment, which made me sound like Marge Simpson. I coughed. Felix laughed.

'The car's parked over there, I'll be along in a sec.'

Gratefully, I sped off towards the Jag, which sat like a disapproving old gentleman alongside the common folk of Metros and Fiat Pandas. I slid into the passenger seat, breathing in that exciting aroma of old leather, cigarette fumes and stale crisps.

'Keep calm, just don't get panicked. I know Emma's not here, but you'll be *fine*.' I've always had a habit of speaking to myself when nervous. And, sitting in the car, I tried to convince myself that the other members of Moja would welcome me into their lives. 'Amber might seem a bit scary but you've just got to befriend her and get her on your side. And Justin seems OK, even if he is a bit arrogant—'

'More than a bit, I can tell you,' came a voice from the back seat.

I screamed and began fumbling with the car door, but hearing giggling from behind me, I turned around and felt sick. My brief conversation with myself had been overheard by Nicky, the drummer, who had been sitting patiently in the back of the car, completely covered by his kit, waiting for Felix to return. Even now I could only make out his shoes and the top of his head.

'Oh my God, I had no idea you were in the car!'

'I don't mind, I'm always talking to myself. Most of the time

I'm the only person who listens to me anyway,' came the voice again with a sniff. 'And I can tell you that the whole experience was weirder for me than for you as I've never seen you before and as far as I was concerned there was a stranger in Felix's car ranting on about the band. I just had to interrupt you before you got round to discussing my performance tonight, which was pretty ropey, actually. Did you see the smoke machine? It was pumping out right next to me and I couldn't see the kit. Then I dropped a stick and couldn't see it to pick it up again. Fucking amateur pub venues.'

It dawned on me that this boy was far more worried about his drumming than he was about my possible insanity.

'I'm Lydia,' I said to the bass drum, which seemed to be obscuring most of its owner.

A hand appeared over the top of a cymbal. 'Pleased to meet you. I'm Nicky,' came the reply. I shook the hand, feeling stupid. There was a pause, and then the drums spoke again. 'You're the girl that Felix took to the fair, aren't you?'

'Yeah, that's right.' I felt encouraged by the fact that he seemed to have heard of me. 'I thought tonight was just amazing. You rocked the place. I can't wait to see you play again.'

'Why, what's the point?'

'What do you mean?'

'That's the seventh time we've played the Lemon this year alone. Every time we play there I promise myself that it'll be the last time before we get a deal. Yet here we are again, same old thing, same old disappointments, no closer to achieving anything worthwhile.'

'How long have you been doing it for then?'

'Three years. Can you believe that?'

'Is that a long time to be trying? I thought that bands had to play for years and years and years before they got the recognition they deserved. I read somewhere that Pulp were together for nine years before they made it.'

'I can tell you right now that there is no way that I'm prepared to carry on doing this for another . . . six years. It's just too depressing.' He sounded as if he had forgotten who he was talking to, forgotten that he didn't know me at all. 'Anyway,' he went on briskly, 'have you been to Stanley Road before? Felix's mum's place?'

'No, never. What's it like?'

'Pretty incredible. Pretty Carolyn Stewart. Very mad, very fashion. You haven't met Val?'

'No,' I said slowly. Val – Felix's *girlfriend*? I couldn't bear it. I felt sick.

'Who's Val?' I questioned, trying to keep my voice light.

'Felix's little brother, Valentine.'

'Oh, his brother!' I exclaimed, louder than necessary. 'I forgot he had a brother. What's he like?'

'Looks just like a mini Felix but he's very different. Very London. He's just seventeen. He's doing some art course some-where at the moment.'

'Will he be there tonight?' I asked, staggered at the thought of a replica of Felix.

'Almost certainly. Carolyn's away in New York most of the time so Val and Felix have free run of the house. But that's great for us too.'

I would have liked to question Nicky further but Felix was back, opening the boot of the car for his guitar. He flopped into the driver's seat and turned round to face Nicky.

'You left your sticks on stage,' he said.

'I know. They were bad luck. I don't want to see them again.' Nicky sighed dramatically. Felix turned back to me, rolled his eyes and smiled.

'OK, Lydia?' he asked.

'Totally. Let's go.'

We listened to the Moja demo again on the way home.

'Take it off!' yelled Nicky from the back seat.

'I need to work out why we can't ever get that solo right in "Dark Soon",' said Felix.

'Must be the crap guitarist,' said Nicky.

'No, the drumming always lets that song down,' said Felix.

'To be honest, the bassist sounds stoned.'

'The singer's shit, too.'

They were laughing now. I just smiled and watched the Marylebone Road spin by. London hugged me tight.

Justin and Amber were waiting outside the house under a full moon when we arrived. Felix chucked Amber the keys to the front door and began unloading the drums with Nicky.

'That's right!' Nicky shouted as Amber and Justin shuffled past the mass of equipment without volunteering any assistance. 'Just leave me to do it as always, you lazy gits.'

Amber looked smug. 'One of the main reasons that I decided to take up singing was because it didn't involve lugging huge instruments around,' she said. It was obviously a well-trodden argumentative path.

'I guess you've got enough to carry anyway, what with your ego weighing you down,' responded Nicky sweetly. I kind of liked him at that point.

Eva Rice

'If *you* choose to play the drums then *you* carry them around, sunshine,' replied Amber, apparently not bothered by Nicky's comments.

This put me in a difficult position. Should I help Nicky with his stuff and endear myself to him, or follow Amber and win her over? My question was answered by Felix.

'Just leave the stuff in the car for now. We'll unload when we've had a drink. By the way,' he added hastily, 'Amber – Lydia. Lydia – Amber.' Amber couldn't have ignored me, even if she had wanted to.

'Hi,' she offered lightly.

'Hello – you were great tonight.'

'I *was* good, I know,' she responded.

Nicky didn't appear remotely shaken by her confidence.

'If you had any idea how expensive these drums are . . .' he grumbled as we made our way into the hallway.

'Oh, blah, blah, blah,' said Amber, pushing past me and into the house.

I had planned to be very cool and unaffected by Felix's house, whatever it was like, determined to show the others that I could handle the glories of the urbane. But when I first set foot in 35 Stanley Road, I stood in the middle of the hallway, gawping like an idiot. The walls were painted a dark crimson and the light of a vast crystal chandelier glimmered down on us as if we were entering a fairy palace. Exquisite paintings crowded the walls, jostling for attention like court jesters all trying to please their Queen. At least a week's worth of unopened mail lay on a table of the smoothest mahogany, much of it addressed to Felix.

I was painfully aware of how at home the members of Moja

were in this palace – as soon as we entered the house they were off all over the place. Justin rushed downstairs.

'Val, what was the score?' he yelled.

'They drew, one all!' came the reply. 'Karl Ready scored!'

I looked questioningly at Felix. 'Is Justin a QPR fan?' I asked.

'Yes. Don't tell me you support them too?'

'They're my local team,' I said. 'I try and catch a couple of games a season.'

'Oh well, we all have our cross to bear,' said Felix. I laughed.

'You not into football?'

'Yes, into football, but not QPR for God's sake! You and Justin will have a lot to talk about. I think you'll be the only other person he's ever met who is into them.'

The house was an opium den of fabrics – orange crushed velvet curtains clashed brilliantly with purple velvet sofas, which seemed to stretch the entire length of the room and engulf you as soon as you sat down. Above the open fire in the drawing room was a huge, framed black and white photograph of Carolyn Stewart with the two boys either side of her. One was Felix with his guitar slung over his shoulder. The other, smoking a cigarette and laughing up at his brother, was Valentine. The overall effect was the perfect advertisement for nineties youth – cavalier disregard for the dangers of smoking coupled with the delight of a mother who was so hip that she didn't care about it anyway.

Carolyn's fame was such that I felt as if I was invading her home uninvited. Further photographs of the boys crowded the mantelpiece and book shelves, as well as numerous shots of Carolyn herself with various film and music stars. A huge white grand piano occupied a corner of the room, offset by the sleeping presence of a sleek black Siamese cat.

'Hello Minxy, my baby,' crooned Nicky, sweeping the purring creature into his arms and flopping on to a thick leopard print rug. I decided to stay with Nicky rather than follow Felix and the others downstairs. Despite our toe-curlingly embarrassing first meeting, I felt more comfortable with him than I did with Justin, and Amber and I were still pacing around each other like panthers. I crouched next to Nicky on the rug, preparing to give Minxy my undivided attention, until the sound of Felix rattling around in the kitchen sent her off out of the door.

For the first time, I saw Nicky's face under the flattering glow of the huge indigo-based lamps that stood like guardsmen in three of the four corners of the room. The thing that I really noticed about him was his nose – long, straight and elegant, the centre point of a face governed by freckles. These coupled with the blue eyes and blond hair gave him a look of innocence, the kind of boy I would have expected to see running through enchanted woods or sailing off on pirate-infested adventures, his gingerbeer by his side. But there was something naughty about him too, an air of chaos and mischief that made his disposition seem more Artful Dodger than Enid Blyton.

'Skin up, will you, Lydia?' Nicky cut into my thoughts with such a blistering lack of romanticism that I laughed in surprise.

'How d'you know I smoke?'

'Why are you laughing?' he demanded.

'No reason, except I was just thinking you've got very angelic looks for a drummer.' How silly I sounded, although Nicky seemed satisfied enough.

'I am the good boy, I tell you,' he sighed, rustling around in his cymbal case for his gear and taking out enough grass to knock out an elephant for several days. In a no-nonsense manner, he rolled while talking to me about Amber. Actually, I guess I started the conversation.

'So, do you and Amber not really get on?' I began hopefully, seeing Nicky as my ally in the event of trouble between Amber and myself.

'Oh no, we love each other desperately,' he said, without glancing up from the task in hand.

'Really?'

(I noticed that he was using the *Kama Sutra* to roll on which made me miss out on the first bit of what came next.)

'. . . even though we argue because she's nothing like how she first appears. You have to give her a chance. She's very switchboard,' said Nicky.

'Switchboard?'

'Loads of issues all going off at the same time. Needs to have her finger on the pulse of everything. Amber's had a weird life. French mum. That says it all, doesn't it? I hate the French.'

'Why? They wear much better clothes and shoes than us.' What was I *saying*?

'Good point. English girls don't know how to dress.' Nicky looked at my trainers without much enthusiasm. 'Cursed be Nike and Adidas for preventing girls from wearing stilettos as they should. Did you really think we were all right tonight?' Nicky steered the conversation sharply back to the gig.

'It was just *brilliant*,' I enthused. 'Didn't you think so?'

'We were OK. I'm pleased you liked it, although no doubt you were staring at Felix thinking, "Oh my God, he's so beautiful!" throughout,' he added slyly.

'No . . . well – yes and no,' I said, grinning.

'You know, Felix needs it more than anyone, if that's possible,' said Nicky, sparking up the joint. 'I need it because I'm fucking broke and I want to buy a flash car and collect Brit Awards like every other tosser in a band. I want the money. I love the music and I love Moja, but I want the money too. Felix – he doesn't give a shit about the money. He's got the money already so he's doubly obsessed by the music. That's his incentive. And he wants his mum to think he's made it,' he added

'Lucky him, not having to worry about money. It doesn't mean he needs it more, it just means, well, lucky him for having it all before you even get started.'

'I guess so,' said Nicky. I was glad he understood what I was saying because I'm not sure that I did.

'What do you all do – you know, when you're not in the band?' I asked.

'We're always in the band,' he replied sharply. 'There's never a time when we're not in the band.'

'OK, OK! Do you have, er, day jobs?' I questioned.

'I'm a session drummer. I go and play drums for other people. It means I get better and I get experience and all that crap.'

'Meet interesting people . . .' I added.

'Oh no, most of them are dull as shit,' said Nicky happily, 'but I get to play drums. And occasionally I get paid. It's what I do. I play drums. Tonight, and forever, Matthew Nicholas Clarke is going to be a drummer.'

'Is that your name? Nicky Clarke? The same as the hair-dresser?'

Nicky looked resigned. 'Hilarious, isn't it? I don't see my parents much at the moment, but next time I do I'll be sure to bring it up with them, although I don't imagine that in 1976 my namesake had quite the following that he does now,' he added. I laughed.

'Go on – what does Amber do?'

'Amber works at Chica – Felix's mum's agency.'

'As a model?'

'No, she's too small and too impatient for that. She's a booker. She books the right girl for the right job.'

'My best friend's a model,' I said smugly. 'She's the new Butterfly underwear girl.'

'She's all over the underground in nothing but her knickers and bra,' said Nicky with mock disapproval.

I chided myself for expecting him to be impressed. We were sitting in Carolyn Stewart's house, for God's sake. 'Does Amber see anything of, um, Felix's mum?' I asked.

'Hardly ever – she's nearly always away. Felix got her the job but she's actually very good at it. We're always trying to think of excuses to come in and see her at lunchtime on the off-chance that we'll bump into the models. "The Girls" as Amber calls them.'

'And Justin?' I asked quickly, horrified at the possibility of Felix lounging around Chica all day.

'Justin,' Nicky said slowly, 'is a law unto himself and about three other people. He's great at playing bass and *so* into his music – and he works in Thomas Cook.'

'The travel agents?'

'Correct.'

'How very unlikely.'

'We had a cheapo holiday in Greece last summer, booked through Justin. He nearly lost his job when they found out he'd been kicked out of the hotel, but he got away with it. As ever.'

'Why was he kicked out?'

'He passed out in the lift wearing a white sheet and nothing else, off his face. I thought he looked rather wonderful, like some entry for the Turner Prize, you know – *Julius Caesar Drunk In Elevator* or something . . .' Nicky paused, remembering the scene. 'We all moved out with him, except Amber who said he was a jerk and she was staying put to enjoy the holiday.'

'Sensible girl.'

'Well, Felix found out that a friend of his mum's lived in the plushest villa on the island so we pushed off there.'

'Did you tell Amber?'

'Yes – she wouldn't come. It got really silly after a while, her sitting in the hotel on her own while we drank champagne all day by the pool, but she's like that. Said that she had saved for the holiday, so she was going to get what she'd paid for.' Nicky shrugged. 'Typical stubborn woman.'

'Has Felix ever had a job?' I asked.

'Not that I know of. Oh yes – he worked in a café in St Ives last summer for a few weeks. He wanted to get away so he took his guitar down there and hung out with the surfers and artists. He just did it for the novelty value. But he came back all nostalgic and theatrical, you know Felix,' he went on, forgetting that of course I didn't really. 'He was ranting on for weeks about wanting to go back, and how he missed the beach and the Tate Gallery and Pirate FM.'

'How adorable,' I muttered. Nicky looked at me speculatively.

'He is adorable. That's half his problem. Too bloody adorable.'

I felt light-headed and thrilled, like I'd won thousands of

pounds on a scratch card. Lounging on the rug in 35 Stanley Road, hearing Felix and Justin shouting downstairs and inhaling the smoke that languished from Nicky's spliff, I felt hugged by richness. I imagined I was wrapped in the softest cashmere, lying on the fluffiest of white clouds. I was falling on to feathers from a great height. I was – I was – I was stoned.

Chapter Six

I could have sat there all night talking to Nicky about Moja and his drum kit. Felix knew I was upstairs, and that made me cloudy with elation. There was a certainty about that night and about what was going to happen.

We must have been on our own for about an hour before the others ventured up to find us. Amber had changed into track suit bottoms and a tiny pink cardigan. She had rubbed off her make-up, and her pixie-like features were accentuated even further by her hair being thrown into a band off her face. Every bit of her seemed so minuscule and perfect, and every bit of me seemed to swell and grow like Alice after a bite of the magic mushroom by comparison. Justin threw himself on to the purple velvet sofa and Amber collapsed beside him, stroking his hair and giggling. I was suddenly deflated. How did anyone else stand a chance when there were girls like Amber in the world? Felix sat down beside me and Nicky instantly moved away.

Following them into the room came Valentine, instantly recognisable as a mini version of Felix. He was entirely at ease with Justin and Amber, and as soon as he sat down cross-legged next to Nicky, he produced a pack of cards from his pocket and began to deal for the two of them.

'What did everyone think of tonight?' he asked, flicking the stereo on with the remote control. Madonna's voice filled the room.

'I thought we were awful,' said Nicky moodily. 'We don't deserve to get a deal when we repeatedly fuck up the opening of each song.'

'We weren't that bad,' protested Justin, sitting up and frowning at Nicky. 'It was a new amp, and I wasn't sure how the levels were working.'

'That's just fucking pathetic!' exclaimed Nicky. 'You should have collected the amp weeks ago, and if you'd practised before we went on stage it would have sounded fine.'

'I can't believe it,' said Justin. 'Another load of hype for nothing.'

'What do you mean?' I asked him. 'I thought you were so good.'

'It doesn't really matter what you thought,' said Justin coldly. 'We're playing because we want a deal. We need a record company to understand us. But it's just the same every time – you spend a week getting ready for the gig, you try to keep calm, but in the back of your head you're always thinking, "this is it! this is it!"'

'And it never is,' concluded Nicky. 'So what the hell is

the point?' He turned to Felix. 'What did the bloke from Quirk say?'

Felix shrugged. 'He said he quite enjoyed it but he thought the songs weren't quite ready yet. Wanker. He said he'll come again in six months time.'

'He wasn't even listening to the first two songs!' said Justin. 'He was talking to that girl from Dizzymusic at the bar. I saw them together.'

'I just don't know how much longer I can go on,' said Nicky. 'It's getting to the point where I don't even want to give a record company the satisfaction of signing us. If they're so fucking stupid that they don't realise how great we are –' he slammed his fist on the floor – 'then they can just get lost.'

'I want to try Conspiracy,' said Felix. 'They've never seen us before and apparently they're all right.'

'Why should they be any different to all of the others?' asked Justin. 'I reckon there's an interview for anyone working for a record company – *Can you guarantee that you will arrive up to thirty minutes late for any gig of any unsigned act? Yes. Good. Are you terrified of music that cannot be immediately categorised? Yes. Good.*'

Nicky joined in at this point. '*Are you more interested in laminates and backstage passes than the music? Yes. Good. Do you agree that talking crap to your colleagues during every gig you go to is the ideal way to behave? Yes. Good.*'

'Well, you've got the job, starting on Monday,' said Felix. 'Oh, and be sure never, ever to return calls. Ever.'

'All *I* could hear were the drums,' said Amber, cutting into the conversation and changing the subject completely. 'And what the hell were you wearing that ridiculous shirt for?' She turned accusingly on Justin who looked furious.

'I have no money to spend on clothes to wear on stage,' he said through gritted teeth, without looking up at her. His tone was dangerously quiet but Amber ploughed on, her voice becoming louder, more pressing, her forehead crinkled in indignation.

'You spend all your money on spliff and alcohol and keeping up with Felix and it's dragging everyone else down, Justin! We need to look good when we perform, and at the moment you look so uncool.' She paused for breath. Justin didn't even raise his head. 'It's been going on for far too long. You're always wrecked when we play, late and hungover when we rehearse – doing *coke* off Nicky's parents' bedside table last weekend!' she added in disgust. Felix giggled. Justin avoided Amber's gaze but looked across to Nicky.

'Yeah, sorry about that, mate,' he said, 'but it was the only surface in the house that I hadn't shagged Amber on.'

With that he stood up and walked to the door. Amber looked mutinous. Felix was laughing even louder, and Nicky was playing cards with Valentine as if nothing had happened.

'And you can shut up!' shouted Amber, turning on Felix. 'You're always complaining about people behind their backs – you never say anything to anyone's face. All of you are just useless because you're always stoned. It's just so *boring*!'

Justin left the room, slamming the door behind him.

'Amber, darling, you know what they say?' said Felix.

'What?' she asked sulkily.

'Hard work pays off in the end.'

Amber looked ready to cry.

'But laziness pays off immediately!' concluded Nicky.

Amber sighed and looked resigned.

'You and Justin need to sort yourselves out because you're both to blame,' said Felix.

Amber stood up, eyes glittering with rage. 'You have no clue about me and Justin – *no clue*.'

'Maybe. But I do know that it's screwing up the band.'

'Justin hates being put down in front of people he doesn't know,' said Valentine suddenly. 'You must never make a fool out of him. He's too insecure for that.'

Nicky made a sound of agreement.

'I'm going to buy some more fags,' announced Felix. 'Look after Lydia until I get back.' He obviously wanted to go alone.

'Get me a Coke and twenty Silk Cut Ultra, will you?' asked Nicky. I noticed that he didn't offer Felix any money.

The front door banged as Felix stepped out into the night, and suddenly the temperature in the room seemed to drop. What was I doing here? I wondered. Without Felix to protect me, I was suddenly intimidated and edgy.

'Pass the wine,' ordered Amber.

'She does have a name, you know,' said Nicky. I felt myself go red.

'I'm not saying she doesn't have a name,' said Amber, 'but do you really think that he gives a toss if – sorry what *is* your name?'

'Lydia,' said Nicky quickly.

Amber stood over me. She looked me right in the eye and I held her stare for as long as I could, then looked away. I could sense her smirking. She addressed the room. 'Do I really care if *Lydia* heard that conversation? I mean, it's not like she's about to have some monumental effect on his life or anything. Sorry to single you out like this,' she added in my approximate direction.

I felt, at this point, that I had had just about enough of Amber, the rude cow.

'I would mind if I was Justin. You made him look like a real idiot,' I said. 'And how do you know that I'm not going to have any effect on his life? What if I hold the key to your success?'

'In what way could you possibly have any effect on Moja? Apart from being another one of Felix's little admirers? Believe me, darling, I've seen more girls come through that front door with Felix than I can name. In fact, let's *try* to name them!' She was on a roll now and in a sick kind of way I wanted her to go on. She had her hands on her hips, very much striking a pose and obviously elated by the high melodrama. Val and Nicky carried on with their game.

'Well, starting from the beginning of the year, there was Samantha Thingy, Nicky's friend—'

'Samantha Harris,' corrected Nicky without looking up.

'Yes, Sam Harris. Then there was Anna – she was OK, I quite liked her. Then there was Olivia Rich and her little sister Jackie, and then Tanya Wills for a week or so, then Sarah the barmaid at the Dublin Castle, then, oh, Claire Stewart-Whatsit, and then – oh, then Lydia. Pardon me for forgetting your name, but believe me, things get confusing. I mean, you know what they say about Felix – low quality, high turnover . . .'

'Amber!' It was Nicky, reacting with suitable disgust to this outpouring. 'That is not true! Tanya Wills was gorgeous, and so was Sarah the barmaid!'

'Oh per-lease!' exclaimed Amber. There was a horrible silence. Then Nicky burst out laughing.

'You missed one out! You might as well know it all, Lydia,' he added in a mock dramatic tone. 'You missed out that girl in

Edinburgh when we played at Andy Jackson's party.' There was a pause while everyone, presumably, tried to recall who he was talking about.

'Oooh, that amazing Puerto-Rican girl who thought it was a Bond theme party and came in the white bikini?' asked Val.

'Stupid cow – she only did that to get attention. Of course she knew it wasn't a Bond party,' chuntered Amber.

'She was pretty amazing looking, wasn't she?' agreed Nicky. 'But apparently a total nightmare. She kept asking Felix to write songs about her. In the end he said, "I can't write anything about you that you won't be mortally offended by", and she decked him, didn't she?'

'Slung a right hook,' confirmed Val. 'Felix thought it was funny, but you had to cancel that gig because you wouldn't let him on stage with a black eye,' he said to Amber.

'Too right,' she said. 'Everyone would have assumed that it was me who had hit him. I didn't want that.'

Nicky looked at me. 'Listen, the reason we can talk about these other girls is that they've all been entirely irrelevant. Don't take it seriously.'

'Oh, right.' What more could I say? Nothing that I had heard was especially surprising; it just made me more determined than ever to keep Felix, and to be the one girl who lasted more than a few days. As if on cue there was the sound of a key turning in the door and Felix was back. He chucked cigarettes and a can of Coke at Nicky and sat down next to me.

'Everything OK?' he asked.

'We were just telling Lydia that there hasn't been that "special someone" in your life this year,' said Amber sweetly, inserting the inverted commas with her fairy-like hands.

'Can't you talk about anything other than my love-life for a change?' yawned Felix, picking up a tattered copy of *Sky* magazine.

'Surely the expression "*love*-life" is pushing it a bit,' said Val. 'There has been precisely no love involved so far this year.'

'Will you all shut up?' Felix was suddenly, heart-warmingly irritated with the conversation. 'Are you all determined to wreck what little chance I have left with Lydia?'

'Quite right,' said Nicky. 'Sort out your own problems, girl-friend,' he added to Amber, who flounced over to the stereo.

'You know what, though?' Felix was talking to me directly. I could feel myself melting. 'You are the only girl I've met in the last year who I really, really want to see again. There's something about her,' he added to Nicky and Val, who turned to look at me as if for the first time.

'Lydia, you are certainly the most *intelligent* girl Felix has ever bought home. And you've got great legs. If you hadn't fallen so madly for him I would have gone for you myself,' said Nicky with a sniff. He turned back to Val and they resumed their game.

'Don't listen to the others, they don't matter.' Felix had moved closer to me, so close that our mouths were only centimetres apart. 'I'm sorry about that. Amber's so ridiculous. She spends her whole time complaining about us and yet as soon as I bring someone back here she sees it as a threat and behaves like a psycho. You know what? I don't give a stuff about anyone else I've seen this year. I really, *really* fancy you. And you know what else? Before you ask, I *don't* say this to everyone,' he murmured. I laughed. Felix was so very sweet. He had a way of looking at me with amused affection which made me lose myself completely. But if I was going to kiss him, I was going to make sure that it happened when we were on our own and not in the presence of the Greek Chorus of Amber, Nicky and Valentine.

The whole conversation had been so weird, and even stranger was the natural way in which everyone had been talking in front of me. Felix's honesty had totally thrown me, but all I cared about was the fact that I had decided to believe him. That was the bottom line. I believed him. Amber began to redo her hair which had escaped from it's pony tail.

'Have you really shagged on every surface in Nicky's parents' place?' I asked, not without a certain amount of admiration. Amber looked thoughtful.

'Yup,' she said after a pause. 'But we kept the noise down.' Suddenly she smiled at me. 'It was lovely. He's wonderful in bed. And out of it,' she added after a moment's thought.

'Justin is *always* out of it,' observed Nicky. Amber laughed, and crossed the room to him.

'You were so good tonight,' she said. 'You're such a super-star.'

'I'm not, sweetheart, you are,' said Nicky.

'I just don't know any more,' Amber said quietly. And for a split second her face was awash with confusion. 'I'm going to bed.'

Felix, Val, Nicky and I sat upstairs, talking and smoking. Valentine was like a little puppy version of Felix, clambering around the room, changing CDs and demanding that Felix teach him how to roll a spliff. Felix handed the job to me and Val crouched at the table like a little monkey, watching me shredding weed into a long Rizla. The experience was rather like *The Generation Game* and I half expected to see Jim Davidson peering over our shoulders with snorts of hilarity.

79

'Too much tobacco,' I said, removing some from Val's effort. He pulled a corner off an errant postcard addressed to Carolyn Stewart to make the roach, and handed it on to me to do the same. I hesitated.

'Go ahead,' said Felix. 'It's from that git Andreas — you can tear the whole thing up.'

'Felix and I are not as fond of our step-dad as we should be,' explained Valentine, his face contorting with concentration as he twisted the delicate paper around the grass and the contents of half a Marlboro Light.

'There!' he said with satisfaction. 'Thanks, Lydia.'

Two hours later, Nicky and Val collapsed under big duvets on the sofa, Minxy the cat purring at their feet.

Felix and I sat in the kitchen, drinking Southern Comfort, of all things, and munching our way through a shared bowl of Crunchy Nut Cornflakes. Felix had led me downstairs, his bare feet completely covered by corduroy flares.

'Justin and Amber are always like this,' he explained. 'They've been together for four years, joined the band together and everything.'

The kitchen was chaotic but full of beautiful things — a blue Chinese-style vase dominated the table, overcrowded with yet more unopened mail. The curtains were a soft, creamy pink, matched by two sumptuous-looking armchairs in the same material. Felix read my thoughts.

'Mum likes to sit down and issue orders in the kitchen,' he explained.

'Nice one,' I replied, thinking how Mimi would react to being ordered around by Carolyn Stewart. Felix went over to the huge old American-style fridge and pulled out some milk for our cereal. Closing the door with his knee, he examined the magnetic poetry stuck on its surface.

'*Wise Men Betray When Drunk To Get Laid*,' he read. 'Ain't that the truth?'

'I presume that's your philosophy,' I said.

'My mum's more likely,' said Felix, sitting beside me. 'Val is the most adorably devoted boyfriend any girl could wish for. Or he would be if he had a girl to devote himself to.' Felix sloshed half the box of cereal into a bowl. He was a messy eater, but I was so entranced that watching the majority of the cornflakes spill out of his mouth and on to the table did little to dampen my spirits. He spoke as he ate.

'Moja are going to be huge, Lydia. That's why Amber and Justin have to sort their Tom and Jerry life out.'

'Why Tom and Jerry?'

'Justin's Tom – bigger and stronger than Amber but not as street-wise. Amber's Jerry – she has to be kicking him down the whole time or she can't survive. But they love each other really. At least I bloody hope they do.' He looked at me and pulled a worried face. 'Nicky is the peace-maker. I generally side with Justin because Amber drives me crazy too, and Val, when he's around, usually sides with Amber, who he will do anything for. Except for tonight – I think even Val thought she was out of line tonight. But Lydia, you should know something. What Amber said.' He adopted an amazingly competent Sean Connery voice. 'There have been quite a few girls this year.'

'Listen, I don't know what you're so worried about. I mean, what's going on between us anyway? We ended up in the same room at Ben's party and I came to see your band play tonight.

81

It's not like we're engaged or anything.' I couldn't believe my own cool, but Felix needed it. How many of those girls that Amber had listed had collapsed into his arms in rapture, only to be brushed off the next day? So he was my dream boy, but if I wasn't the girl that he had been waiting for, I might as well get out now. I looked at Felix defiantly.

'Maybe I should go,' I went on, shuffling around as if I was about to leave.

'Hang on, where are you going to go?'

'Home.'

Felix grinned at me. 'Don't go,' he said. 'It's pointless.'

'Why?' I asked, completely straight-faced.

'Because then we won't see each other again until tomorrow night when I invite you out again, and I want to be with you *now*. Just stay.' He looked at me imploringly, taking my hand. 'That is, if you want to.' His voice faltered a little. I smiled at him.

'Of course I want to stay,' I said, and on impulse I kissed him on the forehead. Felix looked amazed.

'Well, thank God that's settled,' he said. 'I would have lost absolutely all faith in getting a record deal if you'd gone off home.'

'What do you mean?' I asked.

'Well, you couldn't have been very impressed by me or the band if you were planning on leaving now,' he said.

'Ah, is that what you do? Impress girls at gigs then lure them back to bed?' I asked mockingly. 'Don't tell me, they can't contain themselves once they've seen you on stage with your guitar?' Felix had walked right into that one.

'No,' he said. 'Nothing like that. I don't usually get as far as asking anyone to come and see us play. You're a bit of a novelty,' he said.

'Charmed,' I said.

Suddenly Felix dropped his spoon with a clatter and looked at me. I stared into his sludgy, swampy eyes and leaned forward as if magnetised. He dropped a kiss on to my trembling mouth then pulled back and laughed softly. 'You're such a pretty girl,' he murmured.

'Not as pretty as you,' I replied, transfixed. I was surprised that my legs didn't explode; I could feel little shots of adrenalin pricking into my veins. Felix slammed his hand on to the table, making me jump.

'For God's sake let's just go to bed.' He pulled me to my feet and led me upstairs.

I paused in the hallway. I had to get it off my chest while I was still high enough not to care.

'Felix . . .'

'Yes, what is it?' He smiled at me.

'I don't really know what I'm doing here. I'm not a musician, I'm not cool. I work in a museum in the Long Before Man Tour and—' I broke off because Felix was shaking his head in disbelief.

'What are you talking about? I think it's great, really different. I'm *obsessed* by dinosaurs – I had nightmares about Velociraptors for weeks after *Jurassic Park*.'

My jaw fell open. Felix took my hand again.

'Actually,' he said slowly, 'we can talk about this later.' I sighed with relief.

(Later I could tell him that the Velociraptor did not actually exist until the Cretaceous Era, some one hundred and ten million

years after the Jurassic period, but was included in *The Lost World*
for the sake of a gripping plot.)

Maybe the spookiest thing about sleeping with someone for
the first time is letting them inside your bedroom; that elusive
personal space reluctantly reveals more than anyone really wants
it to. Felix's room was right at the top of the house, up three flights
of stairs. No wonder he was so skinny, running up and down to the
kitchen all day. We floated upwards, past soft watercolours and
languid pre-Raphaelites. How could he possibly appreciate such
prettiness when he had nothing to compare it to? Felix seemed to
exist against a back-drop of gorgeousness – an intoxicating, heady
overdose of loveliness.

His bed was enormous, stretching almost the entire length
of the room, unmade and completely covered with clothes,
including a pair of fake tigerskin trousers and a black suede
Gucci jacket. Ashtrays overflowed on to the thick cream carpet
and two half-empty mugs of tea balanced precariously on top of
the stereo. The moon glowed through the open window making
Felix seem like a boy from a fairy tale. Despite the chaos and
carelessness of the room, it felt enchanted. It was the kind of
bedroom that Peter Pan would have chosen to visit, had he been
into pop music. And if he was Peter, then I was Wendy, and
Amber was Tinkerbell the fairy – furious, jealous and selfish.
Maybe, like Tinkerbell, she would come round in the end. The
thought made me smile, and lessened my first-night nerves.

Felix's record collection dominated the room. Scattered on the
floor by the stereo lay CDs, in and out of their cases. The Beatles,
the Spice Girls, the Sex Pistols, the Chemical Brothers and Abba
lay together in bewildering incoherence. There were more piled

high on the shelves above his bed, and 12-inch singles stacked up on the floor to one side. A photo of Carolyn Stewart was stuck above the door. There was only one other picture in the room – a pencil drawing of a boy with bare feet playing the guitar.

'Val did it,' said Felix. 'Isn't it great?'

'He's very good.'

'Course he is – he's my brother,' said Felix dryly.

He shoved everything off the bed and on to the floor. A black T-shirt found itself nestling in a bowl containing dried-up Weetabix. Felix lit a candle and a cigarette. I was nervous. I may just as well have never slept with anyone before that night. Or maybe I was subconsciously aware that everyone else had been a rehearsal and that here, sitting on the bed beside me, was my baby – my boy. He handed me the cigarette and our fingers touched. I wanted him so much that I almost felt sick. Felix chatted easily, soothing me and watching me smoke. When I had finished he passed me an empty bottle of Becks and I dropped the cigarette into it. He lay down on the bed and pulled me towards him. I trembled a little. He moved closer and closer to me until his features were distorted by my eyes being so close. He started to kiss me.

'You're so beautiful,' I whispered. I had to say it. I didn't even really want to say it – why should I want to give myself away that much? But it was as if I had no choice. I *had* to say it.

Felix looked at me through half-closed eyes. His long, long lashes curled exquisitely upwards and flickered against my cheek.

I pushed my hand inside his shirt, feeling his ribs, how real they were, how real he was. He bit my bottom lip and pulled my hair off my face.

'You can tell me to get lost,' he said into my mouth, 'but I wanted to fuck you from the moment I first saw you.'

He wanted to fuck me. No one had ever, *ever* said that to me before.

It didn't take Felix long to take off his clothes. The moon and the streetlamps outside gave him a milky, exotic brilliance, as if nature herself was adjusting the lighting to show him off to perfection. He stood up next to me and kissed me again, slowly, slowly, holding my face in his hands. He pulled my T-shirt over my head, so quickly, as if the most unbearable thing in the world was to break the kiss for even a second. I could see myself in the mirror that hung on the inside door of Felix's wardrobe. I was amazed by how long my hair was, and by how much taller than me Felix was. I moved my hand down to touch him and felt him shiver. I could see my face, my mouth fused on his, my eyes sleepy and drugged with wanting him so much. I wanted to watch the whole thing because I wasn't sure how else I was going to believe it.

I saw myself take his hand and move his fingers down. Still standing, quivering, I felt how hard he was. *He wants me, he wants me*, I thought. I wanted to scream it out, to laugh hysterically. I wanted him to know, more than anything else, how much I wanted him. I kissed him with such intensity, as though someone had poured petrol on to my soul. I had so much energy it was almost unbearable – how could I express it all, how could I show it all? I heard Felix draw in his breath sharply, so quietly, but I knew what it meant and I was ecstatic. He was amazed and surprised by the potency of my reaction to him. How could I make sure that I was the most special, the most remembered? I saw a glass of water beside his bed and I broke off the kiss and picked it up.

I poured as much as I could into my mouth and then spat it all over his face. I had no time to think about what I was doing, I just did it because I knew that I had to make sure I was different, and it was the nearest prop to hand. Felix took it all in his stride, as if he was expecting it to happen anyway, but he kissed me with even more fire.

'You kiss so well,' he murmured. 'I can't wait to be inside you.'

'I want you so much,' I whispered. 'I want you so much . . .' My words faded into my longing. I needed to drink as much of him in as I could, to take from him as much as I could. I could feel what he was taking out of me, this dream boy with his long fingers and skinny body. We melted on to the bed and he kissed me harder and I pulled at his hair and felt my fingernails dig into his gorgeous back, and he sucked all the dangerous thoughts and the longing and the secrets right out of me like a vampire. Even when he stopped to put on a condom I could feel myself shaking and trembling with the loss of myself. I *lost* myself in him.

When he smiled at me and slid inside me, I felt scorching hot tears running down my face. I was entirely conquered and I knew in that moment that everything else in my life would be measured by how I felt *now*. I had found the purest, most raw nerve in my whole body, and in the instant that I had found it, Felix had violated it. I had been touched. He came with a perfect, delicate violence – his eyes closed, his body resigned to its final consequence.

Afterwards, we lay completely still for what could have been hours, eyes wide open, enveloped in silence – a clamouring silence so full of opinion and contradiction that I could hardly hear myself think. Then, without speaking, Felix slipped his fingers back inside me. I was still a little sore and sensitive and it accentuated the longing and the thrill. I pushed against him and drowned in delight.

Chapter Seven

It seemed preposterous to me that I could walk into work the day
after my first proper night with Felix and find everything the same.
Surely the fact that my life had taken this completely unexpected,
unscripted twist would have changed something – anything – in
the odd cast that made up the rigid structure of every day.

I had been at the museum for two years, but without the
familiar structure of new terms and holidays that I was used to,
it seemed much longer. In truth, the routine and the plodding
sameness of the day, the chat during coffee breaks and the cranky
hopelessness of the tube, completely threw me. I needed to
escape – but where to? I felt that there was nowhere left to
go to. Leonard, my boss, was an overtly camp thirty-nine-year-
old on a constant power trip boosted by the fear of hitting forty.
We would have got on better if he hadn't criticised my clothes
every day since my arrival: 'Too sexy, too hippy, too scruffy;

Lydia, what *are* you wearing today?' In fact, that became a bit of a catch-phrase.

So you see, I had my little place in office life. I was the slightly off-centre court jester in maverick's clothes. Really, I was just wearing what everyone else aged twenty-three was wearing. They were the weird ones. I had to keep reminding myself of that.

I set off for work later than usual, smiling at strangers and finding curious beauty in the sweltering streets, and laughing at the way I had so neatly conformed to stereotype when kicked by love. It had taken Felix to make me realise that every cliché ever spoken about love was true.

I spent the first half hour of the working day sitting at my desk, trying to write down how I felt. It was impossible to come up with anything new. I looked across to where Leonard was sitting, head bowed over a spreadsheet of figures. He looked up at me and frowned.

'You were late in this morning – what were you up to last night?'

'I went to see a band playing in Camden.'

'A band?' Leonard sounded thoroughly confused.

'Yes, you know, music.'

'What kind of music?'

'Not anything you'd like – very loud guitars and lots of drunk people in the crowd.'

'Be that as it may, Lydia –' Leonard had an irritating way of speaking as though he was auditioning for a part in a Jane Austen adaptation – 'there is little excuse for your tardiness this morning. You are right, though, in assuming that I would not be happy in Camden. And it clearly hasn't done you any good. There's a young man involved, I presume?'

'Oh, shut up,' I said, smiling.

Leonard raised one eyebrow an impressive distance towards his hairline. 'Hmmmm . . .'

I scrunched up my scribblings and turned my attention to the day's activities. Felix had promised to call that morning to let me know when we could see each other again. I had left him in bed at nine o'clock. When I woke him to tell him I was leaving for work he had looked at me as if I was speaking Chinese.

'Do you have to go? Leave me your number at work,' he had asked. He smiled at me and within seconds was asleep again.

I nearly leapt out of my skin when Leonard's macaw-like voice cut into my thoughts later that morning. 'David Bowie's holding for you, Lydia.'

'Hello,' I mumbled into the mouthpiece, turning my back on a Miss Livingstone and her party of seventeen from Pembridge Place who had arrived for their tour.

'Lydia – Lydia? Fucking crap signal I've got – can you hear me?' demanded Felix.

'Yes,' I squeaked, raising my voice a fraction.

'We're all meeting tonight at Penelope's.'

'Where is it?' I whispered.

'. . . for a drink . . . Justin . . . e . . . es . . . bar . . . li . . .'

'You're cutting out! I can't hear you!' I began to inform him in that all-too-familiar mobiles-got-the-better-of-us way. I put the phone down. There was no way I was going to embark on a farcical telephonic charade attempting to decipher Felix's words. He'd call back.

'Miss Livingstone, I presume.' Leonard had waded through the hoard of school-kids with a joke that failed to endear him to the set-faced teacher. I pulled myself together and began to organise the group. Fifteen minutes into my tour I began to panic. Why hadn't he called back? I ditched the class for twenty seconds and quickly dialled 1471.

'*You were called, today, at 12.47 hours . . .*' began the smug tone of British Telecom.

'*I know I was fucking called!*' I wanted to shout. No number.

I took my lunch break at one-thirty and just as I was opening my Prêt Chicken Club, Nicky walked into the museum. He was wearing the same clothes as last night, pair of shades on top of his head, pushing his sandy fringe out of the way and making him look like Ronan Keating's little brother. He waved at me and came over to where I was sitting. I stuffed the sandwich between my files and pushed back my hair.

'Felix called me when he realised I was just down the road from you and asked me to drop in and give you the message about tonight. Jesus! What a place to work in!' Nicky's eyes widened at the sight of the vast Triceretops skeleton suspended above his head. 'Don't you have a gift shop? I used to love the shops in these places. You'd bunk off the boring museum bit and smoke fags and then you'd meet everyone in the shop and buy postcards with all the shit from the museum all over them.' Nicky looked dewy-eyed with nostalgia.

'How romantic you make it seem,' I said.

'Lydia – no lunchtime visitors without signing them in and checking with me first,' snapped Leonard, sweeping past in a pinstriped haze of CK Be. I rolled my eyes but Nicky held Leonard's flustered gaze and grinned impishly.

'Anyway, you're to meet us tonight at Penelope's for a drink.'

Leonard was looking over at us, his face a picture of fascinated interest masquerading as disapproval.

'Right – um – who is she?' I whispered.

'Penelope's – the club, silly! You must have been there!' exclaimed Nicky annoyingly, peering into a glass cabinet containing fragments of T-Rex eggs.

'Oh, *that* Penelope's!' I said sarcastically. 'Listen, I don't know the place. Where is it?'

Nicky fished a pencil out of his pocket and scribbled an address on the back of a matchbox. 'I've written my mobile number on the back, too. We'll be there from about ten o'clock. Felix is meeting the guys from Element Records this afternoon so we're all getting together tonight to hear what they think of us. He's a member and he's sticking your name on the guest list, OK?' He glanced at his watch. 'Shit! I've got to go, I'm meeting some girl who needs a drummer for a three-day cruise around the Greek Islands.'

'Hey, Nicky, before you go.' I indicated that he should follow me into the museum shop. 'Go on,' I said expansively. 'Choose something. Live out your childhood again.' Nicky chose a huge black marker pen with a snarling dinosaur head on the lid.

'Very Freudian, I'm sure,' he muttered.

Leonard, who was rummaging on the floor looking for his glasses, seemed rather too interested in Nicky's psychology. I pushed Nicky towards the door. The last thing I needed was my boss getting a crush on my new boyfriend's drummer.

'See you later, crocodile,' chirped Nicky in Leonard's direction, picking up his glasses for him and affording him another cheeky smile. Shades back down, he sloped crookedly into the sunlight.

*   *   *

Later that night, there I was, mingling in unhappy alliance with the fifty or so disciples of Penelope's who gravitated towards its discreet entrance in a well-lit door in Soho. Lunch breaks spent jealously guarding their metre of sun in Hyde Park had given the crowd a curiously Mediterranean feel. Guilty tans, I thought. We're not meant to want them any more.

Someone's wooden wedged platform sandal cracked down on to my open toes. I turned to see a radiant girl with short red hair wearing no more than a pale blue see-through T-shirt and matching hot pants, giggling with her boyfriend, oblivious to the damage she had caused to my feet.

I'm overdressed, I thought, as the crowd surged forwards again. Under my white shirt I was wearing a black string bikini top. With as much cool as I could muster, I unbuttoned the shirt and tied it around my waist. I caught a glimpse of myself in a tall boy's shades. I looked all right, I decided. Paler than the majority of those around me, but interesting.

I pushed past the redhead to the front of the queue.

'I'm on the guest list?' I said, foolishly letting my voice rise in a questioning tone.

'Name?'

'Lydia Lewis. I'm on Felix's list – he's a member.'

'Yes, we know Felix,' said the bloke on the door, as if the mere idea of *not* knowing Felix was absurd. 'But there's no Layla on his list,' he said firmly.

'Lydia,' I corrected him.

'I can't see your name, love, you'll have to join the back of the line.'

'But I'm down there, I know I am.' I felt a rapid flush of panic.

Suddenly I noticed Amber walking down the stairs to the club with princess-like authority.

'Hang on,' I said to my pal on the door. 'Amber — *Amber*! Hello!' I shouted to her retreating back. She turned, and I *swear* she saw me before turning around again and whispering something to the girl she was with. They both laughed. Pal On Door smirked in an 'I've seen it all before' manner.

'Sorry, darlin',' he said.

Quite irrationally, I felt my eyes fill with tears. I swallowed hard, but it was too late. A fat tear, weighty and hot with embarrassment and anger, shot out of my eye and landed on the guest list that my pal was holding. It landed on Felix's name. It smudged. My pal looked at me in amazement. Then, with a theatrical gesture that propelled me completely into Penelope's, he smiled.

'Sweet Cinders, you shall go to the ball,' he announced under his breath. 'Just don't let my management know I've let you in or I'll be the bloody pumpkin!' He grinned delightedly at his analogy.

I was in.

I couldn't find the others, of course. And after the incident with Amber, I wasn't even sure I wanted to find them. Why hadn't my name been on the list? Had Felix forgotten? I wandered from room to room, up and down three flights of stairs, and in and out of the Ladies' like I was experiencing the club in virtual reality. Clusters of hyper-cool girls sat round black and white marble tables on black and white striped velvet chairs. The *really* cool people, who never had problems with the guest list and looked as though they had grown up in here, wore long, slouchy trousers and hippy sandals with faded T-shirts and preppy glasses. Most drank vodka with mixers – there was the occasional table of champagne drinkers, but these groups looked less at home and more like they were enjoying an evening out.

The music changed from room to room, confusing me with its diversity. Downstairs, in the den-like lure of the basement, where the crowd collapsed into each other on squashy sofas and huge cushions, I recognised the hypnotic strains of Massive Attack. On the ground floor, where the main bar rose like a naughty treasure chest above a sea of people, the crowd argued, shrieked and shouted over an inoffensive selection of seventies songs – Diana Ross, the Bee Gees and Donna Summer drifted calmly in and out of their consciousness. Upstairs, a tiny area next to the DJ formed a little dance floor for those who were bored with talking. Underworld boomed from the speakers as I stuck my head around the door in search of Felix.

'Is there a VIP area?' I shouted to the barman. He nodded and pointed up with his finger. There was another level to the club, and knowing Felix (or did I?) he would be there. I looked up the staircase and relief flooded over me. I felt that familiar injection of adrenalin. I had spotted him, hands in his pockets, talking to Amber. He caught my eye at that moment and ran down the stairs towards me.

'Lydia! Where have you been? Did you have problems getting in? Your name was down, you should have been OK.' I looked at his face, all anxious and questioning, then at Amber who was picking at her nails.

'I was fine, I got in fine. I just bumped into a couple of old friends on the way up here.' There was no way I was going to let Amber know that I had experienced any trouble on the door. But the closer I looked at her, the more convinced I became that it was she who had taken my name off the list. Bitch. Felix was pulling me towards him.

'Well, now I've found you we'll go back upstairs and carry on with dinner.'

Typical, I thought. Not content with being a VIP in the trendiest club in London, he has to *eat* here too.

'Nicky and Justin are ordering burgers and chips – what do you want? The food's OK here. No candy-floss though.' He smiled at me encouragingly – he wanted me to be all right, didn't he? – then pushed me into the exclusive zone which was a haven of low-key understatement in comparison to the heady mayhem downstairs. Justin and Nicky were giggling together.

'I just can't bear the idea of losing my hair at thirty,' Nicky was saying.

'It doesn't matter about losing your hair, it's the face that counts,' interjected Amber.

'So you're in *real* trouble, Nick,' said Justin. Justin looked odd when he laughed; it seemed out of keeping with his usual impassive countenance. But I learned that night that he was prone to fits of hysterics. His laughter was uncontrolled and infectious and seemed to explode against his will. He was frighteningly appealing when he was smiling, but I still feared him.

I wanted to put my shirt back on, but seeing Amber, smouldering in a clingy black tank top and scarlet micro-mini-skirt, I decided against it.

'What do you want to drink? And how's that gorgeous boss of yours?' Deadpan as ever, Nicky passed me his bowl of chips. I took one and dipped it in tomato ketchup.

'My boss is in love with you, I think, which makes my life very hard,' I replied, thanking Nicky silently for his friendliness.

He looked slightly bored. 'Isn't this place a nightmare? Why the hell we had to come here I do not know—'

'Shut up, Nick, Felix is about to tell us what Element said.' Amber cut into the conversation. Felix looked around the table.

'Listen, should I go?' I asked suddenly. It felt wrong, being included in this conversation. Why me? I had nothing to do with the band, nothing at all.

'No, stay, stay,' Felix said. 'I asked you to come tonight and I want you here now. You saw the last gig so you can tell me if what Hooch Benedict said was true.'

'Hooch?'

'He's the head of A and R at Element,' explained Nicky, 'Very important bloke with a fucking sad name.'

Felix took a deep breath. I listened to him as intently as the others, feeling everything that they were feeling, wanting the story to turn out well for the sake of Moja. Only my emotions were confused by the power of sheer lust. I wanted to kiss Felix the *entire* time.

'I went for the meeting at two o'clock, got there early, so sat in the car listening to the demo to get me in the mood. I walked in at five to two, announced myself to the receptionist, waited for ten minutes downstairs, read the *NME*, and got taken up to Hooch's room. He offered me coffee and cigarettes and then he put on the demo.' Felix paused to light another fag, hands shaking. 'He listened to it *so* loud. I could hear every second of the fucking energy and time and money and sweat that had gone into it just pouring out of his stereo. I wanted to cry. I was like – oh my God, I've never heard this sound so fucking great, and Hooch was sitting there, tapping his feet, swaying in his chair, closing his eyes, staring at the stereo . . .' Felix looked up, shaking his head.

'All I could think was that this is what I live for – this moment, hearing Moja sound like this. I've played the demo three hundred times, but I've never heard it sound like it did in that room.'

'What did he say when it finished?' prompted Justin impatiently.

'He listened to all three tracks. Then he switched off the stereo. And he said, "Well, you've obviously worked hard and there are some good musicians in there, but I just don't think the songs are there, to be honest, I'm really not convinced".' Felix looked mutinous. 'He said that the songs sounded like something that had been released but had made no impact and were on their way to the bargain bin. Then I asked him what he had thought of us live and he said we sounded like – like . . .' Felix stopped, as if gagging on the words. 'He said we reminded him of T'Pau.' There was a horrified silence around the table. Amber stood up and walked across the room, her hand over her mouth. Felix was still going '. . . I said, "Well, actually, I liked T'Pau in 1987, but I don't see how we're anything like them." Then I got up and left. The guy's a wanker, and he'll pay for this.'

Amber looked stunned. 'T'Pau!' she kept saying.

'Fuck it, let's cover "China In Your Hand",' said Nicky. And suddenly they all exploded into fits of giggles. Felix, head in hands, was shaking with mirth at the end of the table. Amber was letting out little screeches of hilarity every few seconds, and Nicky and Justin were thumping the table, practically crying with laughter.

Once again I felt that strange sense of detachment. I envied their confidence, their unity, their conviction. But I had made a decision that was going to change everything. It was going to be me who got them where they wanted to go. I had

99

to be the one to make it happen. I was involved now. No turning back.

When we left, swaying and clattering down the stairs, it was almost light. Amber and Justin took a cab together to Justin's flat in Fulham. Nicky and Felix flagged down the next taxi for me. Just before I stepped in, Felix pulled me back.

'Quick,' he said, 'close your eyes and breathe in. Now pretend that it's a cold morning in October. Can you feel the winter?' I shivered. He was right. I could *feel* the winter.

Chapter Eight

My so-called life, pre-Felix, pre-Moja, caught up with me the next day at work, and sounded mighty annoyed.

'Where have you *been*, Lydia?' asked Alexandra, the pushiest of the All Bar One Fulham crowd. 'Why haven't you been calling back? Where were you on Tuesday night?' I had completely forgotten that Tuesday night was usually reserved for dinner at Alex's, followed by some bar or other until closing time.

'I went to see a band play in Camden,' I said, doodling Moja on the *Daily Mail*.

'A band?' Alex sounded as confused as Leonard had done. 'What do you mean? What about us?'

'I'm sure you survived a night without me,' I said briskly. Then, knowing how to placate her I asked, 'How have you been, Alex? How's your boss been treating you this week?' She was off.

'. . . so Dan and Rachel *both* knew before me,' she finished, fifteen minutes later. 'Can you believe it?'

'No.'

'Well, I just think they can all go off and gossip about me as much as they like, I mean, I don't care. Who wants to sit around all day gossiping?'

'Alex, I gotta go,' I said. 'Leonard's coming. Look, I'll call you later.'

'Well, what about next Tuesday, then?' asked Alex.

'Er, I dunno. Look, I'll call you soon.' I could sense Alex's suspicion.

'Suit yourself,' she said. I could imagine her shrugging as she said it.

'I think I will,' I said. 'Bye Alex.'

Nicky called in again that afternoon.

'Hey girl,' he said, leaning over my desk. I was checking details for our new web-site while thinking about Felix, and nearly jumped out of my skin. There was no warning phone call; Nicky just appeared like the Cheshire Cat, his familiar shades over his eyes.

'What are you doing?' I hissed, 'I'm at work.'

'I can see,' he said. 'I didn't know you wore glasses.'

'I only wear them to watch TV and drive,' I said defensively.

'I think they're great,' said Nicky. 'Ooh, and they're Armani, very posh.'

'Why are you here?' I asked. Nicky made me feel slightly confused, with his habit of materialising out of nowhere. Yet at the same time, he was part of the new world that I had found, part of Felix, and so my uneasiness was coupled with excitement and anticipation.

'I'm doing some session work for a band who rehearse just down the road from here,' he said. 'I thought I'd come and rattle your cage,' he added, peering round at my computer screen.

'*The Tyrannosaurus Rex was the largest carnivorous dinosaur living seventy million years ago*,' he read. 'I mean, we've been looking for a record deal for three years – these guys were kicking around seventy *million* years ago. It puts things in perspective, don't you think? Wow.' It was, as ever, hard to tell if Nicky was being serious or not.

'But I doubt any of them were ever in a signed band,' I said.

'Yeah they were – T Rex had a deal.'

Nicky was one of those people who became even more cheeky and flippant on the buzz of no sleep. I smiled at him.

'Look, I've got to get on with stuff here,' I said. 'I was late in this morning so I've got some catching up to do.'

'OK. I'll leave you in peace for the next five million years,' said Nicky. 'But I'm in this area for the next few days, so watch out.'

Leonard was approaching, quickening his stride as he spotted Nicky.

'Lydia, I really must stress that personal visits need to be restricted to your lunch hour.'

'I was just on my way out,' said Nicky, taking off his shades and winking at Leonard. 'Look after her,' he said ridiculously. 'See you around, hound,' he said to us both. 'Hey, and I wouldn't tell Felix I've been in to see you, he'll probably get in a strop.' And just as suddenly as he had appeared, he was gone.

'Lydia, you really must try to control your new friend,'

said Leonard. But I hardly took in a word of what he was saying.

Nicky *was* my new friend, and nothing could dent my excitement. I didn't fancy him in any way, but he was so different to anyone I had ever met before, strangely asexual despite his flirtatious nature, and singularly unpredictable. The fact that I liked Nicky so much elevated my already rocketing feelings for Felix, and made him even more delectable. Then, in turn, this panicked me because I knew that I had never felt anything like this before, and I knew that I just had to keep him.

I left work still in a daze, running out from the delicious, dark cool of the museum into the August afternoon and feeling the heat hit my body like a fist. London always looked astonished by the summer, I decided. It lacked the relaxed, siesta-saturated nonchalance of the Mediterranean, and felt overheated and claustrophobic, embarrassed by the languid nakedness that came from the heat. I scampered down the steps to the underground. I felt relieved to have left work for the day, relieved to be travelling. It calmed my nerves, my jittery impatience. Clarity seemed to come with movement.

The key thing about Moja, I thought, was their absolute conviction that they were going to be successful. The T'Pau comparison had generated hilarity rather than concern. Justin had commented that he could hear himself relaying Hooch Benedict's words to Q magazine in three months. Three months. That was confidence for you. Felix was nervous, but still entirely sure that it was only a matter of time before the band were recognised. Nicky had told me that Moja were far bigger than just a band who played in grim pubs.

'Lives hang in the balance,' he had said, alcohol fuelling his dramatic hyperbole. 'It's not that we want to make it – we *have* to.'

Until I met the band, I had never known anyone who had wanted to change the world through song. To the outsider (and I was still an outsider) it came down to ego. Amber, for all her luminous cuteness, was intensely selfish. Justin was deeply self-conscious in a manufactured kind of way, and Nicky, audacious, sweet and charming, had no money and had admitted that he was in it for just that reason. Felix was the one who puzzled me most of all. He was generous with his time and money, completely lacking in prejudice and, extraordinarily, showed no signs of vanity. They were the strangest combination.

I arrived home and fumbled around for my keys. I had to call Felix. I had to know his reason for wanting to do it all. He answered immediately.

'Felix, it's me, Lydia.'

'Hello darling, I thought you were going to be the woman from Element calling me. Were you OK last night? You looked so utterly sexy, I wish we could have been alone. Let me take you out soon.' (You had to hand it to the boy, I thought, he was pretty smooth.)

'Um, I'd love to meet later. Listen, there's something I need to ask you.'

'Yeah?'

'Why do you want to get a record deal? Why not just carry on playing for fun? Is it because you want fame or money or what?'

'"I Don't Like Mondays".'

'What?'

105

'"I Don't Like Mondays".'

I took a deep breath. 'The Boomtown Rats. 1979?'

'My God! I am so excited you knew that.'

'What about it?'

'That's the reason it started. I was four years old. The song entered my entire being. It's the ultimate goal – reaching nirvana in three and a half minutes. Not through sex or drugs but through *music*.' It was amazing how Felix could talk like this and sound so convincing. 'That's why I need it, Lydia. To make sure that Moja gets through like that. Because I can't *not* do it. It has to be done. It's as simple as that. No question.'

'You can't just pretend that you know someone to get an interview. People aren't that thick – even people who work in record companies,' said Emma that night as we ate baked beans on toast in front of MTV. I was *starving*, having worked out that I had not eaten a proper meal since I met Felix. I was still completely unable to eat anything in front of him.

Emma, who was applying for a job in public relations, was working with great enthusiasm on my relationship with Felix. I confessed that I wanted to be the one who got Moja their record deal.

'Don't you think that if it's that easy, then all the bands who want record deals would have them?' Emma asked with her mouth full. 'If all you need to do is phone up and say "I manage a great band, please sign them up".'

'But Moja are different,' I said.

'Every manager in the country says that about their band.'

'But you've seen what they're like. They have everything – the beautiful girl, the rock-god guitarist, the druggie bass player and – Nicky. It's already there.'

'I don't know what I think of that Justin. He's a loose cannon. He's got that wild look about him, like he can't be trusted.'

'I would have thought that the last thing he needs to be is trustworthy. He's in a band for God's sake!'

'Look, I'm just giving you my personal opinion, and I don't really know anything about the industry anyway. You have even *less* of a clue, by the way, which makes your plan completely crazy.'

'Just crazy enough to work,' I said grimly. 'I'm going to make it happen for them. They're *artists* – which I suppose goes some way to justifying how mad they are – but they need someone clear-headed, with a business mind, to make the initial moves for them. You're right – I don't have a *clue* about the industry, but this is going to work.'

Emma looked doubtful. 'And you certainly don't possess the business mind,' she said cuttingly.

'Ah, but Moja don't know that,' I said. 'I'm going to call Felix now and suggest it to him. He can say no if he wants.'

'Good luck to you. And please – reserve me a seat on Concorde.'

'Don't be all sarcastic. It was you who took me to see them in the first place, telling me how wonderful they were.'

'Sure, sure, but there is a big, *big* difference between the Lemon in Camden and Wembley Stadium. A couple of hundred thousand people in fact,' she added smugly.

'But it *does* happen. It happens all the time,' I cried, waving my hand towards the television where the Spice Girls were performing their new single.

107

'And what do you suppose the industry is going to think about their privileged backgrounds? They *hate* that kind of shit. They want poverty, rags to riches, ex-addicts, orphans – not the kind of people who loaf around the King's Road in the school holidays, smoking Silk Cut at the Feathers Ball and doing work experience in Kensington Palace.'

'Felix is the only one who went to boarding school,' I explained patiently.

'Bull*shit*! Justin and Felix *met* at boarding school. Justin left in the sixth form to do his A levels in London and dropped out after one term—'

'Great! That's rebellion for you,' I said triumphantly.

'Oooh! Any minute now you're going to tell me that Amber was born in a cardboard box with nothing but her astonishing beauty to cling to.'

'I don't know about Amber, but she's a bitch and she's had loads of sex which suggests that she probably went to a convent in Hampshire. I'll need to investigate there. Metivier is a very exotic surname,' I conceded. 'Now Nicky *definitely* didn't go to boarding school. He never has any money, and he wants to make it for that very reason. He told me.'

'He may never have any money, but I can assure you his family does. Ben and Dan Lawson have known Nicky's family for years. Apparently they threw the most unbelievable twenty-first birthday party for Nicky's sister – Catherine, I think she's called. Anyway, Ben talked about nothing else for weeks afterwards. They had the party at their pad in Suffolk. Ben said there were bouncy castles and vodka fountains and a band playing Abba covers and breakfast cooked at four in the morning in the marquee overlooking the sunrise over the lake.'

Emma's face took on a faraway look. 'Sounds pretty wild, don't you think?'

'Well, why doesn't Nicky ever see his family then? They sound all right to me.'

'There are six kids — Nicky's the youngest, I think. I don't know the full story, I just know that there was some kind of massive falling out and Nicky never really speaks to any of them any more. Or maybe they never really speak to him, I don't know. Maybe they hate the fact that he's a drummer. I'm not sure I'd think it was very cool if I'd sent my son off to the most exclusive school in the country and he turned around and said he was joining a band.'

'Well, I think he's amazing,' I said.

'Is he gay?'

'I don't know that. I don't know him that well.'

'He looks like he could be.'

'Or that could be an act.'

'Unlikely. What you need to do,' said Emma, 'is find out as much as possible about all of them if you want to look after them. What happens if you get them the deal then discover that Justin's got a love-child in Australia, or Amber's had a sex change or something.'

'I wish Amber *would* have a sex change, it would make my life much easier.'

'So, let's summarise,' said Emma. 'You've got a druggie who flunked his exams, a bitch with an attitude, a sexually confused drummer, and Carolyn Stewart's son. Don't worry, it could be worse,' she said with a shrug.

'How?'

'They could be rich.'

'But you've just told me that they're all loaded.'

'Exactly.'

I called Felix at Stanley Road. I could hear Amber and Justin shouting in the background above the faint strains of Robbie Williams.

'Hello, the Savoy Grill,' said Felix.

'Ha, ha. Can I book a table for two for tomorrow night?'

'Lydia darling, how are you, sweetheart? I was about to call you – *shut up, Amber, for God's sake turn it down!* Do you like Robbie Williams?' he demanded.

It was another of those 'important' questions. I had to get the answer right.

'You know what? I like his style but he's not my scene.'

'I bet you fancy him.'

'I don't actually.'

'Yes you do, *everyone* fancies Robbie.'

'I always preferred the little one in Take That.'

'Mark Owen,' said Felix immediately, as if I had challenged him to remember the name. He was full of that – pop-quizzing the whole time.

'Yeah, Mark.'

'I *know* you fancy Robbie. Come on, you can admit it to me.'

I was laughing now at his insistence. And I really *didn't* think Robbie was very sexy. 'Whatever, Felix. You can think whatever you want,' I said expansively.

'Hang on, Lyds, I'm moving phones.' There was a clunk as Felix put down the receiver and I turned to Emma.

'He thinks I'm in love with Robbie.'

'Watch out,' warned Emma, opening a blueberry Fruit Corner

and spilling it down her white T-shirt. 'Oh shit! Who designed these cartons?' she wailed.

'Why watch out?' I persisted.

'Because he's already getting edgy about you looking at other boys. You may think he's joking but he's not, I promise you.'

'Lyds.' It was Felix back on the line. 'I'm in my room. Why don't you come over? I need a break from Tom and Jerry downstairs.' Just imagining him lying on his bed, abbreviating my name and inviting me to his house made me feel dizzy. Or maybe it was the lack of sleep. I had promised Emma that we would watch a video together and I needed to call Frankie in New York.

'I won't come over tonight, but I really want to meet you tomorrow. I've got this idea, you see,' I began.

'About what?'

'I think I can help you get the deal.'

'Oh yeah?' Felix sounded doubtful.

'I want to get a meeting at Conspiracy. I can pretend to be your manager and get the right people along to see you.'

'I don't see why you would have any more success than I've had. Lyds, you don't even *know* anyone at Conspiracy,' said Felix, perfectly reasonably.

'But you can't sell yourselves. I can. I've seen you play. I know how good you are. If you let me try, I really think I could help you – I want to help you. That night at the Lemon just blew me away. You're so much better than every single act on *Top Of The Pops* tonight. You should be writing and rehearsing. Just let me try for you, please Felix. If it doesn't work, that's it, and it's up to you again.'

Felix laughed. 'I'll have to check with the others.'

'Of course.' I sighed.

'Amber?' guessed Felix.

'I'm not exactly her favourite girl in the world.'

'She'll get over it. She doesn't mean half the things she says.' Touched though I was by Felix's loyalty to Amber, I was quick to deduce that even if she didn't mean half the things she said, that still left another half of intentional rudeness.

'Look, I'll meet you tomorrow in Tower Records, Piccadilly Circus.' He could have told me to meet him on Pluto and I would have been there.

'Six o'clock?' I suggested.

'Fine. I'll talk you through Conspiracy then. Hang on, Amber's just walked in.' I could hear her muffled voice as Felix covered the mouthpiece with his hand.

'What did she want?' I asked, trying not to sound too inquisitive.

'Oh, she wants to get out a video but Nicky hasn't returned the last one so she can't. And Blockbuster think that Nicky is me because he's used my account so many times. Apparently I owe them over sixty quid,' he added in a surprised tone.

'So you better get this deal so Nicky can afford to pay off this sort of debt,' I said slyly. 'What is this film that he's had out for weeks anyway?' I asked, wondering if it would give me any insight into Nicky's past.

'*So I Married An Axe Murderer*,' said Felix.

'Oh.'

'See you then, Lyds. Six o'clock?'

'I'll be there.' Clunk. Felix had already hung up. Like American soap stars, he apparently regarded saying goodbye at the end of a call unnecessary.

I went to bed humming 'Angels'.

Chapter Nine

London groaned with sunstroke as I took the number 94 bus from Bayswater and arrived for my meeting with Felix early and sticky in denim mini-skirt and platform espadrilles. What section of Tower would Felix be most impressed to find me in? I wondered, wishing I could sit down. What a place to meet! Tourists gabbled in baseball caps and sandals, flocking from the tube station into the comfortingly familiar mecca of MacDonalds and Burger King. Inside the store, shop assistants sang along to The Cardigans like robots. I mooched into Rock and Pop and flipped through Jamiroquai's back catalogue. I saw Felix come in, wading his way through crowds, talking into the hands-free wire of his mobile, hair tied back in the pineapple again, nails repainted the same shade of green. He wore a pair of faded Bermuda shorts and a T-shirt with 'Enjoy Cocaine' in the Coca-Cola writing on the front. He spotted me and ended his call, switched off his phone and pulled me towards him.

'I was right on time for the first time in my life and you were early,' he said, leading me out into the street again.

'I've only just got here, I promise,' I said, not wanting to appear too eager.

Felix led me to a sandwich bar next to the Café Royale. Even the most mundane of tasks, such as ordering a cheese and tomato bap, were cloudy with stardust when I was with him.

'Why Piccadilly Circus in August?' I asked, peeling my bare legs off the high stool I was sitting on.

'It's important to see London through the eyes of those who come here and never get beyond WC1.' Felix gestured towards two travellers, a boy and a girl at the next table, rucksacks dusty beside them on the floor. 'You in London long?' he addressed them, mid-mouthful.

'Three days,' replied the boy in thickly accented English.

'Where are you from?' inquired Felix.

'Rome,' said the boy, smiling a little smugly, knowing how the rest of the world adored Italy.

'*Ma Lei parla Italiano?*'

'*Certo. Mio babbo e di Cinque Terre.*'

'*Cinque Terre! Non ci credo! La prima giornata a Londra e c'incontriamo con un'italiano!*'

'*Mi manca troppo l'Italia.*'

'*Ehi! Deve ritornare. Presto. Venga da noi!*'

I was smiling and nodding to the girl as if I understood the conversation. I noticed her surreptitiously swivelling her seat round towards the mirrored walls to check her appearance. I had never been out with a boy who had that effect on girls, yet when people met Felix it was instinctive within the female psyche. Meet Felix, check face.

Felix turned to me and explained a little. 'I was saying to Carlos and Marina that they should get out of the West End and stay in Notting Hill or Camden for a few days.'

'Great idea. You don't want to be in the West End at this time of year.'

'Thank you so much for your help, you are very kind!' said Carlos, and I could imagine their relief at having spoken to Felix. They wouldn't forget him now. They were standing and arranging their backpacks.

'*Ciao!*'

'*Ciao!*'

And they vanished, laughing, back on to the streets.

'I love hearing you speak Italian,' I said.

'I knew they were OK because I noticed he was listening to Blondie, *Parallel Lines*,' said Felix. He paused. 'I gave them my number and a flyer for our next gig. I'm so well trained in getting a crowd together whenever we play. There's actually a real talent to it.'

'In what way?' I asked, trying to get a covert glance in the mirror to see how my hair was looking. It had refused to go straight that morning and had fluffed up under the hairdryer.

'Well, we've been playing the same old venues for the past three years so it's kind of hard to fill these places up every time. You have to have very serious strategies for every gig – cool flyers, a change of venue every time so that you can give the crowd somewhere different to moan about, and of course, new songs. We always need new songs. And that's where the weight falls on my shoulders. Justin and Nicky don't have a clue how

difficult it is sometimes. Not that it could ever be any other way
– *I* write and that's the way it is. But it's hard because I write for
a girl, which is strange in itself, and I have to worry about what
Nick and Justin are going to be playing.' He took a large bite of
his roll. 'So you see,' he went on, 'I couldn't really have a proper
job, not really. How could I get anything creative done?'

'You'd find a way if you had to,' I said. Felix looked per-
plexed.

'Of course,' he said. 'But I *don't* have to. So I get to spend my
time working on songs for the band, luckily for all involved.'

'Do you ever write with Amber?' I asked, not really wanting
to imagine Felix and Amber snuggled up together, coming up
with suggestive lyrics and giggling a lot.

'No. Absolutely not.' Felix shook his pineapple violently.
'Never.'

'Is it hard for you to collaborate with anyone?' I asked.

'I don't know. I've never really tried. Amber and I attempted
to write together once but ended up— Oh, it was awful . . .'
He inspected his nails and trailed off.

'Ended up what?' I bleated.

'Oh, we ended up in the most horrendous argument,' confessed
Felix. 'I sound really anal, but she wanted to rhyme "home" with
"alone", which isn't a pure rhyme – and very unoriginal – and I
told her she couldn't and she said that she was singing the song so
I should shut up and listen to her for once, and I said that I wasn't
prepared to play guitar for her if she wouldn't take in anything
I was trying to say.'

'So what happened?' I asked, riveted.

'I just wrote a whole load of new words and told her to
get on with it. She knew I was right. The girl can sing, but

my God, she can't write songs. It's very important to know your place within the band, you know? Amber's the front girl – she's the one that everyone focuses on, and when she's on stage she's so creative and so beautiful, that's when she can be in charge. But I'm the one supplying her with the tunes and the words. I'm the one who gives her what she needs to perform.'

'Don't you find it weird, writing for a girl?' I asked.

'It's not weird because I know Amber so well. I know the way that she thinks, I know the way that she reacts to things. I watch her and Justin and I write about them together. I'm used to it now. Anyway, you know what I think?'

'What?'

'*The early bird catches the worm, but the second mouse gets the cheese.*' We both giggled about this completely random comment for a bit. I could tell that Felix wanted to move on from talking about Amber; he liked to keep any conversation in a constant state of flux.

'Did you find that boy good-looking?' he asked me. 'The Italian boy.'

'Not at all,' I said in surprise. 'Why?'

'I just thought you might like that look.'

'What, the sweaty backpacker look?'

'No, the Italian thing. Girls like that, don't they?'

'I don't know. Why, were you jealous?'

'No,' said Felix defensively. 'Not at all. I just saw you looking at him.'

'Felix, from what I've heard, I have far more to be nervous about than you,' I said.

'That's just not true,' he protested, grinning. Then, changing

117

the subject briskly, 'How's *work?*' He pronounced the word with a flourish of novelty in his tone. I laughed.

'It's OK. I'm still not used to it. University is absolutely the worst preparation for a nine-to-five lifestyle.'

'I just cannot imagine it.' Felix shook his head. 'Wow. Getting up every morning at seven-thirty. I just could not deal with it.' He giggled and took my hands in his. I noticed that his were covered in biro.

'What does it say?' I asked, opening them out so that I could read the words. '*I need to feel each moment* – what does that say? *Magnified?*'

'Yeah, just an idea for a new song.' Felix pulled his hands away and looked embarrassed.

'What moment do you need to feel magnified?' I asked him. My heart was hammering again. Felix pulled the pineapple out and pushed his hands through his hair.

'I thought of it last night,' he said. 'After we spoke on the phone. I went to bed thinking about you. Lydia, this is not normal for me, you have to understand.' He spoke as if he was explaining something very complex and uncomfortable. 'I'm not used to having someone on my mind.'

'What makes me different?' I asked softly.

'I don't know. I'm as confused as you are,' he said, almost in irritation.

'Don't fight it, feel it,' I said.

'Primal Scream, 1991,' Felix said automatically. 'Great track. But you know what? Talking of Primal Scream –' Were we? I wondered – 'I never, *ever* liked "Loaded". It drives me mental. Isn't that just the worst thing to have to admit? It was such a moment-defining record.'

'A moment-*magnifying* record,' I suggested, wondering how to steer Felix off the subject of music and back round to how he felt about me and him. The little café was almost full now. Felix moved his seat closer to mine to allow a couple of students to pass. Outside, the traffic lurched through the lights and swooned in the heat.

'What's the song that you're just too embarrassed to admit that you don't like?' asked Felix, completely missing my hint. I rolled with him.

'It's not that I don't like it, but I never thought that "Imagine" was as great as everyone else did.' I watched Felix's face fall in disbelief. 'I mean,' I added hastily, 'I just feel that John Lennon recorded better songs. Although the song that I *really* never liked that everyone else went crazy over was "Wannabe".'

'The Spice Girls?' asked Felix incredulously. 'Oh, now you're just being silly. *Everyone* loves that song.'

He had that aura of pixie naughtiness about him again, like he had in the bathroom when I first saw him. Maybe it was the way he moved that made me think that. He was always moving, always aquiline – long fingers touching, eyes darting and searching, ears pricked up to catch any conversation he might be interested in, regardless of who it was coming from. He could switch conversation topics without drawing breath. I was to learn that Felix was quite happy to converse with anyone at all – taxi drivers, pedestrians, the homeless guy who he invited into Stanley Road for a whisky one night. You could see it in the way he derived satisfaction from the smallest of tasks – cracking open a Summer Fruits Oasis was pleasing to him. He seemed to be the least cynical boy I had ever met. He not only embraced life, but he clung on to

119

everything in his past with an air of delighted nostalgia – even the bad stuff.

We left the sandwich bar and went to the pub. Felix gave me a pound to choose four songs from the juke box as he bought two pints of Guinness. As I pressed in my selection, I knew that I was adding to the already thriving soundtrack of Felix and I. We had Pulp from Manchester, just before we first met. Then The Beatles from the car journey back to London the next day. There was Madonna from my first visit to Stanley Road, and Robbie Williams from last night's phone call. So I added Catatonia 'Road Rage', The Stereophonics 'Local Boy In The Photograph', 'Teardrop' by Massive Attack, and finally 'All You Good Good People' by Embrace. It was a fairly standard selection, but Felix loved it.

The pub was full, with no common thread running through any of the crowd. There were men and women in smart suits, drinking gin and tonics at the end of a hard day's work; peroxide blonde secretaries drinking Baileys on ice, which looked delicious; old men laughing toothless laughs and guzzling beer; tourists in crisp jeans, their foreign voices chattering by the bar; underage kids smoking Benson and Hedges and loitering by the juke box. Then there was Felix and me.

As 'Road Rage' cut into the babble of voices we danced. It was the perfect song for that pub, that night, that heat. Felix and I sang at the tops of our voices and he grabbed me around the waist and we shrieked with laughter as he danced me around the pub, spilling our drinks down our arms. He was an amazing dancer, kind of like Robbie crossed with Fred Astaire, and he knew every word to every song I had chosen.

By the time we got to the Embrace song, Felix was practically addressing the crowd. *'Lose all your fears they are keeping you down, you won't have to fake it while I'm around,'* he sang, fag hanging out of his mouth, his beauty and his energy glittering in his eyes. It was an extraordinary sight – Felix singing, word perfect, totally unselfconscious. Once again I marvelled that he could pull off such behaviour and not look silly. It was as if he was born to live his life in three-minute pop video sequences.

When the song finished, there was a faint ripple of applause that got louder and louder. 'Go sexy!' shouted one of the peroxide girls, and her friends giggled and nudged her.

Felix grinned at them. 'Thanks very much, but that's it, I'm afraid,' he said. 'But – I am in a band myself,' he added.

'I knew it!' said the barman. 'You're in that Boyzone, aren't you? I saw you on telly last night.'

'Alas, I am not a member of the great Boyzone,' said Felix. 'In fact, my band haven't quite made it yet, but we're playing next week in Camden, and you're all invited!' With that, he reached into his back pocket and pulled out a handful of crumpled Moja flyers for their next gig. Hands reached out and grabbed at the bits of paper. The peroxide babe took about seven.

'Can I buy you a drink?' she asked, swooping up an octave and back down in her questioning tone.

'It's very sweet of you, but we must get going,' replied Felix. 'Songs to write, drugs to take . . .' he added with an ironic shrug of the shoulders.

'Oh I see!' said the girl coquettishly. 'Very rock 'n' roll.'

Felix took my hand and we left the pub. I could sense the peroxide babe's eyes burning into me as she tried to deduce what Felix could possibly want with me when he could have her. But he does want me, I reminded myself. He really wants me. We walked out of the pub like we were famous. Isn't that cool? We left the pub like we were *famous*!

Felix had given me the *Music Week* Directory in the pub and had told me to do what I wanted with it. I got home at two in the morning, reeling off the walls in a haze of vodka, and sat down at Emma's computer to write a letter to a Symon Grills, the head of A&R at Conspiracy. I also noted that the Managing Director was a bloke called Douglas Carter. At that point I was sober enough to realise that the only way I would have the nerve to send such a letter was if I was in a state of drunkenness.

The letter was full of mistakes when I read it back, but spell-check was invented for people like me.

> *Dear Symon,*
>
> *How are you? Douglas has asked me to organise a lunch with you regarding the band I am managing at the moment, Moja. They are quite simply the best new band you will see all year. We have faced considerable recording and publishing interest, but Douglas and I go back a very long way (ask him about that New Year's Eve!) and I feel that it is only right to let you take a look at the band before anyone else. I have heard great things about your considerable talent from a number of close friends in the industry. Moja are great fans of the label and have talked for some time about working with you.*
>
> *Look forward to hearing from you, regards to Douglas.*
> *Yours,*
> *Lydia Lewis, Manager, Moja.*

The letter was bullshit, of course. I was hoping that a) Symon would believe me and call me without consulting Douglas; b)

Symon would consult Douglas who would be baffled and therefore call me himself; c) Symon would consult Douglas who would assume that he had met me before and that it was his memory that was failing due to a large intake of drugs, so would tell Symon to organise the meeting. Whatever happened, I felt it was a win-win situation. I printed the letter off and ran outside to post it before total sobriety returned. Then I drank an entire bottle of Evian and fell asleep.

The next morning I called Nicky and told him what I had done. He was in the studio down the road from the museum, session drumming for a band called Freakease. They were recording 'Early Sex Pistols'-influenced versions of three Beatles songs, introducing break-beats. He told me that he felt like a prostitute, but at least he was being paid. The session would be over in two days time and he owed Felix all of the money he was earning from it. I told him about my letter.

'I've sent off a letter to this guy at Conspiracy – Symon Grills.'

'Does he?'

'What?'

'What does he grill – bacon, toast?'

'Ha, ha, ha. That's his name.'

'Why do all people who work in A and R have such silly names?' he asked petulantly. 'What did you say to him anyway?'

'I made out that I knew the MD of the company and asked if I could come in and meet him. I told him I was managing you and that you're brilliant. It's crap, I know,' I added quickly, 'but I just want to help you get more people along to see you. I had this revelation watching *Top Of The Pops*.'

'Oh yeah?'

'I just realised how bad the charts are and how great you are, and how you need someone to shove you through the door. I don't know anything about the business, but it might work.'

'You're very sweet,' said Nicky with a yawn, 'but I don't think it's as easy as all that. Not to rain on your parade, Lydia –' I could *feel* him inserting invisible quotation marks around that one – 'but I think we had the same revelations as you about five years ago. For Christ's sake, we've been trying to get a deal for three years.' I could hear 'Yesterday' being cheerfully murdered in the background.

'Look, I know.' I was a bit flustered. 'I just want to *try*. I think they'll listen if they think you've got a manager. Why don't you have a manager by the way?'

'We did have one. Richard he was called. Still is, I suppose. He bailed out.'

'Why?'

'Didn't get on with Justin and wanted to sleep with Amber, which I suppose isn't a problem we face with you,' he conceded.

'Who was he?'

'A jerk. Took one look at Stanley Road and saw the dollar signs flashing. Felix kept on defending him – stupid prat that he is – saying he was a genuine guy and we should all give him a chance. Then he tried to seduce Amber after a gig one night, Justin went ballistic, and that was the end of it.'

Typical Felix, I mused, always thinking the best of everyone, however crooked.

'Look, Lydia, it's not a game you know.'

'I know, I know, just let me try,' I repeated.

'Amber won't like you taking on this role,' he warned.

124

'She will if I get you a deal,' I retorted, suddenly exasperated. I wanted to *help*.

'But you're on her turf, girlfriend,' said Nicky in an Al Pacino voice.

'I am *not*. You can't sit around *expecting* it to happen. Let's get this show on the road.'

My God, I reflected, hearing the sound of my own voice. I was already speaking like a manager. Meeting Felix and falling in love had given me this feeling of invincibility. Never before in my life had I felt so convinced that I was doing the right thing. I wanted to prove something to all of them – to make Felix certain that I was the right girl for him; to show Amber that I was different to the Olivias and Claires and Jackies of Felix's past; to Justin, who had put me down with his aura of cool. Most of all, I wanted to prove something to myself. I wanted the band to make it, but I wanted to be part of it.

Chapter Ten

I used to ask my dad about the sixties the whole time. Why was it so great? Where did he hang out? What was Mimi like? And he always had this great answer. He said that in 1965, there were four people, somewhere, having a cool time. Everyone else, he said, was running around looking for them. I felt like that about the nineties. There were the parties, the places to be seen – there was music. But I never really felt as if I belonged until I met Moja. *Nothing rings home enough to dig your heels in.*

Then it all changed, suddenly, in the blink of an eye.

Conspiracy's offices were in Notting Hill, inevitably. My call from Symon Grills' office was hilarious, inevitably.

He left a message on the phone at home that had Mimi and Emma in a state of disapproval and excitement, respectively. Spoken against a back-drop of Simon Mayo's banter on Radio

One, the message went as follows. 'Hi, this is Gaby, Sy Grills' assistant from Conspiracy calling for Lydia Lewis re Moja. Could you call to confirm lunch on Wednesday? Sy has asked me to book a table at Kensington Place at twelve-thirty. Thanks.'

'Go for it!' said Emma. 'You've got this far, and at least you'll get a free meal in Kensington Place. Lucky you!'

Mimi was less encouraging. 'It seems wrong that you're tricking someone into seeing you. It's nothing to be pleased with yourself about.'

I was both amazed that it had been so easy and terrified at the prospect of lunching with someone who spelt his name as Symon did. Kensington Place was just the icing on the cake of deceit. I called Felix at Stanley Road, but to my dismay Amber picked up the phone.

'Hi, Amber, is Felix there?'

'No, who's that?' She knew how to wind me up.

'Jackie, no, Claire, no! I know, it's Lydia!' I said sarcastically.

'Oh, right. What do you want?'

'I've managed to sort out a meeting on Wednesday with the head of A and R at Conspiracy Records. I'm taking the day off work.'

'Oooh, we are brave,' said Amber. 'Felix told me about this plan of yours. I can tell you right now that you can't go near a record company, especially not to represent *us*, looking like you usually do.'

'I see,' I said, with as much ice in my tone as I could muster. 'Meaning?'

'You need to look like you manage a band. At the moment you look like any old student with your floppy hair and your band logo T-shirts. You need to look like you mean business if

this is going to work . . .' I was torn between humiliation at
Amber's comments and relief that she wanted me to go through
with the lunch. Hell, she'd be offering to *help* me in a minute.
'. . . so I think I should come over and sort you out before you
go.' She said it with another heavy sigh, like I should be eternally
grateful or something. What could I do?

'All right,' I said finally.

'I'll come over with some clothes and stuff.'

'If you really think it'll make all the difference,' I said as
witheringly as I could. I was still a little afraid of Amber. She
was so blisteringly honest with her opinions – something I wasn't
entirely used to – and I was still convinced that she was secretly
in love with Felix. Well, who wouldn't be? But oddly enough I
couldn't resist the idea of Amber and me becoming friends. She
fascinated me. Not for the first time, I wished that Frankie was
around. I needed her more than ever.

Amber arrived early on Wednesday morning for our make-over,
carrying a Prada suitcase. She was pouting in faded Levis and
a crisp white shirt with pink-tinted sunglasses, every inch the
Pop Queen. Her tiny face was free of make-up and there
was a feather sticking out of her black hair. I gulped as I
watched her saunter up the steps and ring the door-bell. I
wondered if she was comparing our house to Stanley Road,
asking herself yet again how Felix could be interested in someone
so terribly ordinary. With a sudden rush of disappointment I
reminded myself that the only reason that she was here was
to help get the record deal. She didn't give a stuff about
me.

Emma showed Amber up to my room. She was surprisingly

gracious. 'Thank you. I saw you at the gig, didn't I?' I heard her asking.

And Emma's reply: 'Oh yes, you were fantastic. What an amazing voice!'

Great, I thought. Emma, expecting the rude monster I had described, had been charmed and would call me paranoid for not liking Amber. I welcomed her without enthusiasm.

'What's wrong with you?' demanded Amber, flinging open my window and chucking her bag on my bed.

'Prada?' I asked casually, knowing it must have cost a fortune.

'Yes, Felix bought it for me in Italy.' I felt that awful, churning, knife-twisting jealousy. But Amber didn't seem to be in the mood for her usual character assassinations and rude asides. 'Right,' she said. 'Try these.'

They were a pair of wide-legged combat trousers in a shiny grey material with fluorescent yellow stripes down the sides.

'With . . . this,' continued Amber, burrowing into her bag for a tight, black, extremely low-cut T-shirt. 'And this on top.' It was a Diesel denim jacket. I made a snorting noise and began to change. Amber didn't turn away as I stripped down to my knickers, and I could feel her critical eyes peering at my pale skin. 'You've got good legs and nice boobs,' she said matter-of-factly. 'The trousers are very trendy, and on you they look all right because your legs are long.' It was incredible how she could make even a compliment sound like a criticism.

'Where are they from?' I asked, rooting around for a label.

'I made them,' said Amber.

'Made them?' I asked incredulously.

'Yes, I make all my clothes. Well, all the nice ones anyway.'

'But they're so *professional*.' I was genuinely staggered.

'We're not all made of money,' said Amber pertly. 'I don't have rich parents, Lydia.' She made it sound like it was my fault.

'Neither do I, actually,' I said. 'My dad's a teacher. But I'm still impressed by the clothes.'

'I enjoy it. I've always been good with a needle,' she said.

'Well, Justin's certainly a big enough prick.' I couldn't believe myself. I waited for Amber's explosion, but to my amazement she laughed.

'He hasn't made a very good impression on you, has he?'

'Not really.'

'He doesn't like competing for Felix's dwindling attention span. Now you've hooked up with him, he sees himself drifting out of the picture.'

'But what about the other girls?' I asked, trying to hide my elation that Amber had admitted that Felix and I were together. If *she* thought it, I reasoned, it must be true.

'The other girls didn't last as long as you,' said Amber.

'But I've only been around for a week!'

'Justin must think it's different with you. I don't know about Felix. Now,' she said, 'let's get on with this outfit.'

I left the house half an hour later in Amber's trousers, the tight T-shirt and the jacket, with her mobile sticking out of the top pocket.

'You can't possibly have a meeting with no mobile. I'll ring at one o'clock pretending to be someone from another record company who want us, OK? Don't pick up any other calls,' she warned.

Amber had pulled my hair off my face and had spiked it out from a huge clip. 'I look like Zoe Ball,' I said, not altogether displeased.

'You gotta act like her too. Don't stop talking, just bullshit, bullshit, bullshit. Sell, sell, sell. Push, push, push.' Amber looked me up and down, satisfied. 'Not bad, though I say it myself.' She nosed around my room. 'Who's that?' she asked, pointing at a photo taken of Frankie in Spain last summer.

'My best friend,' I said, knowing how stunned Amber would be.

'She looks like the model who's just done the Butterfly campaign,' she said, scrutinising the picture.

'Oh, she is.'

'Really? What agency is she with?' Amber's instant paranoia overtook her surprise. I could feel her mind working. What if she appears on the scene? What if Justin falls for her?

'She's with Frenches in New York. Don't worry.' I read her like a book. 'She's based over there at the moment. I hardly ever see her.'

'Whadya mean, don't worry?' snapped Amber. 'Anyone who wears a lime green bikini this long after the eighties is hardly a threat.' With that, she scooped up her stuff and swept out of the room.

You had to hand it to her, I thought, pausing to gaze at my new image in the bathroom mirror. She had style.

As I walked into the restaurant the mobile rang, and in my panic I picked it up. It was Amber. 'What the fuck are you doing answering the phone?' she hissed.

'What the fuck are you calling me for?' I demanded, and hung up. All right! I was really coming into my own. I spotted Symon immediately, mainly because he was the only person in the room sitting at a table on his own, but he also neatly conformed to every stereotype I had about a bloke who worked in the record industry. He just *looked* like he spent most of his time in venues like the Lemon. He had stressed-looking brown hair (very short), amazingly blue eyes, (very tired), and a face that looked like it had taken a thousand punches (verbal and literal.) He wore faded khaki Carhartt trousers and a Stussy T-shirt, and was strangely attractive in a boyfriend's best mate kind of way. There was a lot of faffing around as the waiter pulled out my chair, produced the menu and asked what I wanted to drink. 'I'm on the wagon,' said Symon grimly. 'Virgin Mary.'

'Oh, I am too. I'll have the same, but with the alcohol,' I said cheekily.

Symon laughed softly and nodded knowingly in a 'you kids' kind of way. His voice was nice – soft and hesitant, gently northern – and sat most extraordinarily with what was coming out of his mouth. 'I was so fucked last night at Matrix finishing the mastering of Geejack's remix of Laily's single. I'm off the booze but it's the white lady that's doing my head in.'

I tried to make a noise that sounded sympathetic, amused and/or surprised – surely one of these reactions was correct? It came out as: 'Ahhrow.' A good start. I wished he came with subtitles.

'So,' said Symon, stretching in his chair, 'I'm having the omelette. Tell me about your band.'

It wasn't nearly as scary or as difficult as I thought it would be. Symon listened to everything I said in a way that made me feel simultaneously as though he didn't give a damn, and was hanging on every word. At my description of the band – 'They're all beautiful, of course' – he stared down at the table, nodding rhythmically as if listening to a walkman, and inserted 'Mmm, Mmm' into my sentences whether what I was saying required agreement or not. When he heard that Felix was Carolyn Stewart's son, he became possibly animated, fingers drumming the table, gulping down his drink, ordering the waiters around with panache.

'I'd heard that her son was in a band, but I don't think I've ever seen them. We'll have a bottle of still mineral water and an ashtray, cheers. Of course,' Symon said slowly, 'it's a great selling point for any band, but if the songs aren't there it doesn't matter if you're royalty, you won't get a deal.' He lit a Marlboro Light and offered me one.

But I was like a runaway train once the Bloody Mary had relaxed me. Munching my way through *omelette de fine herbe*, I found that I couldn't stop talking. Symon asked me what other bands I had worked with and I led him carefully away from the subject by telling him that I had spent the past few years abroad recovering from a doomed affair with a comedian.

'It's a difficult time to be looking for a deal, what with the changes,' he said as I paused for breath.

The changes. Help. No one had said anything about changes. Symon had spoken with a whisper of inevitability, like he was discussing the menopause. 'Well,' I said, taking a wild stab in the dark, 'my view is that this is *exactly* when to sign, and the record company that goes with this band is going to be laughing.' I had switched the phone off and had missed Amber's call – it was already one-thirty.

Symon took out a wad of tenners to pay for the meal. 'Could you come to the office now and play me what you've got on demo?' he asked.

'Try and stop me!' I was having too much fun. The tape rattled reassuringly in the pocket of Amber's trousers.

*   *   *

Conspiracy Records looked like a toy company – a caricature of itself. Symon swept through the huge double doors and signed my name into the visitors' book. I tried to look as cool as I could as the sunlight reflected off the gold discs hanging on the walls in the reception area and hit my eyes. MTV was playing silently from a huge screen; I was mildly encouraged to see them playing 'Road Rage', which I took as a good omen. Radio One pumped from a huge stereo. The girl on the reception desk, telephone head-set providing her with instant authority, looked identical to Baby Spice. Every three seconds the phone would ring: 'Conspiracy, can you hold?' she chanted like a mantra. Symon shooed me into the lift and up to the fourth floor.

When we stepped out it was like entering a Magic Kingdom. The vast expanse of office (I couldn't even see the end of the room) was so mesmerising that I forgot my cool demeanour for a few seconds and just stared. It was a bit like a space station – computers sitting like little Buddahs on the edge of each desk, phones ringing insistently like hungry, exotic birds. As I followed Symon across the room, the music I could hear changed with every step as we passed someone else's stereo. He walked quickly; I guess he assumed that I must have been to the office before. I was suddenly filled with panic that Douglas Carter would appear and reveal that he had never met me in his life. I just had to play the tape before we got to that point.

Symon's office was tucked away at the back of the room. Tapes, CDs and paperwork littered every surface. An ashtray had overflowed on to a pile of letters. I managed to read the first few sentences of the letter on top of the pile: *'We are a pop band influenced by Bewitched and Billie, but we all play our own*

135

instruments.' No wonder talking to someone in A&R was so hard when they had this to deal with all day. On the wall behind Symon's desk was a huge poster of Laily Winter signed: *To Sy, my Number One, Thanks for taking care of me, always yours, Laily Winter.* Cute, I thought. Symon shoved two files off the only chair in the room and indicated that I should sit down. There was a sharp knock on the door and a livid-looking girl wearing practically exactly the same as me stuck her face inside. 'Coffee?' she spat tersely.

'Thanks, Gaby. Grumpy cow,' he added under his breath. 'Let's hear this tape then,' he said, relighting a cigarette that had been balancing, half smoked, in the ashtray, and smiling a little. His face was lovely when he smiled. Weary, troubled, cautious – but lovely.

He listened to the three songs without comment. Amber's voice sounded much more fragile without her beauty to support it, which worried me, so I got out the photo and placed it carefully under his nose. He ignored it until the tape had finished.

'Right,' he said, pressing stop and picking up the picture. 'Is this the same line-up as on the demo?'

'Yes,' I said.

'Pretty boy – is that Felix?' he asked, pointing at Nicky. I was startled by the fact that anyone could notice Nicky before Felix. 'No, that's the drummer, Nicky.'

'Obviously, the girl is very beautiful,' said Symon annoyingly.

'Yes.'

'Carolyn Stewart's son,' he mused. 'Interesting. I'd like to come and see them. It's all very interesting.'

'Does that mean good or bad?' I asked. Symon sighed.

'A band like this are a developing act – I'm sure you know that

– and the important thing is that they are given time to grow in the right environment. It's a very organic sound, very real . . .' I nodded ferociously. '. . . I just don't know if we have the right people at this stage to take on this kind of band. But I will come and see them. Let me know when they're playing again.' He handed me the photo. I was desperate to convey how I felt about the band, and was expecting Symon to understand. But how could he? He wasn't in love with them all. 'Are you showcasing them anywhere?' he asked.

Shit! 'Well . . . it depends what you mean by showcase,' I said slowly. Symon looked confused.

'If you're scared of putting them through that, I understand,' he said. 'The most important thing is that you keep it real for them. If they work best with this line-up, then that's how they have to work on it. Good luck, Lydia, I'll see you at the gig,' he said. 'And don't worry – believe it or not, you can actually rely on me to be there.'

'Oh, I believe you,' I said. I shook his hand and stepped out into the Magic Kingdom again. Halfway towards the lift I realised that I had left my tape in his room. When I slunk back in to pick it up, Symon was already on the phone. He raised his eyebrows and smiled at me without stopping his conversation. 'So, tell me about your band,' he was saying. I allowed myself an ironic shrug of the shoulders. Maybe they were right. Maybe it really was as tough as they made out.

As I left for the second time I could hear Gaby on the phone. 'Symon asked me to say don't bother calling again . . .'

We met in a pub in Notting Hill after work the next day, much to Nicky's irritation. 'I hate this area,' he stated moodily.

'For God's sake, why?' asked Amber. 'It's famed for its cosmopolitan, free-thinking residents – very much up your alley I would have thought,' she added cheekily.

'Cosmopolitan, my arse,' replied Nicky. 'Every time I've been around here in the past few months I've bumped into Julia Roberts and Hugh Grant doing that new film.'

'*Notting Hill*,' said Felix promptly, pop-quizzing as usual. 'Stop being so bloody boring, Nick.'

'I don't see what's so great about W11 – the place is stuffed full of pretentious twats all thinking they're the next Andy Warhol,' persisted Nicky.

'Well, the sequel to *Four Weddings* wouldn't have the trans-atlantic impact if it was called *Putney*,' snapped Amber.

'What have you been doing all day, anyway?' asked Felix.

'Working with that band Freakease,' said Nicky. 'The lead singer is the most pretentious man I have ever met. He said that he could tell that I was a session musician because I had no soul for funk. I told him to funk off.'

'At least you haven't spent the entire day consoling Della Gee because they're not renewing her contract with GemStone Watches,' said Amber gloomily.

'Wish I bloody had. I can tell you that spending the day with Della Gee is precisely what I feel like doing at the moment,' retorted Nicky. 'Della's one of Chica's most delicate models,' he explained to me. 'She's over here from Georgia, USA for a year. She came to a gig once and got absolutely off her face afterwards. Then she was sick all over Justin in Felix's car on the way home. We kind of went off her a bit after that.'

'I was never on her in the first place,' said Felix with a shudder.

'And they're aren't many girls you can say that about, are there?' said Amber smoothly.

'Please,' said Felix. 'There must be some new angle for your hilarious wit, Amber. We've had the same line of jokes for at least the last year and a half.'

'You ask for it,' she retorted. I felt myself growing cold again but I knew that was what Amber wanted to see so I tried not to show it. Felix squeezed my hand tighter.

Justin returned to our table with the drinks. It was the first time in weeks that anyone had considered drinking indoors. August was drawing to a close. Felix sat next to me, chaotically gorgeous, nail-varnish chipped, green eyes flashing. Moving, moving, always moving. I drank Guinness. Moja and me. Still the outsider, still the listener, the odd one out. Justin still treated me with pointed indifference, glazing over when I spoke, turning his back to me when he laughed with Felix. He was the most intimidating character I had ever met, not least because he looked so formidable with his black hair and pallid countenance. He was wearing a green T-shirt and Felix's frayed denim shorts which looked wrong on him — as though Dracula had dressed in the dark. Felix kept hold of my hand but was very much in Justin's gang.

As usual, Nicky was my rescuer. Always considerate, always funny, touchingly insecure and exasperated by Amber, he was on my side. Sometimes, when he thought that no one was looking at him, I sensed his frustration with life. Felix was his saviour, the person he owed everything to. I wondered to myself if he was in love with him. They were like brothers, never having to prove anything to each other, relaxed in their completely different ways. Amber was like a firecracker between them — demanding, tempestuous, volatile. The banter between Amber and Nicky, though was based more on habit and genuine affection than anything really damaging. Just as it was essential for Justin and Amber to remain in love but in denial. They all had their roles and they were quite happy to play them out. So I was a disruption. The way that I was with Nicky disrupted Amber and Nicky, and the fact that I had taken up with Felix came between him and Justin. It was Nicky who spoke up now.

'OK – Lydia's been for a meeting with this guy and this –' he paused as if speaking into a camera – 'is what happened. Over to you, Lydia.'

'He liked it,' I said carefully. 'But he needs more. He needs to come and see you play. He thought it was all very interesting.'

'Did you tell him about Felix's mum?' asked Amber. Carolyn was only ever really referred to as 'Felix's mum'.

'Um – yes,' I said. Felix groaned softly.

'Great. Why did you do that?' It was Justin.

'Why not?' I inquired.

'We're not some gimmicky band who want to get a deal because of our guitarist's mum, Lydia. We want to get there on our own.'

Something snapped, as it is always doing in books, but Amber was too quick for me.

'Justin – you want to do it on your own, why don't you? What have you ever done on your own?' Nicky gave a snort of nudge-nudge type laughter. 'Ignore them, Lydia,' said Amber. It was more of an order than a suggestion of kindness. But Felix was looking disturbed. He was staring down at the table, shredding a beer mat into pieces.

'What is it? Was it a real mistake?' I asked him.

'Don't worry. Just don't worry,' he replied. But I had lost him for a moment and I hated it. I felt numb. They agreed that

Symon should attend the next gig and we all went back to Stanley Road. Amber and Justin argued gently while watching *Blackadder* on video, Val joined Nicky for cards, and Felix and I sat downstairs in the kitchen communicating through the magnetic words on the fridge. We were laughing all the time but the shadows under his eyes were more indigo than ever. He opened a bottle of champagne. Within minutes I was swaying, overcome by the heady mixture of intense fatigue and alcohol.

'This Symon Grills bloke. Is he attractive?'

'Yeah, quite. Not my type though. Not compared with you.'

'You always say that,' said Felix.

'I always mean it,' I replied.

'You're so sweet,' he said. 'Don't worry about anything – you don't need to. You're the best thing that's happened to me in fucking ages.'

I felt tears prick my eyelids. Felix was so unexpected. His disarming honesty was something that I felt he was not entirely comfortable with. He looked confused by his own candour.

'I don't mean to freak you out or anything. I mean, I'm just saying that you're cool. And so pretty.' He kissed me, closing his oceanic eyes and stroking my head.

'You're so cool, Felix,' I murmured. I read out the messages we had written on the fridge.

Use Wine To Face Heat I had spelled out.

Keep Music Free From Egos Felix had responded. We crawled upstairs and he played guitar to me until I fell asleep.

Chapter Eleven

Friday Night, the Lemon, Camden. Just over a week after my meeting with Symon Grills. Nine o'clock, and Moja were due on stage in half an hour. No sign of Symon. I hung out with the band backstage, rolling spliff for Nicky and Justin and telling Amber that she looked beautiful. She did too. She was wearing a pink leather mini-dress that barely covered her bottom and a pair of white fluffy moon boots that she had customised herself with silver sequins. She had glitter in her hair and all over her legs. She was at her best before she went on stage – psyching herself up and looking forward to being the most important person in the room. She was electric and her spark reacted with everyone around her. Justin was drawn to Amber almost against his will before a gig. They played together in the corner of the room, Justin on the acoustic guitar, Amber singing along while applying her mascara. Nicky and Felix sat at the bar.

'I always end up inviting people to gigs just to get a bigger crowd, then I have to fucking well *talk* to them afterwards,' Nicky was saying, waving his 'One Free Beer' token at the suicidal-looking barman. Amber strutted up, a glitter ball of a superstar.

'Hello boys,' she said breathlessly, putting her arm round Nicky. 'Lydia – and sign of Grills?'

'Not as yet,' I said. 'He'll be here. He promised he'd be here. He'll be here. There's no doubt, he *will* be here,' I stated firmly.

'Can I get a Moscow Mule with my beer token?' Amber was asking the barman.

'No.'

Felix pulled me towards him. 'You know you asked me why I want to do it?' he said. 'It's for this feeling. *This* feeling. Now. Knowing that for this moment, we are the most important people here. Waiting to go on stage. Writing out the set list. Drinking with Nicky at the bar. Amber and Justin getting on for once. This is it, Lydia.' For a moment I thought he was going to burst into tears with the sheer emotion of it all. The Lemon was a grim place but it made Felix happier than anywhere else on the planet. I grabbed Amber's mobile and dialled Symon's number.

'Where are you, Symon?' I shouted.

'Across the bar from you,' boomed the voice in response. And Symon was indeed sitting opposite me. Clearly he had that incredible A&R ability to sneak in anywhere without being noticed. He grinned at me, crinkling up those incredible blue eyes, and loped over to us. 'Yeah, the usual, please, Gary,' he said to the barman, who cracked open a Coke. 'I'm driving,' said Symon. 'Got to rush off to the Forum after you lot have finished.'

144

'Oh,' I said. (Well, I wasn't about to leap for joy.) He turned to the boys.

'Nervous?' That was the first word he ever spoke to them. It seemed to encompass everything that I had felt in the last few weeks in its two syllables. Nervous about the band making it, nervous about the band *not* making it, nervous about me and Felix, and nervous about tonight.

'No – are you?' Nicky asked him.

Symon looked thoughtful. 'Do I have any reason to be?'

'I don't know,' said Nicky. 'You tell me.' He was looking at Symon in the same mocking way he had looked at Leonard that day in the museum. I didn't get it. I couldn't read Nicky at all. He was chameleon-like, yet a completely closed book.

'We're on in five, Nick, go and get the others ready,' said Felix sharply.

Symon looked at Felix for the first time. 'Good luck. If I don't see you afterwards, I'll speak to Lydia tomorrow.'

We moved away from the bar and into the band room where Felix was tuning his guitar. I took in the crowd. There were the two Italian backpackers, Carlos and Marina, and the Peroxide Babe from the pub with a number of her friends, all squealing with laughter and trying to catch Felix's attention. He looked up and waved to them.

'Oh my God, he smiled at me!' hissed Peroxide Babe to her friend, who giggled doubtfully.

'I'll buy you a drink when we're through!' yelled Felix, doing a 'drinky drinky' sign with his hand. Peroxide Babe and her friends looked ready to explode. I thought it was kind of funny, but only kind of. Carlos was next to me, tapping me on the shoulder.

'Oh, hello! When are you returning to Rome?' I asked. It was the only thing I could think of to say. Carlos only had one point to put across. 'Your boyfriend, *che simpatico! Grazie!*' he yelled over the opening bars of the first song. Everyone was in love with Felix, I thought. I noticed that Carlos was holding Marina's hand very tight, like he was trying to keep a naughty puppy in check. Marina looked sensational – not a bit like the greasy traveller I had first seen. She was pouting up at Felix through layers of candy pink lip gloss, boobs exploding out of a low-cut black T-shirt. Great, I thought. Another one in the bloody queue.

To my utter amazement and disapproval, Leonard had showed up with his brother and his brother's wife. They looked absurd in their suits, especially as Leonard was carrying his lap-top under his arm, no doubt convinced he looked like Pierce Brosnan. 'Lydia!' he hooted awkwardly. 'Over here!'

'So you are!' I replied. I didn't care if he was my boss, he wasn't cool and it just was *not* on, him turning up to investigate Felix and probably Nicky too – like a Headmaster at a casino.

Holding a beer and smoking with his friends at the back of the room stood Valentine, almost pointedly ignoring the fact that the band had started. Symon was standing next to Val, fiddling with his mobile in an annoying way. I crossed my fingers behind my back as they played through the first song. It was the same song that I had heard that day I had spent with Felix in the car. Every time I heard it it seemed to splinter my senses afresh. I found that I knew all the words. Almost without realising I moved closer to the stage, wanting to see more, wanting to be closer to them.

Amber, on top of the world because the engineer had said to her during the soundcheck that she had a great voice and why didn't the rest of the band play more sympathetically, was giving the performance of her life. Justin and Nicky, high as a kite on my spliff and drunk on free beer (respectively), were playing with an urgency and soul that was enough to convince even me that they were capable of sympathy and genuine emotion (respectively). And adorable, dangerous Felix, looking like a cross between David Bowie and Sebastian Flyte, with his nail varnish exploding from the strings of his guitar, velvet trousers low slung over his hips, and ripped T-shirt. They finished the song and the crowd went mad.

It was just how it should be. The crowd went *mad*.

Symon was just as distant and evasive as he had been before the gig, only this time there was the unmistakable glint of genuine interest in his eyes, and I could see that he was trying to keep himself in check. There was no doubt at all that he loved Moja. When the gig was over and the band started to pack up, he was right next to me, buying me a pint and ushering me to the quietest corner of the room to talk.

'I really am very into this band,' he said. He looked behind him as if he expected the room to fall silent. It didn't. Most of the people who had seen the gig were now getting happily drunk at the bar. Carlos and Marina were laughing with Leonard, an extraordinarily unlikely alliance, I thought.

'They were absolutely fucking great. Can you bring them in to meet me properly tomorrow?'

'Tomorrow?' I had a vague feeling in the back of my mind that this evening was going to be one of those occasions that was going to provide conversation for years to come. I could almost hear them all now, pulling out the story with the smug certainty that it was going to amaze. 'I saw Moja at the Lemon and there were only about fifty people there.' It was a text-book scenario.

'I really would like to talk to them all, and to you too,' he added.

Felix was at the bar buying drinks for everyone and throwing the odd searching look in my direction. Justin was deep in discussion with Val, and to my surprise, Amber was helping Nicky with his kit for once. Remember it like this, I found myself thinking. It might not ever be like this again. I wondered whether Felix would fall in love with the bigger venues like he had done with the Lemon. I got the feeling that one of the reasons he loved it so much was because he was part of the crowd here. Everywhere else he was Carolyn Stewart's son. Here, they couldn't care less. He was just the guitarist. It struck me that the people he was buying drinks for now had no clue about his background. Peroxide Babe, Carlos and Marina – completely random strangers, picked partly through his curiosity and natural friendliness, and partly because he needed to know that he was something more than a name.

Symon told me to bring the band into the office the next day at ten o'clock.

'Can we make it eleven?' I asked, thinking ahead to the inevitably late night at Stanley Road.

'No.' Symon gulped down the remainder of his pint. 'Bring them all in at ten. Believe me, that's the earliest I've got into the office for years. It has to be a good sign.' He smiled. 'This is a really special night,' he stated firmly.

Chapter Twelve

Carolyn Stewart called when we arrived back at Stanley Road. 'Pick it up would you, Lyds?' asked Nicky, setting up the PlayStation.

'Hello?' I said.

'Who's that?' came the instantly recognisable rasp.

'Um, hello, I'm a friend of Felix's. Would you like to speak to him?' I spluttered. Nicky, who had been talking to me, could tell that I was panicking and laughed at me. Carolyn ignored my question.

'How many of you are there staying in my house now? Jesus, those boys treat the place like the Four Seasons. I really should send Andreas round to check up on you guys. I guess they've got the whole band and all of Valentine's little art school friends staying there? No, don't tell me, I think I'd rather stay ignorant. Who are you, sweetheart?'

'I'm, my name is Lydia. I'm just, er—'

'Beautiful name. Are you Felix's or Valentine's?'

'I guess I'm Felix's,' I mumbled. Nicky was howling with silent mirth and had scribbled 'meet the mother-in-law' on a piece of paper. I waved him away furiously.

'So what are my boys up to? Tell them they both forgot Andreas's birthday, and what a night! Tell Felix we ended up at Spy and saw Rachel and Buzby. They sent their special love to the boys. I said, my *God*, I haven't spoken to them for so long I'm sure they're married with kids now. Oh, and Marion, my Head Booker at Chica NYC is leaving to have a baby with Joel so I passed on congratulations from the boys and sent her champagne from us all – just so they know. I hope Valentine is looking after Minxy. Where is she?'

'The cat?' I asked dumbly.

'Sure.'

'Er – the cat's fine. She's right here.'

'OK, Lydia, I gotta go.'

'Don't you want to speak to Felix or Valentine?'

'Well not now that I've passed on all I have to say to you. Why would I want to say it all over again? Tell them I love them, miss them, you know the stuff. And look after my goddamn house.' There was a clunk as she replaced the receiver. Then, on cue, Val and Felix walked into the room.

'. . . I've worked out that I've broken an average of two guitar strings per gig,' Felix was saying. He turned to Nicky. 'Who was that on the phone?'

'Mama dearest,' said Nicky dramatically. 'On form, as ever.'

For a second I registered the passionate interest in Felix's expression. Then in a moment it was gone and his face became a mask.

'What were the messages?' asked Val.

'Lydia fielded the call,' said Nicky.

'God, I'm sorry,' said Val. 'How very unsatisfactory for you. Was she terribly dull?' I had thought they might have been upset or surprised that their mother hadn't had the time to talk to them, but it didn't seem to be an issue at all.

'Some brothers do 'ave 'em,' said Nicky.

Amber and Justin reappeared from the shower. Amber was wrapped in a huge white dressing gown embossed with the Four Seasons Hotel logo, which was funny in the light of my recent conversation with Carolyn Stewart. A matching white towel formed a turban around her wet hair. She had a pot of fire-engine-red nail polish that she began to apply to her toenails.

'Ooh, will you do mine next?' asked Felix. 'Where did you get that colour from?' He picked up the bottle.

'Miss Selfridge,' said Amber. 'And leave off. You nicked my last pot of *Sorcerer* and that was Chanel.'

'Look, enough avoiding the issue,' said Nicky. 'What did Grills say?'

'I wish you wouldn't call him Grills all the time,' said Amber. 'His name's Symon.' Nicky looked at her quizzically.

'Are you *trying* to wind me up?' he asked. 'Lydia — for God's sake. What did he say?'

'He wants you to go in for a meeting tomorrow morning,' I said. 'Ten o'clock.'

'That can't mean much,' said Justin. 'He probably just fancies Amber.'

'He really, really liked it,' I said. Felix was sitting next to me, stroking my leg. I felt on fire. 'He loved it.'

Felix looked at me as if he was sitting in a doctor's surgery, receiving worrying news. 'I don't understand,' he said. 'A and R people never say that. What did he mean?'

'It means he fucking *gets* it, that's what,' said Nicky.

'I don't believe it. I can't believe it,' said Justin.

'Look, this sounds like it's as close as we've ever been to getting a deal,' said Amber. 'So I'd like to go through what everyone's going to be wearing tomorrow, because I am quite sure that it could tip the balance.' She pulled a 'so there' face at Nicky, who shook his head.

'Stuff that,' he said. 'I think I'm in love with Symon Grills.'

'Look, there's no point in getting excited now,' warned Justin.

'Well, I think that you deserve to be a *bit* excited,' I said.

'No,' said Justin sharply. 'The amount of excitement that you allow yourself to feel is in direct proportion to the amount of disappointment you feel when it all goes wrong,' he snapped. But none of the others were listening. Amber had turned the stereo on full blast and the inappropriate wails of Radiohead filled the room. Felix and Nicky were discussing what they wanted to happen after the meeting at Conspiracy.

'I just want to get into the studio and make an album, not just bloody demos all the time,' Felix was saying. Nicky raised his eyes to the ceiling and switched on the PlayStation.

'I don't want to go to the bloody studio,' he said. 'I want some recognition when we play. It's time to get famous, mate!' he shouted, chucking a cushion at Felix. They both exploded into giggles. Amber was dancing around the room with Minxy, her dressing gown opening at the front to reveal a pert pink Wonderbra and a pair of Justin's Star Wars boxer shorts.

'So, Lydia,' said Nicky, 'does this mean you're our manager forever?'

'God knows. I don't know what the hell's going to happen if Symon expects me to carry on with all this.' I just had not thought this far into the future. All I had cared about was helping Moja to get the deal. But maybe I was in too far to back out now.

'You may have to leave the dinosaurs,' said Nicky, cracking open a beer. 'Would you be prepared to do that?'

'It depends if you all want me to.'

'Listen – we couldn't organise a piss up in a brewery,' said Nicky. 'You came into our lives and we've practically got a record deal within two weeks. It says it all, don't you think? Justin's too caned, I'm too lazy, Felix gets distracted at every turn, and Amber – well, she pretends to be in control but she's really not.' I didn't dare look at her. 'My gut feeling at this precise moment in time is that we need you, darling. You can't desert us now.' Nicky looked into my eyes, his sandy hair flopping over his face. He was like a golden Labrador. He brushed his hand against mine. 'You're so lovely, Lydia,' he said dreamily. 'I wish you were my girlfriend.'

I laughed. 'Do you want a girlfriend?'

'I do. Quite badly.'

I looked across to Felix who was looking like thunder. 'For Christ's sake, leave Lydia alone,' he snapped. He stormed out of the room. I looked at Nicky, horrified. He shrugged.

'Nice one! I can't remember the last time a girl had this effect on Felix. You've got him acting all jealous. It's classic! No, don't go after him,' he added as I scrambled to my feet. 'It's good for him to feel this. He knows he's being a dick.'

153

'But I don't want him to think—'

'Just chill, just chill. Stay with me. If you want to keep Felix you've got to be tough with him. It's like training a puppy. Then you'll have him forever.'

'Has anyone –' I gulped – 'ever got this far with Felix before? I mean, has he ever had a proper girlfriend?'

'Yes. An American girl called Holiday.'

'Holiday?'

'Unreal, isn't it? She went out with Felix for a year about three years ago.'

I took several deep breaths to stop myself from shaking. 'What happened?'

'Turned out it was Holiday by name, Vacation by nature. She went to France one summer and never came back. Met a French architect and got married within two months.'

'She left Felix?' I asked incredulously.

'Yes. He was gutted. Couldn't do much about it though.'

'Was she utterly beautiful?'

'In a very boring way,' said Nicky kindly. 'Very perfect, very precise, with a fucking irritating accent – totally *not* Felix. Since her, there's been no one. Well,' he added as an afterthought, 'there's been everyone, but no one. You know what I mean?'

To be honest, I had no desire to think about what 'everyone but no one' meant.

'Does he still love her?'

'I very much doubt it. He's still very anti-American, but I see no reason to suspect that that is anything to do with Holly.'

At that moment, Felix stalked back into the room.

'Stop being such a wanker,' said Nicky. 'Lydia's worried about being our manager. What do you think?'

Felix looked like a grumpy little boy for a moment. Then he seemed to pull himself together. He sat down next to me and took me into his arms. 'She *is* our manager. End of story. Sweetheart, you'll have to finish at the museum,' he said. 'If we get this deal it's thanks to you. You got Grills down to see us.'

'We've got to be in Symon's office at ten tomorrow,' I said a little cautiously.

'We?' said Justin. 'What – us and you?'

'Symon's expecting me to be there. To get him to the gig I pretended I was your manager. He thinks I know the Managing Director of Conspiracy.' I looked helpless. 'I could just come clean about everything . . .'

'And screw up the deal – are you crazy?' cried Amber. 'We *need* Lydia, you twit,' she said, turning to Justin in exasperation.

'She hasn't got a bloody clue about the industry!' he shouted. I wished that for once they would have these conversations without me in the room.

'Ooh, and you're *really* best friends with Rob Dickens,' retorted Amber.

'Wh— who . . .' stuttered Justin in sudden paranoia '. . . the hell is Rob Dickens?'

'O, E, fucking D!' yelled Nicky in delight. 'You walked right into that one, mate! He's the guy who everyone thanks at the Brits.'

'I bet Lydia didn't know that,' said Justin defensively.

'Oh, for God's sake,' said Felix. 'The whole point of any industry seems to be to just bullshit your way through. Lydia's obviously got that talent. But she also believes in us, she believes in the band, and I really, really think that's the most important thing. Far more important than knowing who's who in the

155

NME, and the phone extensions for the whole of Conspiracy Records.'

'There goes the attitude of someone who's never done a day's work in his life,' sighed Nicky.

'I just think that she can do it.' He turned towards me. 'I had this feeling you were different from the moment we first met. I don't know what it was.'

'I imagine it was the fact that you actually had a conversation with her before you slept with her,' said Nicky dryly. Against my will, I giggled.

Felix looked resigned. 'I just knew from the way she looked in her Blur T-shirt,' he said.

'Oh, how *romantic*,' sighed Nicky.

'This is all completely irrelevant,' said Amber, wading back into the conversation. She flopped down on to the sofa and flashed her eyes about. 'Lydia got us here – I say we keep her with us.'

'You realise that as our manager she's entitled to twenty per cent of our record deal?' said Justin. 'Does anyone really think that's fair? I mean, we've been struggling with this circus for three years, she comes along for the ride for two weeks and she's running away with a nice little package.'

'This is no time to discuss Felix's private parts,' said Nicky smoothly. He lit a cigarette and winked at me impishly. I laughed helplessly.

'I'm not sure that's very fair,' I admitted. 'I really wasn't thinking about making money from this. I just wanted to help.'

'Oh, very cute,' said Amber, 'but I'm afraid I've got to say, bollocks. Look, you got us the deal, you take the percentage and keep your trap shut about the music business until you've learnt a bit more.' She looked at Justin challengingly. 'Come *on*,' she said irritatedly. 'Richard never got us into a meeting when he was our manager. Give the girl a bit of credit for striking lucky.'

'Twenty per cent of the deal won't be very much,' observed Felix.

'But if we keep her on then she's going to be entitled to a lot more than that,' said Nicky. 'And why not?'

'Look, let's not get ahead of ourselves,' said Amber, which strangely was exactly what I had been wanting to say. 'Let's just wait and see what happens tomorrow. They might tell us to get stuffed. Then there won't be a percentage for anyone. Who's got an alarm for tomorrow morning?'

'Ask Lydia, she's the manager,' said Justin. Then suddenly his countenance changed from bitchy pain-in-the-arse to bewildered delight. 'We're gonna get a deal. This is it! Let me phone Rick, man, we gotta celebrate.'

In the end, we didn't need an alarm. We stayed up all night. Rick turned out to be Justin's dealer, and he appeared at 3 a.m. in pin-striped trousers and a pink tank top. Felix set up some decks and DJ'd for most of the night.

At nine the next morning, I had to kick him out of the door at the same time as getting the rest of the band together. Feeling guilty, I called work and said I was coming down with flu. Leonard sounded suspicious. 'Come on very suddenly, hasn't it?' he asked. 'You seemed fine last night.'

'Did you enjoy it?' I croaked unconvincingly.

'It was a delightful evening,' he said inappropriately. 'But that doesn't change the fact that I have three schools booked in today. Who is going to take them?'

'I'm really sorry. I just can't come in. I'll call in later.' I put

157

down the phone. Felix wandered up to me and kissed the top of my head.

'Let's go then,' he said.

'I want to leave this building with the keys to a Porsche in my hand,' muttered Nicky as we walked through the doors of Conspiracy.

'Get real,' said Amber, who looked even more lustrous and lovely for no sleep. As she swept through the door I noticed that Justin was holding it open for her. What a strange set-up those two had. Felix was wearing his stiletto boots again and had splashed glitter on his eyelids to cover the indigo shadows. As we walked into reception, the Baby-Spice-a-like practically spat her coffee all over her copy of *Music Week*. Felix was as oblivious as ever to the chaos his radiance had caused.

'We're here to see Symon Grills,' I said.

'Hold on, I'll just call him,' she said.

Justin looked green. 'I feel like shit,' he groaned. 'Does anyone have a fag?'

'For God's sake!' I hissed. 'Here you are, closer than you've ever been to getting a record deal, and all you can do is moan about how crap you feel.' He glared at me.

'Quite right, Lydia,' said Nicky. 'You tell 'im.'

'Sign in, please,' said the girl. I wrote Moja in big letters. 'Go on up,' she said. 'Fourth floor.' As if I could possibly have forgotten.

When we stepped out of the lift, Symon was waiting for us. 'Welcome, guys,' he said. 'Great gig last night. Let's have a coffee and a chat.' He led the way to his office and we all followed behind him like kids on the Long Before Man tour, Nicky and Justin giggling at the back. I found myself really hoping that they were going to behave. Felix was clutching my hand and staring round the room in much the same way as I had done two weeks ago.

'I want to sign to this label,' he breathed.

Symon led us to his room and, realising that it was too small for all of us, hastily unlocked the boardroom next door. I was so spaced out with tiredness and nerves that the big chairs round the huge oval table looked like the most inviting things in the world. Justin collapsed into the nearest chair and lit a cigarette. Symon produced a complicated-looking ashtray in the shape of a spaceship, with flashing lights all over it. Justin looked at it resentfully, as if it had been placed there to test him. 'Where does the ash go?' he asked Symon irritably.

'You press the top of the ship down and it opens up,' explained Symon, who was looking even more stressed than usual. He was wearing a crumpled grey T-shirt and the same trousers as when I first met him. Stubble had spread across his jawline and his brown hair kept falling forward and obscuring his blue eyes, as if embarrassed by their incongruous elegance. Nicky and Felix sat down between Amber and Justin, and I sat next to Symon on the other side of the table. Nicky grinned at me reassuringly.

Symon opened his mouth to speak just as Gaby came in with a big pot of coffee and a tray of mugs. She looked as grumpy as she had last time, but when she clocked Felix and then Justin and Nicky she afforded the room a brief smile. 'Cheers, Gab,' said Symon as she backed out of the room.

Justin took the biggest mug, which had the Radio One logo round it, and helped himself to a black coffee. Spooning four sugars into the cup he looked across at Symon. 'I'm sorry, mate.

159

I just have to get this down me before you can expect any sense to come out of my mouth,' he said.

'Even then, you're struggling,' piped up Nicky. Felix giggled nervously.

'Relax everyone,' said Symon. 'We're gonna take everything very easy today. I just want to get to know you a bit, I need to know where you see the band going, what you felt about the gig, that sort of thing.' He looked at Amber. 'What's it like for you being in a band with three boys?'

For a moment I thought that Amber was going to cry. 'It's the best thing in the world,' she mumbled.

'At this stage, you've got to start thinking of the band as your second family,' said Symon seriously, nodding at me.

'I'm quite happy to disown my first family if that makes things any easier,' offered Nicky. I tried to kick him under the table.

'The gig was really, really great,' said Symon, smiling at Nicky. 'There's a lot of work to be done, but essentially the vibe is there. Believe me, I've seen more gigs than you lot have had hot dinners,' he went on, 'and last night blew me away. I know we can do something amazing with this, and I know how hard you've all worked. I was in a band once – I know how it is. I hated the industry by the time we split up. We were signed to a major label who dropped us after our first album wasn't quite as successful as they had hoped.' Even as he spoke, Symon's features were contorted with bitterness. 'We thought we were just getting started. I promised myself when I got into this job that I would never, ever sign an act that I didn't have one hundred and fucking *ten* per cent faith in. I've been with Conspiracy for two years and I've only signed two new acts in that time – Laily Winter –' Amber squeaked in excitement – 'and Yeti On Blow.' Justin inhaled through his teeth and raised his eyebrows. That was it; Justin was sold.

'It's like a marriage, you don't go into it lightly. You don't run out on your bands. You don't let anyone *else* run out on your bands,' added Symon. 'Now you know where I stand. I'm not doing this because I think it might work out. I'm doing it because you left me feeling desperate for more.'

'Good thing we didn't do an encore,' whispered Felix to Justin.

'I think we need to get you back into the studio as soon as possible,' continued Symon. 'I've got a fantastic engineer I'd love you to work with and I'd like to discuss a few ideas I've got for a producer.' He looked at me for a reaction at this point and I must have looked terrified because Justin coughed pointedly and Felix quickly spoke up.

'We've got some ideas on who we want to work with. Lydia tends to let us get on with things on our own in a studio – er – scenario,' he said brightly. 'To be quite honest, we all feel that most producers are completely overrated. I mean, any old person can rock up at the studio and claim to be producing something without understanding the slightest thing about recording. As long as we have a good engineer—'

'Now hang on a minute!' interrupted Nicky. 'I wouldn't boot William Orbit out of the studio.'

'I would,' said Felix, 'if he started screwing up my songs.'

Amber coughed. 'The boys get a bit overexcited sometimes,' she said to Symon. 'As if William Orbit would *ever* produce us,' she added with a laugh.

'Well, it's not out of the question,' mused Symon. 'Maybe the second album—'

161

Justin got the giggles. 'Sorry, sorry,' he mumbled. 'It's just that one minute we're playing the Lemon, the next day, literally, we're talking about William Orbit producing us.'

'Forget William Orbit!' cried Felix. 'Producers get away with murder. I want to do it all ourselves. The *song* is the most important thing in any situation.' There was a terse pause. Justin suppressed another snort.

'I think I've got the perfect guy for you,' said Symon. 'You do need some kind of direction. Have any of you heard of Joss North? He worked with Laily when I was demo-ing her. I'd like to get you into the studio with him as soon as possible. Then we can get the rest of them here to come and see you play.'

Amber then completely unnerved the entire room by bursting into tears.

'Jesus, Amber!' exclaimed Nicky. 'What the hell is wrong?'

'Nothing, I'm just so overwhelmed, I just can't believe it. I've waited for so long for someone to have a little faith in us and now it's happening and it's only just beginning to sink in.' Nicky had told me that, working at Chica, Amber was used to tears. There was nearly always a scene of some sort happening, and it was she who was always expected to be strong, picking up the pieces when models were rejected or out of favour. As a result, all her emotions tended to flood to the surface with Moja who knew how to handle them.

Symon, clearly used to dealing with Laily Winter's well-documented hysterics, rose to the occasion with peachy calm. Thrusting a packet of balm-infused tissues at her he ordered Justin to pour her a strong coffee. Justin, for once intimidated and impressed himself, hardly dared say that Amber loathed it.

'I can really imagine how this feels,' Symon was saying with compelling empathy. 'Sometimes when we've waited for so long to hear good things, it comes as a shock because we're just so accustomed to the bad stuff. Don't worry, love, have a good cry.'

Amber blew her nose with surprising force and looked around the room. 'I know we haven't actually signed anything,' she said, 'but it just feels so right here.' She held Symon's gaze for a moment. '"*I have spread my dreams under your feet*",' she quoted softly. '"*Tread softly because you tread on my dreams*".'

'That's beautiful, is that one of your lyrics?' Symon turned to Felix.

'No man, that's W. B. Yeats.'

'I think my mate Emily just signed him to Independiente,' mused Symon.

Amber was off again. Justin took her hand, suddenly oblivious to everyone else in the room. 'It's amazing, isn't it, baby?' he said softly. I had never heard him speak with such gentleness. It was an extraordinary show. Only he and Amber could feasibly have got away with the whole thing. Symon's eyes had softened like butter in the sun. Felix and Nicky were shaking their heads and laughing. I have to leave my job, I thought. I have to be with Moja. I have to be with Felix. Everything that was wrong was coming right.

Chapter Thirteen

Mimi and Dad were appalled. 'Leave the museum?' asked Mimi in amazement. 'Why?'

It was a silly question, I reflected. Mimi knew that I was unhappy in my job, and had been ever since I started there. There were a hundred reasons why I should leave. The fact that every other member of staff was over forty; the fact that I had no friends in the office; the fact that it was not what I had *ever* wanted to do. I had fallen into the job because my university degree meant that it was an obvious choice for me. Also, I had been desperate for money.

'I don't *want* to work there any more. I'm not happy there.' I really had to spell it out to them, I thought. I took a deep breath. 'And something else has come up.'

'Ah – the truth comes out,' said Mimi tartly.

'What is this other offer, Lydia?' asked Dad in a concerned tone.

'Well, this band that I've become – um – involved with . . . they need a manager. They're about to sign a record deal and they want me to look after them.'

'It's Felix, isn't it?' asked Mimi, relieved at finding an obvious point of criticism.

'I thought you liked Felix?'

'Well, he's very charming and sweet now, but Lydia, *please*, ask yourself how long you think this is going to last? It's a golden rule of life, isn't it – never date *anyone* you work with.' She looked at Dad for confirmation.

'It's a dirty old business, Lydia,' he said ignoring Mimi's rantings. 'Music's all a far cry from what you're used to.'

'Don't you think I know that? I don't want to be dragging twelve-year-olds round the museum all day. I'm twenty-three! I want to do something bigger. And I *know* that I can do this. I'm being given a chance here.' The confidence that came with the indignation of my parents suggesting that I wouldn't be able to handle it was unbelievable.

'Your degree was in archeology,' Dad pointed out unnecessarily.

'And?'

'You didn't do any music when you were at Manchester.'

Funny how whenever I thought about my time at university it was *all* music. Music had got me through the whole experience.

'I wash my hands of the situation, Lydia. You do what you think is best,' said Mimi. The idea of her letting anything like this lie was preposterous.

'But Mimi – you were a singer. You must understand how it feels to be in a band?' I pleaded.

'But you're *not* in a band,' she replied blisteringly.

166

'No, but I've got a chance to be with a band who could be huge. I've got a chance to help them.' I turned to Dad. 'A chance to say *I was there!*' He was staring out of the window.

'I understand. You have to do it. I never thought much of Leonard anyway,' he added.

Mimi looked livid. 'Throwing away a good degree on some tin pot pop group,' she said.

Something inside me knew that Mimi was only behaving like this because she was burning up with jealousy. She may have squashed her high hopes for a glittering career as a singer as small as she could when she married Dad, but deep inside her it was always there. She resented me that night. Her own daughter was representing a part of her that she was afraid of.

'Just give me a few months to prove it,' I said to Dad of Moja. 'Anyway, blame Emma for all this – she made me go to Ben Lawson's party where I met Felix,' I added. Mimi always found Emma easier to deal with than me.

'Don't blame your sister,' she said with a ghost of a smile. 'You're out on your own with this decision.'

That was as good as it was going to get, I thought. When I told Emma later that day she was so excited and encouraging that I knew I was right.

Two days later, Symon (who had told me to call him Sy), rang to say that he had booked a studio in Islington for a week to demo the band. He said that he would be taking on a very active role and would be down to see us whenever he could. He was sending Joss North, the producer he had talked about at our meeting, to work with the band.

I decided to go to Stanley Road to tell the others. I hadn't seen Felix since our meeting at the record company, having felt nervous that he might suddenly be regretting taking me on. But he had called constantly, trying to persuade me to go over and see him. I had told him that I had to sort out my job at the museum. Maybe I was crazy, I thought, as I hurried through the mid-day streets to meet him. There was no security with Moja, no contract had been signed, no guarantee of any reward. But there was the beautiful boy and the captivating band. What chance did Leonard and the T-Rex stand against them?

Stanley Road was completely different during the day. It was a place for the night-time, enchanted and magical. I remember it best with the streetlamps outside casting a dim yellow light through the cracks in the curtains, candles flickering, Minxy sliding around the house like a witch's cat. When the moon was full, as it had been on my first night in the house, it flooded Felix's bedroom and threw strange shadows over his face as he lay in bed.

Felix buzzed the door and I let myself in. The daytime lifted the veil of mystery away from the house. The sunlight's unforgiving glare showed up a thousand drink rings on every dusty surface, cigarette burns in the beautiful rugs, CDs glinting naked with no covers. I noticed the remainders of last night's drug quota lying carelessly on the *Kama Sutra* – tiny crumbs of the weed that Justin had been smoking. 'Lucky Man' by The Verve blasted through the house.

Felix appeared, yawning. 'I will never write anything as great as this song, Lyds,' he said. 'It's the most amazing album I've ever heard.' He kissed me and laughed. 'Justin and I stayed up until six this morning. He challenged me to Brian Lara Cricket on the PlayStation. I'm telling you, we played much better than most of the England team ever do. Justin kept bowling no balls 'cause he was so stoned. They even had the commentary going off the whole time. '*Ooh, that was a sloppy piece of cricket*', that kind of thing. Justin said they should base a game on being in Moja. You go around attacking record companies with guitars and playing gigs. You can select which venue you want to play at, you know, the Lemon, the Falcon, Wembley Arena . . .' He looked at me. 'I think it seemed like a better idea when we were stoned,' he concluded sheepishly.

'Once your album hits the top of the charts you are going to have all kinds of Moja merchandise clogging up the high streets. Amber dolls maybe,' I suggested.

'Yeah, and if you press a button on the back of the neck they say "*You're playing too loud, you're playing too loud*",' said Felix. 'And we could have a Justin doll that says, "*Mate, I need some cash*",' he went on. 'And a Nicky doll that wets itself every time you put it on stage.' His tired azure eyes were sparkling with amusement.

'What would the Felix doll be like?' I asked.

'It would have great hair,' he said firmly, 'and a velcro belt that is permanently attached to the Lydia doll who has longer legs than Barbie and the sweetest nose.' He kissed the tip of my nose to prove the point. 'And the Lydia doll would outsell the Amber doll because she looks true and perfect in the *real* girl way, not in the pop star way.'

I was so touched by the way that Felix spoke that I glossed over the facts of what he was saying. He was telling me that Amber looked like a pop star and I looked like a normal girl, but that was all right with him so it had to do for me too. He cracked open a Coke and a packet of crisps and curled up on the sofa, long track-suited legs tucked underneath him. 'I missed you. I've been watching something on ITV about new ways to beat stress at work – so unbelievably tasteless, that kind of thing. I don't like you not being here. Have you sorted out *your* job stress?' he asked, spotting the bag of weed and emptying what was left of it into a crumpled Rizla.

'Yes, I think so. I'm leaving the museum. It's something that I was going to do anyway,' I said in half-truth. I didn't really want Felix to think that I was jacking everything in for him. 'Symon wants everyone in the studio next week,' I added. 'Will Justin be able to get out of work?'

'He left already.'

I was a little taken aback. Felix had said nothing to me about this.

'When? Was it all OK?'

'He was sacked,' said Felix dismissively. 'He was shit at the job and he arrived at work at eleven-thirty yesterday – which seems to me a very reasonable hour to start work in the mornings – but Thomas Cook and co clearly think differently.'

'Was he upset?'

'Hardly, Lydia, we're going to be signing a record deal in the next few weeks.'

'But has he got enough money to be going on with?'

'He never has enough money.'

'So are you going to be looking after him?'

'I look after Nicky most of the time. What the hell is the point in having money if you can't spend it on your friends? There's no better way of getting rid of the guilt that comes with all this,' he waved his hand around the room, 'than sharing it.' Felix sparked up the spliff.

'Do you ever worry that they rely on you too much?'

'Everyone relies on everyone too much. When we get the deal, they can pay me back. I've never had any doubt that they will. They're my mates, I'm not exactly going to chuck them on to the streets, am I?'

'Of course not, but do you ever wonder what they would do without you?'

'No, but I'd be lost without *them*.' Felix inhaled sharply. 'Isn't that the most noticeable aspect of my character? That I couldn't live without them?'

He asked it as a genuine question. Well, was it, I wondered?

'What exactly do you mean?'

We were interrupted by Felix's mobile, as usual. It was Amber. I talked to Minxy until he hung up, but was miserably aware of him making plans to meet her later. I had hoped that, for once, Felix and I could see each other without the rest of the band.

'That was Amber,' said Felix unnecessarily.

'What did she want?'

'She wants us to meet her tonight at this new bar in Islington.'

'The studio's in Islington,' I observed.

'Great, we can check out this bar for next week.'

'Listen, Felix, don't pretend to me that Amber wants me there. I bet she can't wait to see you without me, having had me around so much in the past few weeks.'

'Well, here's the thing. She *does* want you to come along. In fact, she specifically mentioned that you should be there. I'm as surprised as you – I don't think she's ever invited one of our girlfriends along to anything.' Felix was looking bewildered. 'She must *like* you,' he added, as if the mere possibility of such a thing was completely alien.

'No! What reason could she possibly have for liking me?' I said sardonically. 'All I've done is get you a meeting with the head of A and R at one of the best record companies in the country!'

'I'm amazed Amber didn't hate you even more after that,' said Felix in all seriousness. 'She's so jealous, and it takes over every rational thought in her body. She wouldn't be thinking it was great that you got Symon along to the gig, she'd be thinking "Bitch! Stay away from my boys!"'

'But you're not "her boys",' I said in exasperation.

Felix looked thoughtful. 'Well — we are in a way,' he said. 'Nothing can ever really take away the power that Amber has over us.'

'Meaning what exactly?'

'Meaning that without her Moja wouldn't exist. She's a pain in the arse sometimes, and a real cow when she wants to be, but she's the one they all come to see.'

'That's not true! The first time I came to see you Amber was wonderful, but I couldn't stop gazing at *you*. Like *all* the girls who turn up. She's nothing without you! And Nicky and Justin! Isn't that the whole point of being in a band? Being together and equal?'

I had never spoken to Felix like this, and I had no idea how he would take it. He offered me the spliff and I shook my head violently.

'It's very hard to explain, Lyds,' he said. 'I've seen Amber be outrageously rude to every single girl I've ever introduced her to. What about the first time she met you?' he added by way of a convenient example.

'I know, I know!' I cried.

'But there's this little feeling inside me that understands it all.

She's always going to be a nightmare with my girlfriends.' Felix flicked on the TV and picked up Amber's copy of *Vogue* that had dropped off the sofa.

'But why? It's not like you used to go out with her and broke her heart,' I persisted, determined not to lose Felix to the heady world of Condé Nast as usual. He was studying an advertisement for Clinique mascara but tore his eyes away.

'Sorry, what was that, Lyds?'

I knew that he didn't mean to annoy me. His brain had a mechanism within it that switched off whenever he felt that he was being pressed to answer something difficult. Despite my annoyance, I felt that this characteristic was instinctive, not deliberately vindictive.

'I said that it's not as if you've ever been out with Amber, not like she has any reason to be so over-protective, like some mother hen on acid.'

Felix looked up at me. 'I know. That's the point. She hates the fact that she *hasn't* broken my heart. That's what she can't deal with. The fact that I never wanted her.'

'Why didn't you?'

'She's really not my type.' We were entering dangerous ground. I should have just shut up and accepted that Felix wanted me, but there was still something so uncertain about it all, so confusing.

'I helped the band because I wanted to be with *you*. I've never come close to feeling this way before. I've laid myself open now, I can't turn back.' It was almost as if I was speaking to myself. 'I don't care about Amber's hang-ups. It's just *you*.'

Felix looked enchanted by all this, genie-like on the sofa, smoke swirling around him like a prop for his elusive complexion.

173

'Let's call Amber back then, and tell her we'll be there,' he said.

After leaving Felix, I went to a second-hand shop on Portobello Road and spent what little money I didn't have on a black leather corset top with a red star on the front and a pair of pink and white tie-dyed jeans. Together the two items of clothing looked artistically punky and definitely rock 'n' roll. Then I spent an hour roaming the shops for make-up, asking the girl behind the Mac counter to show me how to put it on. I was amazed at the results. Pre-Felix I wore very little make-up except for mascara and lip gloss, relying on the ideal that nature had ways of making the face beautiful through the sheer force of youth. That afternoon, make-up was my ammunition.

Felix, Val, Justin and I made our way to the newly opened Gina's Bar in Islington. September lurked round every corner. Justin, who was quite happy to spend thirty pounds of Felix's money on drugs and cigarettes that night, pointedly refused to take a taxi with us and opted for the tube. It was pouring with rain. When we arrived, Amber and Nicky were already there; I could see them laughing together in the corner of the room.

'Felix!' shouted Amber. 'Over here!'

We pushed our way through the chattering masses to their table. Amber was looking a little more tired than usual, but still gorgeous. Rain had drenched her hair and her T-shirt. Just the right amount of mascara had run under her eyes and she looked like every boy's fantasy. I wanted to gnash my teeth. She turned to me, radiating friendliness.

'There's someone here to see you, Lydia,' she crowed. Not knowing what Amber was up to, and not trusting her an inch, my

174

eyes darted suspiciously round the room, but Nicky was smiling. Then I saw who they were talking about. Walking back from the bar, struggling with three pints and turning every head in the room, was Frankie. My adorable best friend Frankie. Intense relief that she was here battled with confusion that she was with Amber. When I looked at Felix he was smiling at me.

'Is it a good surprise, Lyds?' he asked. I just stood there like a dummy. Frankie had no such reticence. As soon as she noticed me she slammed the pints down on the table and smiled her huge smile that hurt my soul because I had missed her so much.

'You are here!' she cried, hugging me into her skinny frame. 'I wait and wait and Amber tells me to wait more for you, and I don't believe these people who say they know you, girl!' Frankie was oblivious to the audience she had captured – not just our table but the entire bar. Her long, glossy, russet-coloured hair fell immaculately straight to her tiny, perfect chest which was encased in a tight chocolate brown scoop-necked top, showing off her impossible model's figure. Her dark brown eyes with their long lashes were heavy with mascara.

'How come you didn't tell me you were here?' I bleated. 'I've missed you so much and you never called to say you were coming over!'

'I got a call from Amber,' explained Frankie in her curious Mediterranean, American lilt, a result of her childhood in Spain and her work in the States. 'She says she knows you, and asks am I coming over to London because she has seen my Butterfly campaign and wants to know if I have a good agency in London because she is a booker at Chica and they are the best.' Frankie turned to Amber and laughed. Amber smiled at me in triumphant satisfaction. 'So I say OK, I'll come over

175

and see the agency and do the shows, and Amber said I should surprise you.'

Did she really? I thought. But I was overwhelmed by the solace of Frankie's presence and the exhilaration that came with her being back. She sat down and extracted a small black box tied with white ribbon from her bag. 'For you, Lydia,' she said, 'because I've missed my friend so much.' Her voice broke at this point and she clutched my hand, her eyes welling up with tears.

Justin, who probably felt that he had experienced enough girls blubbing for one week shot a sidelong glance at Nicky, who grinned and raised his eyes to the ceiling. 'Here we go again,' he muttered to himself.

Felix pulled me on to his lap. 'Come on, open it!' he demanded impatiently. It was a tiny silver telephone on a chain.

'Because we have both spent so much money on our phone bills,' said Frankie with a sheepish smile. She pulled out her rolling tobacco and Rizlas which instantly impressed Justin. 'But we're together now, and I need to know *everything*.'

There was so much to tell her. I had held back from calling Frankie over the past few weeks because I was afraid that talking might make everything too real. I was in my own little bubble of Felixness and one of the best things about it was the fact that no one could get to me there. I had found him on my own, and I had entered into his world without anyone else. He was my private enigma. I had often wondered how Felix would fit into Girl Talk, especially down a telephone line. There were so few adjectives that captured him. But now that Frankie was here, physically beside me, and her eight o'clock was my eight o'clock, I was desperate to tell her everything. Felix was stroking my hair.

'Frankie,' I said. 'This is Felix.'

Frankie leaned forward and whispered to me so that no one else could hear. 'You must be very afraid of losing him, because you are wearing make-up,' she said. I blushed a little.

'I *hate* it when women do that!' Nicky was saying. 'What did you say that you can't say to the rest of us?' Frankie looked amused.

'I say she is so pretty that she can have whoever she wants.' I laughed. 'But you know what?' she went on, 'The *weirdest* thing about this place. The guy behind the bar is a model from my agency in Milano.' Nicky looked marginally more interested.

'Oh yeah?' he asked. 'So what's wrong with him?' Frankie had everyone's attention now. She flicked back her hair and flashed her eyes round the table.

'I met him on the catwalk – he walked past me in the Versace show. I'm thinking, like, he is very pretty, maybe something good can happen for us. We go out after the show and he buys me cocktails. Then he takes me to his room and he says he is in love with his best friend – another model – and he needs to talk about it. So we are like, talking, talking, then he say: "But he is too beautiful for me". I say "He?" He says "I am in love with a guy". I'm like thinking, "Great! Not only is this amazing boy in love with someone else, but he is in love with a boy!" I can't compete with this irony, but he says "Come out with me to the Dario Kenyan party tomorrow, I'll introduce you to him".'

'Who's Dario Kenyan?' interrupted Justin.

'The designer?' explained Frankie with a questioning tone to her voice that suggested Justin would suddenly click. 'Anyway,' continued Frankie, noting Justin's blank expression, 'I say I'll go along and see the party, just for a little time, and the guy is there and he introduces me to the boy he is in love with and he is my ex-boyfriend, Luke!'

'Luke?!' I screeched. Frankie had been obsessed by Luke for two years. We had always been confused as to why he had ended it so suddenly. Now it seemed all too clear. 'And,' she finished, 'they get together that night. In front of me – and Luke dares to thank me for helping get them together.' Frankie looked momentarily distraught, then laughed. 'And I walk into the bar tonight, and Luke's boyfriend is serving me drinks.' She broke out into peels of laughter. Only Frankie could sit down at a table full of people she had never really spoken to before and relay such a story.

'Let's get out of here then,' said Val, who was downing his pint and gazing at Frankie.

'Let's head back to Stanley Road,' Amber added to Felix.

'You know what?' said Frankie. 'I would like to go out to dinner with Lydia. We have to talk. Maybe we could meet you guys later on? I should not stay up too late tonight because I have to be in the agency at ten-thirty tomorrow,' she added regretfully.

'Don't worry about that, you can come in later if you like,' said Amber smoothly, pulling on the Diesel denim jacket that I had worn to meet Symon. It looked so much better on her.

'Would that be OK?' asked Frankie. 'I have loads of stuff to sort out, it would be better for me to come in later.'

'That's absolutely *fine*,' said Amber. 'Take your time.'

What the hell was she up to? I wondered as we left the bar. But as Frankie and I headed off in the direction of Café Rouge, I soon realised. Frankie thought Amber was wonderful. Not only had Amber poached Frankie from her previous London agency, which would be great for Chica *and* for Frankie, but she had also ensured that my best friend thought that Amber was the nicest girl on the planet by treating her like a princess and getting her to surprise me by turning up with her at the bar.

'Isn't Amber so lovely?' said Frankie as soon as the others were out of earshot. 'She has just been so great to me. You are so lucky to have found another good friend, Lydia. And I have been missing you so much.' It was all too bewildering and too ironic.

'Frankie, I have *so* much to tell you . . .'

Chapter Fourteen

Moon Valley Studios (abbreviated to MVS) was rather less like the Abbey Road I had envisaged and more like a converted garage jammed full of equipment. There was no cafeteria or bar, only a grimy-looking kettle and a packet of stale Ginger Nuts. It was divided into three rooms, Felix explained to me – a vocal booth, a live room and a mixing area.

When I arrived with the band on Monday morning, nursing the inevitable hangover from the weekend, I wondered whether Symon had been taking the piss. The charming thing was that Felix seemed to think he had landed on Cloud Nine, marvelling at the amount of gear in the studio and throwing a string of questions in the direction of Mick, the engineer, who was trembling with cold despite the warm September morning and wrestling with the answerphone.

'Fucking machine's broken again,' he muttered in despair. Justin sped over and plugged it into the phone.

'Should be all right now, mate,' he said cheerfully. 'Although Christ knows how he's planning on engineering the studio if he can't even deal with that,' he muttered, preparing to skin up.

'He'll be fine,' said Nicky confidently. 'The more incapable they seem at first, the better they are.' I presumed Nicky was right because he had spent more time in the studio than any of the others due to his work as a session drummer.

Mick was small and skinny like a ferret, with long dyed-black hair, an ageless face and an expression of permanent bewildered agony. His sidekick was a fifteen-year-old boy called Elliot who was on work experience and was gazing at Justin's stash of weed in dazzled reverence.

Amber had walked through the door, sighed in resigned disappointment, and had vanished to the Tesco Metro across the road. By the time she arrived back, twenty minutes later, no real progress had been made. Symon, who had claimed he wanted to be with us on the first day to introduce the producer, Joss North, was yet to arrive. Felix tore open a packet of crisps and cracked open a Coke. Nicky was rummaging around in Amber's Tesco bag for something to drink.

'Cranberry juice!' he exclaimed in disgust. 'Is that all you got? What's this?' He pulled out a packet containing two custard tarts. 'I love these, can I have one?' he asked.

'Get your own,' snapped Amber.

'At least let me read this,' he said plaintively, whipping OK magazine out of the bag. Amber rolled her eyes.

'I'd forgotten what a strain it is to be ensconced in a studio with you. I've already got cabin fever,' she said, snatching the magazine back again.

'Amber, you love me really, and you know it,' said Nicky

sweetly, reading over her shoulder. 'Ooh, is that Robbie's new girlfriend?'

'I like her trousers,' observed Amber. 'I might try and copy those.'

Felix was restringing his guitar. His hair flopped over his eyes as he pulled the old strings out and examined the guitar for new damage.

'Lydia, have you got a hair band I can borrow,' he asked, without looking up.

'Here, catch!' Amber had pulled her own hair free and was chucking her silver elastic band over to Felix.

'Thanks.' He whipped his hair up into the familiar pineapple with the speed of a girl. Typical, I thought. There was something infuriating about Felix wearing anything of Amber's. But then it was only a tiny hair band. What was coming over me? Tiredness had distorted my sanity.

Symon arrived with Joss an hour later. Felix had put 'Motor-cycle Emptiness' by the Manic Street Preachers on in the studio and had been lecturing Mick on what a clever record it was. Every so often he looked over to Amber or Justin and shook his head in disbelief. 'We are in the process of getting a record deal,' he kept repeating, trying to convince himself that it was real. His excitement was magnetic. Of all of the band, Felix was the one who lived for the music. Nicky had told me that when I first met him. 'Amber just craves attention and she likes singing and she's obsessed with being in the band,' he had said. 'But she's not really that worried about how she gets noticed. The actual *music* is the least important part of the equation. She could just as easily be an actress or a dancer.' Justin loved the lifestyle, the freedom, the drugs, the street-cred that came with the band. Nicky wanted money and had so much to prove. But Felix was all music. The fame part for him was really to show Carolyn that he could do it. It was entirely separate from the music. I loved him for it, for his simple addiction.

When Symon walked in, Felix was lying back with his eyes closed letting the record fill his entire being. Nicky was sitting cross-legged on the floor sharing a spliff with Justin and Mick and chatting about amplifiers. Amber was curled up on a big coffee-and-nicotine-stained zebra-print velvet sofa reading *Marie Claire* and fielding calls from Chica on her mobile.

'Sorry I'm late,' boomed Symon over the noise. 'Joss's car broke down and we had to take the tube in the end.'

Joss, I presumed, was the bloke standing next to Symon. He was tall with thick, blond wavy hair which rippled down past his shoulders. With the exception of his clothes, he looked rather like how Samson was always depicted in a children's Bible. He was wearing a pair of clean, pressed trousers and a spanking new pair of DKNY trainers, with a pair of shades nestling into the wild jungle on top of his head. He looked highly delighted with himself. I remembered that I was the band's manager and leapt to my feet.

'Hi Joss, I'm Lydia,' I said. 'We've just been, er, chilling.'

'Good to meet you, Lydia,' said Joss. He nodded round at the band who waved a spliff at him (Nicky), flashed a divine, accommodating smile at him (Amber), nodded curtly (Justin) and stood up to shake his hand (Felix).

'Peace,' offered Elliot from under the mixing desk. Mick was rooting around with leads and mumbling to himself. He clearly had not noticed that Joss and Symon had arrived until Joss slapped him on the shoulder and he nearly hit the roof with shock.

''kin'ell man!' he cried.

'Mick,' said Joss. 'Good to see you again.'

Mick nodded at him slowly, recognition spreading over his rat-like face, then launched himself into action and took orders for tea and coffee. Symon sat down next to Amber who offered him half of her Twix.

'Thanks, love, I'm starving,' he said, shoving it all into his big mouth at once.

Joss was prowling round the studio, peering at the mixing desk and making incomprehensible comments about the gear. 'You've got the TLM103 mike set up, have you?' and, 'That's the TC Electronic Reverb unit you've been using, is it?'

Mick became positively animated when talking about the studio and even laughed when Joss asked him about some new sampler. 'In my dreams, man,' he said.

Once everyone had their hands cupped round their mugs of tea and coffee, Joss, who seemed to like the sound of his own voice, launched into his 'pre-production chat'.

'Today we are simply going to vibe, guys,' he told Moja.

'Typical,' murmured Nicky, who was dying to play his drums. 'Get your pillows and duvets out.'

'It's an important part of recording,' said Joss, sensing Nicky's irritation and the rest of the band's impatience. 'I want to vibe with all of you, spend some time just jamming and getting the right groove. We'll listen to some tunes and get to know each other. I need to make sure that we're all *au fait* with everything before we start. I know that you've got a great sound,' he went on, 'but we need to find out how to capture that in the best possible way and show you off to your best advantage. You have three and a half minutes,' he went on, as if outlining a mission

185

to James Bond. 'Three and a half minutes to get the attention of the listener. There's no room for wanking around with solos and self-indulgent introductions –' Amber looked as if she was warming to him – 'We just need to hit the listener with a great tune and a great vocal. Bam! Wham!' He hit his hand into his fist to emphasise this bit. 'And you've got your listener captured. I want to create something different, something *avant-garde*.' I could hear Nicky making a snorting noise. 'And I am very, very excited about working with you. It's hard work but I know we can do it. Now, let's settle down, have a smoke and get vibing.' I wondered if Joss, like Samson, would lose his guru-like stance if he were to cut his hair.

We left the studio well past midnight. Opinions on Joss were divided but it was generally agreed that he had been right about the pre-production day being a necessary part of the recording. The song that Moja now planned to record had been cut in half and had a completely new chorus.

'It sounds a million times better,' said Amber, who was delighted that Joss had told the band that they should all abide by his 'Slave to the Vocal' rule.

'I don't know,' said Felix. 'It's very cheesy now. I wanted it to be much harder than it is.' He frowned. 'I guess we just go with what Joss thinks at the moment.'

'Incredible skunk he was smoking. I've asked him to get me an eighth for tomorrow,' said Justin.

'Great. Good to know how concerned you are about the recording,' said Amber sarcastically.

Nicky took my arm. 'You were getting on well with Sy today, Lyds,' he said loudly. Felix looked furious at the implication that

Symon and I were getting along well, and at the 'Lyds' that Nicky had stolen off him.

'He's actually a really interesting bloke,' I said, wanting to reach out for Felix but trying to heed Nicky's previous advice about being strong. 'He's travelled loads.'

'What idiot likes travelling?' demanded Felix.

'I do,' I said quickly. 'And you travel to Italy every year.' I was a little afraid that I was being too aggressive with him.

'Italy's my second home,' said Felix. 'That's not travelling. Travelling is what people do when they're bored with their own country. How can anyone get bored with England?' It was an astonishing outburst, even by Felix's controversial standards. England didn't really look at her most lovely either; a thin veil of rain sprinkled the streets as we stepped over drunks in alleyways and slippery leaves.

'You're just being obnoxious, shut up,' said Nicky. 'Only a real twat would say something like that.'

Felix stopped dead in the street and for a moment I thought he was going to hit Nicky. Then, shadows flickering over his haunted eyes, he laughed. 'I know, I know,' he said. 'Just get off my girl!'

Nicky smiled slowly. Amber looked livid. 'It's not like you to mind, Felix,' said Nicky. Nicky was a trouble-maker, I decided, but such an appealing one.

I borrowed Felix's mobile and called Frankie. She sounded very low and announced that she had eight castings the next day, all of which were going to be hell. 'Chica is a great agency, though, Lydia,' she added, remembering that I was with Amber. 'They really are lovely. But I need some work.'

'I'll come with you tomorrow,' I said. 'The band are quite OK

187

without me.' When I switched off the mobile, Felix was looking ashamed about his outburst.

'Are you going casting with Frankie tomorrow?' he asked.

'If that's all right – I guess you lot will be "vibing" with Joss and Sy,' I said.

'Take the Jag,' said Felix.

'I can't!'

'You can drive, can't you?'

'Well, yes, but your beautiful car! What if something happens to it?'

'You're insured, don't worry,' said Felix, looking relieved at my expression of excitement. 'Much nicer than the underground.'

'How would you know?' cut in Justin. 'You haven't been on a tube for about five years.'

'That is because you,' said Felix in a dangerously calm voice, 'owe me enough money for me to take taxis everywhere for the rest of the year.' Because he so rarely spoke up about Justin using his cash for drugs, alcohol and accommodation, it was an ugly moment. If Justin hadn't been so stoned he would certainly have reacted more than he did. As it was he merely shrugged.

'Rick needs to bring his prices down. If I can score off Joss for less money then he's out of a job,' he said in all seriousness. I looked across at Felix, who was trying not to laugh.

Chapter Fifteen

Frankie's arrival meant we had stayed up most of the weekend. Half of it had been spent at home where she caught up with Mimi and Emma and we bought ingredients for tortillas and Sangria. Mimi had insisted that Frankie stay with us and not in the apartment that Chica had found for her. Frankie was touchingly grateful.

'The model's apartment is just so horrible,' she said with a shudder. 'There are five other girls all living there, too. There's three girls over from Paris who are new faces at Chica and this one girl who I kind of know who I just can't *stand*. We never, ever speak, it's just the *worst*.' Frankie had always had a regular supply of people in her life (nearly always girls) who she 'couldn't stand'. Most of the time the reasoning behind the animosity lay in something quite ridiculously trivial – she had made a sworn enemy of one girl who had borrowed her hairdryer and forgot to return it for a week, but I had to remember that this kind of thing really mattered to Frankie. It underlined once again how very different we were. I had a feeling that if we had met for the first time aged twenty rather than twelve, then we would never have become friends.

I was pleased that Mimi had invited Frankie to stay, but at the same time I had been spending most nights at Stanley Road and was unsure as to how Frankie was going to fit into my new world. And I was still confused by Amber and why she had wanted Frankie over here in the first place.

Home seemed so *still* compared with the constant action in Stanley Road. Mimi loved Frankie and had been in an excellent mood, not even minding when I talked about Moja. She loved hearing about Frankie's world – the catwalk, the tantrums, the travelling. Frankie knew how to tell a story to Mimi and she exaggerated the bits that she knew Mimi would love, and played down the loneliness, the self-doubt. Later, as we sat outside wrapped in big jumpers and drinking Earl Grey tea (Frankie's favourite drink), she admitted that she had grown bored and disillusioned by the whole thing.

'It's so easy to say, Lydia,' she said, peeling paint off the bench, 'but I am not happy any more. I need something else. I don't want to be treated like a stupid model any more.'

'Why don't you give it up? You could do anything you wanted,' I said with perfect truth.

Frankie smiled. 'I need money,' she said. 'I need security of money. It is addictive,' she added, her eyes widening. 'I get good, good money from my Butterfly campaign. I will take a few months to work, I need another campaign. I go to castings.' She paused. 'I *hate* fucking castings.'

'I'll come with you, I'll keep you company,' I said. 'The band will be working in the studio, I'll have time next week.'

'You are doing what you want to do. You're so lucky.'

'But this is what you always wanted!' I said. 'You're a successful model – you've done what you always wanted to do. Frankie, you've made it. You're always going to be OK now. You've realised everything that you always dreamed about. You know, when we were little and you used to say that you wanted to be like Cindy Crawford. Well, you're nearly there.'

'And the most scary thing of all is finding out that what you've always wanted isn't actually so great after all. You know, when your band make it, they will feel this too. It's just like everyone says. You work and work for something and then when you get it, it's kind of empty. Not really how you imagined it at all.'

'All that Felix really cares about is the music,' I said. 'He's not really obsessed with fame.'

Frankie laughed. 'He may tell you that – who knows, he may even believe that himself – but you have to be pretty mad to want to do what he wants to do. He wants fame as much as I did – as much as everyone in a band. He's just better at disguising the fact.'

I was taken aback by Frankie's directness. She had hardly even spoken to Felix.

'What do *you* really think of Felix?' It had taken me long enough to ask her. I had told her everything, the story of how we met, the nights in Stanley Road, the gigs.

'How can I answer that?' reproved Frankie. 'I don't know him.' She grinned mischievously. 'But wow! He is so, *so* pretty. And there is something else about him, some kind of dangerous charm

– something that maybe even he is not completely aware of. He has secrets.'

I shivered. Frankie had an uncanny way of hitting on the truth.

'And his brother!' she added. '*He* should model. Dario would kill for his face for his new collection.'

Every second that I was with Felix seemed suspended in new sensations. We walked through Hyde Park one afternoon, to the cinema in Kensington High Street. Felix loved the cinema and tried to catch a new film once a week. Sometimes he walked with his arm around me and sometimes he walked very much on his own, hands in his pockets. He was comfortable with silence in a way that I found unusual for a boy so full of opinion. It was in these silences that questions raged in my head. I wanted to know what was filling his thoughts and felt impatient with him for not revealing everything to me. That afternoon in the park, I took a deep breath.

'Do you think you like the cinema because of your mum?'

'No.'

'Well, it must have been cool going to watch her in films when you were little.'

'It was all right.'

'God, Felix, she's so famous, don't you find it weird?'

'No. Why all the questions?'

'You never really talk about her.'

'She never really talks about me.'

'How do you know?'

'Listen, Lydia, if you're trying to get all psychological with me then don't bother. So my mum's a famous actress, and I never see her – we don't even live in the same country – but I'm no more fucked up than the next person.'

'I'm not saying you are! I'm just interested.'

'It's really pretty boring.' Felix kicked an apple along the path.

I had one last try. 'Do you think that you want the whole fame thing because you want to prove to your mum that you can do it?'

'Of course I want to prove to Mum that I can do it!' He stopped in his tracks and looked at me. 'But big deal! Don't you need to prove something to your mum? Or Emma or your dad?'

'Kind of. Look, let's forget it.' I kicked the same apple further along the path.

'You're a frustrated footballer,' said Felix lightly.

'No, I just like kicking things.' I lunged at the apple again, but this time lost my balance and fell over completely.

'Oh baby!' Felix was next to me, half laughing, half concerned.

'Ow!' I moaned. 'Oh my God, how uncool was that?' And we started to laugh until Felix collapsed on the ground beside me.

During the two weeks that followed, Frankie and I went casting almost every day, sometimes on the weekends. On her first day we checked in with a new booker at Chica, which was based in South Molton Street, as Amber was away in the studio. Kelly, whose hippy-style plaits and nose-rings belied her incredible organisational powers and snappy telephone manner, was terrifying. This meant that for the first time in her life, Frankie was on time for everything. That first day we arrived in the Jaguar, Frankie was still frantically applying make-up in the front seat of the car as we drew up outside the agency, her hair still wet from the shower. Kelly read out the list of people she had to see and places we had to get to, and I scribbled them down as Frankie went through her portfolio and checked her chart for options, requests and work.

It was exhausting, strangely enough. Kelly was also responsible for getting Frankie to attend various hip parties given by people who needed beauty to wallpaper their events.

'There's this restaurant opening in Soho tomorrow night. You're down to go,' said Kelly, sifting through a wad of invitations.

'I don't think I can make tomorrow night,' said Frankie, who had an unhealthy obsession with English soaps and feared missing the *EastEnders* hour-long special.

'There'll be free booze and canapés and Robbie Williams is going.'

'Oh, all right then.'

Once she was ready, we set off again, music blasting and arguing about the best route to Kingsland Road. The traffic was terrible as we navigated our way across London from the West End to Battersea, from Docklands to Shoreditch.

When we arrived at her first casting there was a huge queue. I felt so sorry for the girls, pale and unnervingly unsexy in their uniform of trainers, boot-cut black trousers with cropped T-shirts, and jagged hair – none of whom looked anything like their pouting images on the front of their cards. Many of them had terrible skin from smoking so much and wearing inches of make-up. They all carried rucksacks over their shoulders, out of which came mobile phones, well-thumbed A–Zs, bottles of water and tattered copies of *Memoirs of a Geisha* and *Midnight in the Garden of Good and Evil*. They spoke in a curious jargon of postcodes and tube stations.

Frankie inevitably knew everyone every time we arrived anywhere; it was highly unlikely that she recalled their names, but they all hugged and greeted each other like sisters.

'Have you got the L'Oreal PR in W8?'

'No, but I've got a commercial request for Oreo's Cookies in WC1.'

'I've got a three o'clock in Perseverance Works.'

'Are you doing Fashion Week?'

'I've got show castings in the agency.'

'I'm testing this weekend for my new card.'

'The agency want me to go to Milan for catalogue work but I don't want to leave my boyfriend.'

'My God! You've got a new boyfriend?'

'Yeah, he's a model but he's trying to get into acting. He's in that new BriteWash ad, you know, the one where the guy spills the coffee when he sees that girl and—'

'Oh my God, he's amazing!'

'No, he's not actually the guy who spills the coffee – he's the guy who's drinking coffee behind him?'

'Oh, riiiight.'

'He's so talented. This really hot new agent saw him in the ad and wants to take him on.'

'Wow.'

'Milan is just so crap. I want to go to Paris. There's so much shit there I want to see.'

'Everybody's a number, Lydia,' Frankie said grimly as we sat in Vogue House flicking through *House and Garden*. She pulled

out her hairbrush and her lip gloss for the fourth time that
day.

How was it possible to be a model and retain your grip on
normality? I wondered. Frankie seemed the same as ever on the
surface, but there was more manic insecurity, a constant need to
hear that she looked beautiful, and more gloomy despondency
when she had a bad day.

'I felt so horrible yesterday, it's hardly surprising I didn't get
called back for that Colgate casting,' she said. 'My skin has just
gone so, *so* bad, and I'm just eating so badly and not drinking
enough water—'

'Frankie, your skin's *fine*, what are you talking about?'

'That man casting for the TV ad this morning was horrible –
he really tried it on with me.'

That was the strange thing. Frankie's manic insecurity was
apparently negated by her absolute conviction that she was the
most desirable girl that any man could ever hope to meet. She
pulled herself down but then buoyed herself up again through
the force of her looks. She was older than many of the girls, and
because she had done the Butterfly campaign she was recognised as
someone who had made it, but conversely, this seemed to increase
her paranoia.

Then, from out of nowhere, there were flashes of a more
positive Frankie – the girl I used to know who was quite willing
to stand up for herself and the other models if they were kept
waiting for too long or treated like they were stupid.

'You don't keep girls waiting this long,' she had reprimanded
one potential client when the casting had started forty-five minutes
late. 'It's not easy being a model, and lots of these girls are just
starting out. Why do you have to make everything more difficult

for them just because you want to have a nice long lunch break and can't start on time?'

Frankie missed out on that job and the client even complained of her rudeness to Chica, which she seemed to enjoy.

'At least they had a good reason for not wanting me,' she said. 'They didn't say that I was too short or too fat or whatever.'

It seemed that the band were very happy to keep Frankie at a distance. There was no novelty in hanging around with a model for any of them. But no amount of logic could stop me worrying about what Felix thought of her.

'Felix wouldn't go *near* a model,' Nicky said to me when I asked if he had ever been out with a girl from Chica. 'You can tell. He's been surrounded by stick-thin, gorgeous girls all his life – it's not what he's looking for.'

'Great!' I said. 'You really know how to make me feel better, Nick.'

'What's wrong with what I said?' he demanded. 'You're lovely because you're a bit *different* and you don't talk about Clements Ribiero and Jimmy Choo like they're your best friends. Felix can't be bothered with all that shit.'

'Yeah, but you're basically saying that because I don't look like a model, I'm not, by your definition, gorgeous.'

Nicky looked at me wearily. 'Women!' he exclaimed. 'I'm just not going to open my big mouth ever again.'

So Frankie and I were out all day, and Moja were in the studio from eleven in the morning until about 2 a.m., sometimes even later. When Frankie and I had finished for the day we returned home and I would talk on the phone to Felix while Frankie had

197

a long bath and changed for the evening. She took hours to get ready, even if we were only going out for a pizza. Perversely, the more time she spent on her make-up and her hair, the less interested I became in my appearance. Frankie was always going to be more beautiful than me, no matter what.

Nearly every night after I had checked in with Felix, we went over to Stanley Road, arriving at around the same time that Val came back from college. Felix liked me and Val as a combination, and loved the idea of me being in his house without him, waiting for him to return from the studio later on.

Those evenings were drenched with magic. One night, Val opened a bottle of champagne and we sat – just the three of us – and watched TV for an hour in the kitchen. The tiniest details were what made them these nights so perfect for me. The fact that I now knew the phone number for the local Chinese takeaway that Felix loved, or the fact that Minxy recognised me, or that I knew to draw the downstairs curtains when it started to get dark outside and to light the scented candle in the hall. (I was less romantically inclined when I discovered that the candle was perfumed with amber.) I wasn't spending as much time with Felix as I wanted to, but because I was in his house, associating myself with his life and his brother, I felt closer to him than ever. There was still the constant sense of delicious expectation which was addictive.

Frankie, Val and I were a strange trio. Val was only seventeen and clearly knocked out by Frankie but trying not to make it too obvious. This had the disturbing effect of half amusing and half irritating me. I couldn't really understand myself. Why was I upset that Felix's little brother was interested in my best friend? Surely it was a good thing? But there was a discerning voice in my head that suggested that if Val found Frankie so lovely, then surely Felix would too. Then there was the fact that Frankie's arrival had burst the bubble that I had created around myself and Moja. Although I had longed to talk to Frankie about Felix, I wasn't altogether certain that I wanted her to be a constant presence in our story. I hadn't imagined that she was going to become part of it all and it made me uneasy. My jealousy disgusted me, but was very difficult to control.

'But I knew Val before you!' I wanted to shout, stamping my feet. 'He's *my* friend!' I realised suddenly how Amber must have felt when I first appeared. You can be as rational as you like, but no amount of clear-headed discussion can make you understand jealousy. Particularly your own. I just wished that I could make Amber realise how little she had to fear in me.

Val made me feel better without even realising it, because he repeatedly criticised Felix, which made him seen more human.

'Felix needs to prove himself to Mum, but he just can't admit it,' he said as we lay upstairs watching *Blind Date*. 'He loves her so much, he wants to please her so much, but there's something in him that can't forgive her for taking an interest in us only when it will help her. Jesus! He chose Number One. Bad choice, mate, she'll ruin you.'

'He never talks about her to me really,' I confessed. 'I just don't know how he feels about her.'

'Well, you never really know anything with Felix, do you?'

'Do you feel the same way?' I asked him.

Val considered. 'No,' he said after a pause. 'I don't want to waste my energy worrying about her. She's a silly woman, and unlucky for us that she's our mum, but we get all this –' he waved his arm around the room – 'and in some ways I would rather have the house and the money and the freedom than the real mother figure.'

'How can you say that?' cried Frankie, flinging her hands into the air, dark eyes flaming. 'Money means nothing, *nothing* against love.'

'Oh, I believe that,' said Val, looking directly at her. 'And I will make sure that I get it right if I ever have kids. But I'm OK with the way things worked out between Mum and us. I have never known any different, so I don't really give a fuck. Felix does though. Maybe it's because he's older. I don't blame him, I just don't want him to get hurt any more.'

'You make her sound like a woman,' said Frankie.

'She *is* a woman.'

'No, I mean a *woman*, not a mother. Someone who has broken Felix's heart.' Even in this context, I winced.

'She has,' said Val simply. 'Broken it and jumped up and down on the pieces.'

'Ouch,' I said. It was hard to imagine the ever-ebullient Felix hating anyone. 'Felix says Carolyn's been through a lot recently.'

'The only thing she's been through recently is the first-class lounge at JFK,' said Val scornfully.

'Felix loves Dad,' he conceded. 'But he's never really *needed* Dad. He really needed Mum, but she never lived up to his expectations. And nothing blackens the soul like disappointment.'

Val had a big photo of his parents hanging above his bed, black and white, taken just after he was born. 'I like the photo as a picture, as a work,' he said to me, taking it down off the wall. Bizarre that he felt he needed to justify having a picture of his parents. Carolyn looked so like Felix then, languidly beautiful with the same sludgy eyes and perfect cheekbones. She lacked the charming, slightly chaotic look that Felix had – her features were much, much harder. Paulo was a gentle, dark-eyed man who looked nothing like either of his sons, except that they had both inherited his big mouth and, according to Val, his artistic nature.

'Mum is no artist,' he said. 'She hung out with them all, she inspired them all – singers, painters – but she's a business woman. Every move calculated. Good on her,' he added wryly.

'Was she very in love with him?' I asked, gazing at Paulo and wondering if I would ever meet him. He looked so young, it was impossible to imagine that he was a father at the time the photo was taken.

'Very,' said Val. 'For a time. He was obsessed by her, surprise, surprise, completely wiped out when she came back to London with us. Still is. God, I hope I don't end up with a woman like that.' He shuddered.

'Why don't you see him more?'

'It hurts him too much. We look just like Mum, for better or for worse, and he still can't deal with it. We just make it harder for him. He would never say that, but it's so obvious. He loves us though, and he makes that clear when we go out to Italy. He always wants us to be OK. That's the most important thing, isn't it?' He sounded suddenly vulnerable, needing reassurance.

'Of course it is,' I said. 'You can tell just by the photo that he would never want to hurt anyone.'

'He's a great artist,' said Val. 'I'll show you some of his work, if you like. He gave me an incredible pencil drawing for my last birthday – the most amazing detail in the work – and he did it especially for me.' He sounded so young, proudly talking about his dad's work, wanting us to be impressed. I saw Frankie's eyes filling with tears. She turned away so Val wouldn't see. He would be mortified if he thought for a second that she pitied him. He left the room to fetch the painting.

'I want to look after him,' she said in a shaky voice. 'I want to hold him and tell him he is loved.' Then she bit her bottom lip and considered for a moment before adding wickedly, 'But before all that I want to sleep with him.' I burst out laughing. Val came back into the room with the drawing under his arm. 'It's beautiful,' gasped Frankie in genuine delight. 'What a genius he is.'

'Why were you laughing?' asked Val.

'I just told Lydia I wanted to sleep with you,' said Frankie promptly. It was typical of the atmosphere in that house, some things kept so hidden and other more intimate issues discussed with disarming honesty.

Val didn't miss a beat. 'Fine by me. Would tonight be OK?'

'It would be . . . the best,' said Frankie. I knew that Val was obsessed by her and I only hoped that she was just as in love with him. She talked about him endlessly but I hoped that she meant it. Frankie fell in love with the frequency that most people catch buses, each time declaring that the one before had meant nothing compared to 'this new feeling'. I admired her for her ability to see so much to fall in love with in so many different people. Val would be the easiest person in the world to fancy – but he was five years younger than her. I had a nasty feeling that it might make all the difference.

At about eleven that night, Felix called, jittering with irritation that Val had a monopoly on me, and told me how the day had gone in the studio.

'Frankie and Val have gone to bed,' I said. 'Together.'

'Oh for God's sake,' Felix snapped. 'What a pathetically predictable cock-up.'

'What do you mean?' I asked, full of fear that Felix was jealous of Val. 'Why shouldn't they?'

'He's too young and she's too insecure to cope with herself, let alone any normal human being,' said Felix.

'Give them a chance,' I protested, not entirely sure that I didn't agree with Felix.

'I want Val to be happy but I fear for his heart,' he said. 'Anyway, enough of that bollocks –' was it? I wondered – 'we did loads today. Joss gets right up my nose but we really get things done. I can't bear the way that Justin sits there like a stoned monkey all day, agreeing with everything he says. Amber really likes him too. Of course, he fancies her which I find even more annoying—'

'Why?'

'Because he's spending time going through stuff with her that he doesn't need to do. It's a bit of a joke really. But that *feeling* when you listen back to something that you think is good – that's all I want. You get to this time and you could put on *Dark Side of the Moon* and be sitting there going, "Well, I don't know about the drums on this track", and you realise that you've lost all concept of what you're trying to do. Anyway, what does it matter? We sit there for hours on end, eating crap and smoking endless fags, and all that we can possibly produce is something that someone might sing along to. It means everything to us, but it won't mean much more than a three-minute sing-along on the way to work to the rest of the world.' While I was relieved that Felix was displaying a rare humility concerning his craft, it bothered me that he sounded so down.

'Every time I hear Moja I want to go mental,' I said.

'Are we really that bad?'

'No, because you're so good! You fill up my whole soul with your music.'

'I wish there were more people like you out there, Lyds,' yawned Felix. 'I'll be back soon, anyway.'

I crawled into his bed at midnight and was awakened as he crept through the door, four hours later. The next morning he told me that he had heard the sound of the shower going in Val's bathroom at eight o'clock and had stormed in, assuming it was Val. He had been hit by the sight of Frankie shampooing John Frieda Frizz Ease into her hair, eyes shut tight, completely unaware that he had opened the door. He crept out and relayed the story to me, giggling. Frankie, who had spent half her life backstage at shows and had the model's ability to drop her clothes in a room full of people without the slightest embarrassment, merely shrugged when I told her. I found it quite amazingly unfunny, despite the fact that Felix claimed to find Frankie profoundly unattractive.

'She looks like a horse,' he announced to me one evening. It was so unlike him that I laughed, assuming he was joking. But Felix and Frankie were an uncomfortable combination. She sometimes spoke to him in a way that suggested that there were many things she wanted to say to him that she was afraid I wouldn't really like. And I think Felix was jealous of me and Frankie – jealous of the idea that there could be anyone else in my life who deserved attention when he was around. The two of them made me nervous, and the tension was increased when Val tackled Felix about the fact that he never made an effort with his girlfriend.

'She's a model – I can't relate to that world,' Felix said bluntly, which, bearing in mind the fact that his mother had been a model before she was an actress and ran an agency, was by any standards a pathetically flimsy excuse. Then, when I thought about it later on, I decided that maybe that was exactly *why* Felix didn't like Frankie – or indeed any of the models at Chica.

Deep down, however, I knew that there was another reason why Felix would never be very interested in Frankie. Her knowledge of music was limited to the latest Simply Red album and a collection of dodgy South American dance tracks that she would play in the Jaguar and sing along to, astonishingly out of tune. Ridiculous though it was, it was enough to put him off her.

'Frankie's taste in music is fucking awful,' he complained. He gave her an Elvis compilation to educate her rather than endear himself to her, and was horrified when she gave it back saying it was 'out of date'.

'She's Spanish, give the girl a break,' said Nicky on hearing the story.

'How can you even *speak* to someone who doesn't like Elvis?' asked Felix.

'You can overlook such issues because she's so pretty,' said Nicky.

'Oh, no you can't,' said Felix.

Everything in my life had changed. There was never any doubt in my mind that I had made the right decision in giving up the museum, but it frightened me a little too. I was on a roller-coaster ride, and sometimes it made me feel sick, just hoping that I would get off OK at the other end.

Symon had become almost as obsessive about Moja as the band themselves. It was essential that Douglas Carter and the rest of Conspiracy were as charmed by them as he had been at the Lemon.

Frankie and I dropped in to see him after a morning of casting. The record industry was hardly Frankie's scene but she felt that she owed it to me to come along as I had spent long hours trailing around London for her. Symon seemed separate from the rest of the staff at Conspiracy. Symbolically, his office was the only room in the building that had a desk facing towards the window, and not inwards towards the rest of the room. He seemed to be in constant battle with the marketing department, the press and publicity people, and most of all Douglas Carter, for whom he held a deep-rooted respect fraught with constant frustration.

Symon, Frankie and I crossed the road to Ricky's Sandwich Bar where we crowded round a tiny wooden table and Symon ordered enormous chicken mayo baps and bottles of Coke (Diet Coke for Frankie.) I found Symon endearing because he listened carefully whenever anyone was speaking and was incredibly earnest. He also appeared to be giving Moja as much time and attention as he did to his established acts, Laily Winter and Yeti On Blow.

'It would be great to get Moja a support slot on Laily's tour next year,' he said thoughtfully. I gulped, recalling Laily's recent *FHM* cover backed up with the quote: '*I'm anyone's after a Vermouth on ice.*' She would love Felix, naturally. But how could I object to the incredible opportunity that Moja had? As their manager, I needed to be the first person to encourage this.

'That would be just amazing,' I said. 'I think Amber would love that. She's a massive fan of Laily's.'

'Everyone loves Laily,' said Frankie.

'She's a bit of a nightmare at the moment,' confided Symon, who as usual looked exhausted. 'She sacked three of the session musicians I had flown in from New York to record the last track on the album. I hope Amber won't start behaving like that,' he added, looking worried.

'Oh, she'll be far worse—' I began, then remembered that I should be promoting the band's best interests. 'No, I'm joking,' I added unconvincingly. 'Amber – she's very real. Very unspoilt. I can't see her turning into a difficult case. She – she makes all her own clothes,' I went on feebly. 'Anyway, the boys all keep her in line.' I sucked the rest of my drink up through a straw, eyes wide, looking at Symon.

'Well, that's all right then,' he said, wiping a blob of mayonnaise off his chin. 'Yeti can be very difficult too, but then of course they've all been to heroin and back.'

'Have they?' asked Frankie in amazement, leaning forward towards Symon. I was secretly gratified that Symon showed very little interest in Frankie's flirtatious behaviour. But then he had never shown the slightest bit of interest in any female and never, ever presumed to ask me about my relationship with Felix. I wondered why this was, until I realised that for him Felix and I had always been together.

There was something almost child-like about Symon and his straightforward belief that you stood by what you believed in and worked with people you respected.

'Douglas sees me as the trouble-maker in the office at the moment,' he sighed. 'He doesn't trust me on principle. Ever since I passed up signing HotBoy Five—'

'Thank God you did!'

'Yeah, but that's where the market's going at the moment.

Pure pop. Boy-bands, manufactured bands – Steps, Spice Girls, Boyzone, Bewitched – but I can't get into all that. I have to work with something that I truly believe in.'

'That's why you're so great.'

'And so totally fucking unsuccessful,' said Symon. 'Moja have a lot to prove,' he went on. 'They're pop music, but they're not instant hit, throwaway pop. They're not MacDonalds pop. They're more grown up.'

'Do you really think so?' I asked doubtfully, thinking of Nicky and Justin still relying on Felix for financial support, and Amber's child-like mentality concerning certain issues.

'Oh yes. They've got brains which makes them different instantly. Their music says more than "wave your hands in the air—"'

'Like you just don't care?' I suggested.

'Exactly. Once we've got Radio One, we're OK.' I looked at Symon's face, tired and worried. How insane to imagine that some bloke at a radio station or two held his entire sanity in the balance. And it was up to Felix, Nicky, Justin, and Amber especially, as the front person and the girl, to seduce the radio. I never doubted for a second that they would do it. It was lucky that all of Moja were so concerned about themselves that they were oblivious to the fact that they had such terrifying responsibility.

I tried to drop in at the studio every other day, when Frankie was working rather than casting, and could understand why Joss was bordering on the frustrating.

One day I arrived to find Nicky and Justin up a step-ladder stringing a huge purple sheet across the room like a vast curtain. Amber was pulling Indian Spice scented candles out of a big box on the floor and lighting them with individual matches. Elliot, the work experience boy, who had decided from the moment he met the band that recording studios were great because they contained fit girls and a seemingly endless supply of spliff, had broken his silence of the first few days and was talking at Amber without drawing breath.

'My mate Steve and me — we saw Richard Ashcroft the other day and he looked, like, *really* fucked off. They say that The Verve are breaking up but I won't believe it till I, like, see it.' He finished rolling a very lumpy-looking joint, lit it and passed it to Amber with a self-conscious pout.

She took a drag and the roach fell off in her mouth. Poor Elliot, I thought. Amber passed the spliff to me. 'Fix this, will you?' she asked.

'Do you smoke too?' asked Elliot, who had gone red with embarrassment.

'A little. Depends who I'm with,' I answered. 'It's actually very boring after a while but it's something everyone has to go through.' I completely rerolled the spliff. Elliot looked at me with new respect. How easy it is to impress fifteen-year-olds, I thought. If only I'd known at the time.

'I mean, I don't smoke that much,' he said. 'I just think it's quite a laugh, like, when you're in the studio, to get a bit stoned.'

'Good boy, you're learning fast,' said Justin from across the room.

'Oh shut up,' said Amber. 'Remind me never to let my kids near you.'

'What? Never let them near their own father?' asked Nicky in mock horror. Amber grinned.

'Are you two gonna have like, kids?' asked Elliot. 'They would

be so fucking *out of it, man*! How like, rock 'n' roll would they be?'
His eyes were so wide I thought they may pop out of his head.

'It's the Charge of the *Like* Brigade,' muttered Felix. He was
playing the riff from the song they were about to record and
looking resigned. 'Hello baby,' he said, seeing me and patting the
floor beside him. 'They're vibing. Getting the right atmosphere
for the next song.'

'Which song are you doing next?'

'"Heavy Traffic".'

'Isn't that a really punky tune?'

'Joss thinks there are "hidden fragilities and sweetness in the
chorus" so he wants to set the mood for that. As I wrote the
fucking lyrics I wouldn't mind being consulted for once. The
whole point of the song is that it's rude and nasty, and as we
don't do that much, we should just leave it like that.'

Joss came bustling over, golden mane tied back in a big band,
carrying a sequin scarf which he suggested should be draped over
the drum kit.

Nicky looked quite pleased. 'Frock and roll,' he said with a
shrug, kissing me hello.

Joss put his arm around Felix's shoulders. 'Listen, darling.
Felix. I know this is your song, your baby. What we are doing
is trying to bring out the best in it. Like we did with "Better"
and "Make it all right". You may not trust me now, but just roll
with it for the moment – take it as it comes. All right?'

'Let's just get on with it. The studio looks like something out of
Changing Rooms. I'm just waiting for Carol Smillie to walk through
the door,' grumbled Felix, not without reason I thought.

'We're right on schedule, Lydia,' said Joss, turning away from
Felix and speaking to me in a low, careful voice, rather as a

teacher-to-mother at a parents' meeting. 'They are all doing great. We've had some very memorable times over the last few weeks. They're a tricky bunch when they want to be, but they've learned to *think* –' he tapped the side of his head to emphasise the point – 'and to *listen* to each other.' He clutched at his ear. 'It's been a tough final day, *comme toujours*, but we're really getting to the stage where we're ready for a big group hug.' I wanted to laugh. 'Justin, are you ready? I want to try and get the drums down so can everyone get ready to do a guide? Lydia, come through and sit with me.'

Joss, Elliot and I sat behind the mixing desk watching Nicky, Justin, Amber and Felix through the glass panel as they prepared to start recording. Joss pressed a button to talk to them.

'Nicky, I don't want anything crazy going on here, just keep it very simple for the moment. I don't want the drums distracting from the rest of the song. I'm gonna try you without the click just to see how it goes. Amber, how are you doing?'

'Mick, can I have a bit more of me in my cans?' asked Amber. 'Can Elliot get me some water as well?' she added.

'Elliot, get some water for Amber,' ordered Joss. 'Right, we're gonna go for a runthrough so Mick can get levels up etcetera, etcetera, etcetera.'

'One, two, three!' began Felix. They played along so that Nicky could record the drums, following Amber's lead and Felix's guitar. Halfway through Amber burst out laughing and the drums ground to a halt. In the control room, Elliot, Joss, Mick and I could not hear what they were laughing about. I could see Felix giggling and talking with Justin, Nicky and Amber, who was doubled up with mirth.

'OK, are we ready to go again?' asked Joss. He pressed another button so that he could hear what was going on.

'Sorry, Joss,' said Amber, regaining her composure. 'It's just this ongoing Moja joke about a line in this song,' she explained.

They started again. I had never seen them more together, more sympathetic towards each other, more in touch. Elliot sang along with the recording with astonishing confidence for someone with no obvious musical talent. He had formed his own interpretation of what the words to the song were, and whenever there was a break in the singing he leaned over to me and said, 'I love this tune, man. When they were rehearsing it this morning I was just, like, wow, that is so fucking amazing. It's like Radiohead meets Catatonia meets Underworld.' It would have been a challenge to come up with a description of the song that was less appropriate. I looked at Elliot in amazement.

'Are you joking?' I asked.

'No, I just really thought that that was the vibe.'

'Shut up, Elliot,' said Joss.

Elliot looked crestfallen. 'I just think this song has this wicked cross-section of influences,' he said.

'Then you're shaping up to be great A and R man,' muttered Joss.

At the end of the song Joss looked pleased.

'Great, come through and have a listen,' he said. But when he played back what they had recorded so far, I wanted to cry. It was so perfect, such a far cry from the clunking, badly recorded demo that had been on permanent play in the Jaguar and in my head since I had first met Felix. It was just so *professional*. They were a proper band now. Everything was refined and polished and

Amber sounded like a different singer. While it shocked me, how much it had changed, I realised in that instant that they were going to be bigger than I had ever imagined. Now they had everything. The performance and the beauty, and the *songs*, which sparkled like the sequins on Nicky's drums. 'We need to bring the bass up in the mix,' said Joss, turning to Justin. Amber picked up *Cosmopolitan* and sighed.

'I think the vocal needs to be higher in the mix, too,' she said. '*Plus ça change* . . .' whispered Nicky to me.

Chapter Sixteen

It was strange, my new life. There was always a plan, always someone organising the seven of us. The seven of us consisted of Moja, Valentine, Frankie and me. It seemed that most of the scheduling came from Amber, but had to be approved by Felix. Nicky was disconcertingly easy-come, easy-go, and was always happy to go along with whatever the arrangements were for the evening, making his own fun as he went. Because Frankie and I were usually out during the day, she at her castings and me at the studio with the band or at meetings with Symon, we didn't tend to hear of the arrangements until we called Val late in the afternoon. No two nights were ever the same, or even close to being the same, which was odd because we were frequently playing against the same back-drops. Amber favoured Gina's Bar for a drink after the studio, and if enough of us could be bothered we would share a cab to Penelope's.

I had all but abandoned the crowd that I used to spend so much time with, although Alex managed to reach me by getting Felix's mobile number off Emma. We were discussing whether the eighties had been musically more impressive than the nineties.

'You see, you associate the eighties with crap fashion, but there was some amazing, ground-breaking music out there,' Felix was saying.

'But maybe you just prefer the eighties because it's got that nostalgic glow around it,' I said.

'Probably,' he conceded. His phone rang. 'Felix speaking. Who goes there?' he asked. 'OK, she's right here.' Felix lobbed the phone across the room to me. 'Someone for you,' he said, pulling the 'mysterious caller' expression.

'Lydia? It's me.'

'Who?' I asked, knowing perfectly well but irritated by her presumption.

'Alex, of course. My God, you *have* changed. What's all this I hear from Emma about you resigning from the museum? She said something about you managing a pop group, which I found hysterical. I said to Emma that the Lydia I know couldn't organise her way out of a paper bag.'

I should have made some cutting reply to this, but I couldn't think of anything scathing enough, so I did something really naughty.

'What's that, Alex? I can't quite hear you, I think the mobile's losing reception!' I shouted.

'It should be fine,' muttered Felix in surprise. 'Bloody phone.'

'I just said that you couldn't organise your way out of a paper bag. I heard from Emma about—'

'Sorry Alex, IF YOU CAN HEAR ME, I CAN'T HEAR YOU,

YOU'RE BREAKING UP!' And I pressed the button to end the call. Then I switched the phone off.

'That does it,' said Felix, 'I'm changing network. We're in central London for God's sake!'

I giggled. 'Felix, I deliberately cut her off. She's a nightmare friend of mine, I just couldn't cope with her right now.'

Felix looked slightly bewildered. 'God, Lyds, don't ever do that to me,' he said.

'Don't be silly! I just didn't want to speak to her, that's all!'

'Yeah, but it freaks me out that you can act so well.'

I loved the people that made up my cast, and for the first time in my life I felt part of a gang. Yet being involved in such a close group was not something I felt entirely comfortable with, especially where Amber and Justin were concerned. The politics were unbelievable and overwhelming and I was glad to have Frankie around on the occasions when the two of them were either arguing or causing problems with the rest of the band. My favourite time of day was always when Felix and I could be alone together, ideally in bed. We had sex that blew all previous experience off the scale. And as if the thrill of being with him on his own was not enough, our pillow talk was addictive. The daytime gave me time to contemplate what we had talked about in bed the night before.

'Sometimes I really worry about myself,' was a favourite opening line of Felix's. Then he would laugh. We joked about him always bringing the conversation back round to Moja. 'I mean, we mean nothing to anyone. That's what I have to keep reminding myself. We are irrelevant musicians. Why does everyone behave like the world's going to collapse around our heads if we don't get this deal?'

217

'You *are* going to get the deal,' I said automatically.

'Yeah, but even so. We're not doing anything different. No one can ever do anything different. It's all been done before. *None of us are original.*'

'But you are to each new generation that you seduce,' I said.

'Maybe,' said Felix.

We laughed and laughed about nothing and everything – old TV shows we had both watched as kids, Elliot and Joss in the studio, Felix's occasional stutter when he spoke too fast. As the nights grew colder, we snuggled down deeper. I drove Felix mad because I was incapable of whispering.

'You can tell you never went to boarding school,' he said. 'Whispering is an art. Let me teach you.' His mouth was close to my ear. 'You hardly have to speak at all,' he whispered so softly that I had to strain to hear him.

'Ooh, Felix, you're making me ticklish!' I squeaked.

'You're impossible,' he sighed.

'It's getting really wintry now,' I observed. We lay silent for a few moments. I could hear Val and Frankie watching *Vertigo* downstairs.

'*A sad tale's best for winter*,' Felix murmured. '*I have one of sprites and goblins.*' He looked like a little goblin. In the dark his eyes looked a deeper, more swampy green than ever.

'Tell me a story then,' I begged. And he did.

Most of the time he made the stories up as he went along. Sometimes he would play the guitar too, lying down with it flat on the bed. He told stories of his childhood in Italy and of the first band that he joined. He told stories of his days at school and of the beginnings of his friendship with Justin.

He told stories of his mother.

*   *   *

September elbowed the last remaining fragments of summer away and it became colder. Frankie, for all that she complained about English weather, was showing no signs of moving back to New York. Every so often, Felix tried to talk to me about how he felt about her.

'I know she's your friend, Lyds,' he would always begin, 'but she's so one-dimensional, so un-Val. Why the hell can't he see that? She's just going to get bored and dump him and the whole thing will be hell. I give them three months, max.'

'Listen, I know that Val seems very young to us, but he can look after himself. Nothing that you say to him is going to make the slightest bit of difference about the way he feels about Frankie.'

'Watch This Space,' said Felix grimly. 'Jesus! I should be in bed.'

'Why are you drinking champagne then?'

'I know that I don't stand a chance of getting to sleep so I thought I might as well stay up. There's a series of cult eighties movies on Sky at two in the morning all this week. It's *American Werewolf in London* tonight.'

This was normal. Sleep was little more than a dream. Felix, who regarded moderation as a deadly sin, drank and smoked more than ever. Every day I felt that he was pushing things as far as he could. It was as if we were killing time at an airport, and nothing really mattered except where we going to be next. But with Felix, we were definitely in the First Class Lounge.

I went up to bed thinking about what Felix had said about Frankie. I desperately wanted them to become friends, but at the same time I was experiencing a secret relief that they didn't want to get any closer. I passed Nicky on the way upstairs. Sometimes

making my way up to Felix's room took longer than necessary
due to the amount of band clobber blocking the way. I climbed
over a bass amplifier and encountered him on the other side.

'What's up?' he asked. He was carrying a snare drum and was
wearing a dark blue shirt of Justin's and a pair of grey cords. With
his sandy hair falling long over his eyes, he looked about fifteen.

'What should I do about my boyfriend and my best friend not
liking each other?' I asked him.

'Come up to my room.'

Carolyn Stewart's spare room *was* Nicky's room really. He
had spent every night there for the past year and a half. It was
opposite Carolyn's first-floor study – a room that I had never
seen. Nicky's room was directly below Felix's so had the same
outlook on to the street below. Unlike Felix, Nicky was rather
tidy and had very little cluttering up his room, except for his
drum kit, a neat stack of *Rhythm* magazines, and a rail of clothes.
A big photo of the band was blu-tacked above the single bed.
The light pink painted walls, and the heavy silk saffron curtains
complemented Nicky's delicate little-boy-off-fishing features. I sat
down on the floor.

'My advice to you,' he said, 'is not to rock the boat. Just let
them get on with not liking each other. I don't think Felix likes
the idea of anyone captivating Valentine like Frankie has. Just roll
with it.'

'But I want them to like each other,' I protested.

'No you don't! Why should you? The last thing you need is
for Felix to prefer being with her to being with you – not that
he ever would, of course.' Nicky crossed over to the window and
opened it to smoke his cigarette.

'I'm not asking him to like her *better* than me, for God's sake.

I just want to know that they are all right in each other's company.'

'Well, go out in a little threesome then,' said Nicky. 'Give them a chance to talk to each other without seventeen other people being around. If that's what you really want to do.'

'I think I might do that, actually. I just want them both to realise why I like both of them so much.'

'Who do you prefer?' asked Nicky.

'What a ridiculous question! You can't ask that!'

'Why not?'

'Because I don't prefer either of them. I mean, that's like me asking who you like better – Amber or Justin?'

'Well they *both* irritate the hell out of me,' sighed Nicky. 'But if I had to be stuck on a desert island with Felix or Frankie, well, I know who I'd choose.'

'You'd only choose Frankie because she's beautiful. You don't know her at all,' I protested.

'I wouldn't choose Frankie, actually,' said Nicky in surprise. 'I can only discuss the latest Calvin Klein ads and who's on the cover of *Vogue* for so long.'

'But she's a girl! You could have babies and everything.'

'Sod that,' said Nicky. 'If Felix brought his guitar we could have some seriously good jamming sessions. I could make some amazing percussion instruments out of coconut shells and animal skins. Now *that's* rock 'n' roll.'

So I met Felix and Frankie at Notting Hill Gate tube at four o'clock. Frankie was half an hour late as she had been at a shoot in East London, which wound Felix up.

'Doesn't she have a mobile?' he asked me.

'It's switched off – ah, here she is.' I waved to Frankie as she crossed the street in her black leather mini-skirt, stopping traffic and turning heads.

'About time,' muttered Felix.

'Sorry I'm late.' Frankie was contrite. 'The photographer was so slow! Every five minutes he took a break, and we were, like, drinking coffee for most of the day, then he suddenly remembers that he is actually shooting for British *Elle* and he needs to get some pictures done. I'm *so* tired,' she went on. 'I spent the whole day standing under the wind machine and my eyes are so sensitive that they started running and they kept having to redo my eye make-up. It was a *mess*.'

'Well, thank God for Photoshop then,' said Felix briskly. I was annoyed with him. There was still no tangible reason that I could grasp that would explain his dislike of Frankie.

'Where are we going?' she asked.

'The Churchill Arms. It's this great pub, does amazing Thai food,' I said.

It was the coldest day that I had ever spent with Felix. There was a strong wind that blew flyers out of the hands of the people campaigning for Greenpeace, Help the Aged and Eat as Much as You Want at Pizza Palace. The roads were heaving with rush hour traffic. Pedestrians raced between the cars and buses at the lights. People seemed reluctant to leave the summer behind and were wearing shorts and trainers with heavy coats on top. A couple emerged from Snappy Snaps, laughing at their holiday photos and asking, *How come the summer went so fast?* Well, it had gone even faster for me because it had only really begun when I met Felix.

We walked past a man selling the *Big Issue*.

'Hey, Lydia, have you got any change?' asked Frankie. I rummaged in my bag. 'No, I need to go to a cash-point, ask Felix.'

'Felix, will you buy the *Big Issue*?'

'No. It's a load of crap.'

'All right then, will you give this man some money for the homeless?'

'Oh, for God's sake.' Felix dropped a pound coin into the bloke's hand. 'Sorry, mate, but I hate your magazine,' he said.

'Fair enough,' said the man. 'Take care of yourself.'

We walked on. Then, suddenly and without warning, Frankie stopped in the street and pulled Felix back by his jacket.

'What's wrong?' he asked.

'How dare you treat that guy like that!' Her face was flashing anger.

'Like what?' asked Felix. His face had fallen; he looked like a little boy being told off for something that he had no idea he had done wrong.

'Saying you hate the magazine, making out you're so important that you don't need to buy it,' she said. 'You think you're so much better than him, don't you?'

'Will you shut up?' said Felix.

'You just go back to your beautiful house and your car and your cat and your friends and carry on living in your own little dream-world. Do you have any idea about the world outside your own?'

'Frankie, chill out—' I began.

'It's all so easy for you. Just dismiss those who haven't got what you've got because – hey – why do you need to worry about them anyway? I've never met anyone so oblivious to the

223

rest of the world in my whole life!' Frankie was really shouting now. Felix's expression changed from one of bewilderment to one of absolute disgust.

'You know what? I always suspected that models were as thick as posts, and you've just confirmed that theory.'

'Are you saying I'm stupid?'

'Only a model could be so fucking smug. You spend every day of your life panicking about your hair and whether you have a spot on the end of your incidentally rather large nose, and you think you have the right to tell me how to behave?'

'I came from nothing. I had *nothing*!' exclaimed Frankie, stamping her kitten-heeled boot into the ground. 'I fought my way here. You had everything to start with, *everything*, and you can't even buy a magazine to help a guy who sleeps on the streets and has nothing more than the clothes he is wearing.'

'Unlike your good self, I doubt he shops at Prada,' snapped Felix. 'For God's sake, just leave it out.'

But Frankie was not to be stopped. I had seen her like this many times before, and what frightened me was that her behaviour, however much she genuinely believed in what she was saying, was always employed when she was trying to impress someone – trying to make her impassioned presence known. She was very big on the fact that her parents had never had any money, and relished the telling of her impoverished childhood. She loved the girl-from-nowhere-does-good form that she felt her life had taken. But Frankie had what Felix had never had, which was a mother who adored her. I could see Felix's face taking on the appearance of a thundercloud. We were still standing in the middle of the street, which I imagined suited Frankie's need for theatrical abandon. Felix couldn't have cared less where he was.

'Everything is so easy for me, isn't it? Do you have any idea how it feels to be me? I make the most of what I have because I want to. You think that you fought your way here? Jesus, do you have any idea how it feels to have a mother who sees you as a fashion accessory? I have my house and my friends because they're *all I've got!*'

'And a never-ending supply of money!' retorted Frankie.

'What do you suggest I do, give it all away?' yelled Felix. A couple of passers-by were staring.

'Lovers' tiff?' suggested an elderly man with a toothy grin.

'She's not my fucking lover!' yelled Felix, drawing further attention from a crowd of fifteen-year-old school boys.

'I wouldn't mind her!' piped up one of the kids to much hilarity.

Frankie was still going strong. 'At least don't treat people who have less than you as if they're less important than you! Never forget that at the end of the day, you've got a warm bed and a roof over your head.'

'No!' shouted Felix. 'At the end of the day, I've got Lydia!'

'Ooooohhhhh!' hissed the old man. 'Another woman involved, I might have guessed.'

'Stay out of it, man,' warned Felix. Frankie pouted at him.

She's actually enjoying this, I thought numbly. I had never seen Felix so angry. Come to think of it, I had never seen him angry at all.

'You know why I hate that magazine?' asked Felix. 'Because they were fucking rude about my mum's last film, that's why. You see, I *have* got a reason, I'm not just some awkward bastard who wants to make a point of not liking it. But then you wouldn't have any idea how that feels, would you? To read that some little jerk who works for some irrelevant paper thinks that your mum should give up acting because she was never any good in the first place, and should start acting her age and stop trying to seduce her much younger co-stars. Don't even dare t-to fucking try t-to p-p-presume that you know how that feels.'

I had wanted Felix to tell me about Carolyn for so long, but never like this. It had been my intention to encourage Felix and Frankie to be friends, but it was perfectly obvious that there was no connection between them at all. Instinctively, I wanted to protect Felix.

'Felix, please, let's not talk about this now,' I begged.

'Why not?' He turned to me, ablaze, his green eyes suddenly full of tears.

I saw Frankie catwalking off in the opposite direction.

'Let's go home,' I said. I put my arm around my boyfriend and hailed a cab.

'I just don't understand what's come over her. She never used to be so aggressive. I mean, she always had a pretty frightening streak, but I've never seen her behave like that.' I reported Frankie's behaviour to Nicky that night.

'People do change, and you can't just hang around wondering why,' said Nicky. 'Move on. I knew it was only a matter of time before she and Felix came to blows. *Hakuna Matata.*'

Just before I went to bed, Frankie came to say good-night.

'I'm so sorry, Lydia,' she said. 'I'm really stressed at the moment, but I totally overreacted. It's the, er, Spanish blood.'

'Frankie, you really upset Felix,' I said. 'I don't understand why you got so wound up. He's not what you think he is at all. You have to give him a chance.'

226

'He won't give me a chance.'

'You won't give *him* a chance.'

Frankie shook her head in disbelief. I felt irritated. Why was it that everything she was doing and saying seemed so forced and contrived?

'Lydia, I was so much looking forward to coming back to London to work, to see you, but I just feel like I'm getting in the way of you and your new boyfriend.'

'That's not fair!'

'That's how I feel. It's like you've moved on, like you're leaving me behind—'

'What about you and Val?'

'Look, you were always saying to me that friends would be around forever and that boyfriends come and go—'

'I hope you *will* always be around, but I really want Felix to be around forever, too.'

'My God! She wants him forever now!' Frankie rolled her eyes at an imaginary audience.

'Frankie, I love him. I don't just fancy him for a few weeks or want to be with him because I'm lonely without someone. This is nothing like any of that. It's impossible to explain—'

'To someone like me who's never held a boy down for longer than three months?' finished Frankie bitterly.

'You never wanted anyone to hold *you* down for longer than three months,' I pointed out.

'I love Val,' said Frankie defensively.

'I hope you do because he's crazy about you.'

'Look, Lydia, I don't know. Maybe I just feel jealous of Felix because he has you so completely – I don't know. I just wanted to say I'm sorry and can we forget about it?' She looked at me with big, hopeful eyes. I wanted everything to be all right.

'Of course we can. I can understand how freaky it must be for you to see me with a boyfriend that I actually *want* to be with.'

As she hugged me and chattered on about her castings the next day, I knew that the thing that had made her most confused was the fact that I had the boy who would usually have been reserved for her. I imagined her thinking that if she and I had met Felix at the same time, there would have been no competition for his affections. Sure, she had gone for what she considered was the next best thing in Valentine, but she was certainly thrown by the situation.

The new recordings took everyone a little by surprise. I don't think that any of the band expected Joss's influence to have altered their sound so much, while at the same time keeping the original feeling of each song.

'The guy's a fucking genius,' proclaimed Justin after the final day of mixing. 'I will never, ever, underestimate the importance of a good producer.'

'Bollocks – we could have done just as good a job without him,' said Felix, who remained unpredictable on the subject of Joss's talents. 'He'll spend the rest of his life taking credit for songs that he didn't write. The thing that I find so alarming is the fact that I could have done his job in half the time. And I don't like people finding alternative meanings in my lyrics, it's so ungracious.'

'Will you stop moaning for five minutes?'

Amber had handed in her notice at Chica, so convinced was she of success with the band. We were experiencing the curious limbo that Symon had warned us we would feel after recording and before signing the deal. The premonition of what was to come hung in the air like smoke. Stanley Road was a refuge for the strange feelings that everyone had. We spoke about unimportant things, and even more was left unsaid. A couple of nights a week I would return home to Emma because I found the atmosphere around the band exhausting. They were under starter's orders. Felix was shattered by tiredness, unable to sleep and suddenly electric with nerves. He told me that he felt as if some extra-terrestrial force was flying down to get him, like a thing from space. It was typical of Felix to imagine that an alien creature would choose to take him away, rather than anyone else on the planet.

Chapter Seventeen

A week after the recording was finished, Symon took us all out to Pharmacy in Notting Hill and we drank champagne cocktails while staring at tubes of Canesten and the periodic table. Symon had invited most of Conspiracy along to meet the band. Having heard the demo and taken on board the fact that Felix was gorgeous and had a world-famous mum, most of the female staff had turned up to check him out. It wasn't usual procedure, Symon informed us, but he really needed to push Moja forward and show that he was determined to make them a success.

My God, I thought, everyone was so ridiculously trendy. Even Symon, with his slightly anguished face and blindingly blue eyes, was just so very *in*. What was it about people who worked in the record business that they managed to look so superior to anyone else? Most of the time it was with very little justification. A skinny blonde girl wearing a pale suede jacket and smoking Silk Cut was chatting at the end of the table to a rather curvaceous brunette about a recent holiday in Ibiza. I recognised her as Gaby, Symon's assistant.

'I was like – I'm not fucking paying to see him DJing, I had it all day every day for three months for free anyway. I would have paid *not* to hear him again in fact, quite frankly. Then, after his set at Pacha, he came back to our hotel and we were talking in the bar until, like, nine o'clock in the morning, and I was like, well, he's not coming up to my room and there were these girls hanging around him who were all "Oh, we love you so much", and I just thought I can't be fucked with these E heads any more. Seriously. I just want to go to Devon for my next holiday and chill out, because it really does my head in, and what's the point of going on a holiday when you need another holiday to recover? And I don't want him to think that the only reason I went out there in the first place was to see him – I just wanted to go and keep Karen company, and she was all over that bloke from the Aqua Bar she met in Space on the first night.' The second girl nodded sympathetically.

'Come down to my place in Devon,' she said. 'Anytime you want.'

'Thanks Gem,' said Gaby, her voice cracking. 'Who needs men anyway?' she added.

I sat next to Felix, whose languid beauty answered that very question. He lolled gorgeously on the table beside me, playing with a box of matches. Symon, relaxed and in control, was smothering a ciabatta roll with butter and grinding black pepper on top.

'You won't remember who everyone is and what they all do straight away,' he was saying to Amber, who was holding Justin's hand under the table. 'But I thought we could all get to know each other tonight. These guys –' he waved his hand around the table – 'will be responsible for making you the biggest band in the country, or just another band who sink without trace.'

'I would have thought that our creative input has just a *little* to do with our inevitable success,' drawled Felix, lighting a Silk Cut Ultra Low.

'Of course. The idea is that you all work together, as a team,' said Symon. Then he banged on the table with his mobile for silence. 'Right – I'm going to go around the table introducing everyone,' he said, 'and we'll take the evening from there. First, we're all so excited to have Moja recording for us.' There was a cheer from Nicky and Justin. Amber clapped coquettishly. 'The one thing that we all have in common before we even *begin* is the fact that we all love the songs and we all want to make this huge. Because it has the potential to be fucking massive, and we all believe that it's going to take off and make it big-time. So without going on for any longer I'll hand you over to Felix.' I saw Symon glance round at the band and look suddenly overwhelmed. It was a big moment for him. Nicky gave him that slightly mocking look again, smiling his naughty school-boy smile. He whispered something to Justin and they both began to giggle until Justin picked up a glass of water with a shaking hand to try and stop himself. I was furious with them. If it wasn't for Symon there was no way that they would have been there. Symon was the kind of bloke you wanted to hug constantly and stroke his hair and tell him everything was going to be OK. Felix rose to the occasion.

'We're so excited that Symon is so into us,' he said. 'In fact, it's by *far* the most exciting thing that's ever happened to me in my entire life, and we just can't wait to sell millions of albums.'

I could see the women round the table behaving in the usual Felix Effect way – flicking hair, pouting and shooting each other amazed looks. His face was so pretty, but when he spoke he became more magnetic. Even the most cynical of girls had to admit that Felix could bewitch when he spoke to them. Now he was smiling and talking about Joss.

'We all loved what we did with Joss North, even if he did have the most bloody silly haircut of all time.' Symon roared with laughter. 'And we worked really hard with him. So it's up to you lot, apparently, to make us superstars. And I can't believe I'm making this historic speech while staring at a tube of Anusol,' he concluded.

'I can't believe you're admitting to *knowing* what Anusol is used for,' chirped up Nicky.

'Hey – even rock stars need to clean their teeth,' replied Felix smoothly.

'God, I love him,' I said to Nicky.

'You just *fancy* him. That's the most powerful thing in the world,' said Nicky, who was a constant observer of the Me and Felix thing. '"*All beauty is fleeting, take us as souvenirs*". You can forgive anyone anything when you know that they can make your heart thump and the butterflies go in your stomach.'

'What do I need to forgive him for?' I asked. 'He's perfection in human form.'

'Oh that's bollocks,' said Nicky, matter-of-factly.

'OK – is there not one single person in this whole world who you think is perfect?'

'Yes.'

'Who?'

'Can't tell, can't tell!' Nicky wailed. 'But there are demons in my head all the time. *And* they play drums better than me,' he added, deadly serious.

'No one could play drums better than you.'

'Do you mean that?'

'Of course. You rock, boy.'

'Now I *know* we're drunk,' said Nicky. 'Aren't we lucky to be young and drunk and pretty?' I wasn't listening any more. I could hear Amber talking to Felix.

'Why are you such a bastard to Frankie?' she was asking. Good question, I thought.

'She's a pain in the arse model. Not that Val gives a stuff.'

'You only do it because you want her yourself,' Amber replied smoothly.

Suddenly my red wine tasted like blood. I realised I had bitten my lip in horror.

'Oh please!' Felix snarled at her. 'Why are you always stirring? I've never met a girl I find less attractive than her.'

'Except for me,' said Amber.

'That's what this is all about, isn't it?' asked Felix.

'No. I just know that you would only get so wound up about Frankie if you wanted her yourself. Men are so predictable.'

Felix was no man. He was a boy, my boy.

'Lydia!' interrupted Symon from the other end of the table. 'This is Douglas Carter, MD of Conspiracy – you've already met, haven't you?'

I wondered if I could run out of the room. Everyone fell silent at that moment, as they tend to do when you know you're blushing. I already thought I was going to pass out with anger over the conversation I had just overheard. I waved noncommittally.

Then Nicky saved me from any further humiliation and awkward questions by breaking into song very loudly.

'*Hello Douglas, my old friend!*' he slurred to the tune of 'The Sound of Silence', then passed out, right under the table.

The Sunday after our night at the Pharmacy, Symon arrived at Stanley Road to tell us that Conspiracy wanted the band to play a showcase gig for the rest of the record company, a kind of presentation event. He walked through the front door pretending not to be overwhelmed by it all, as I had done weeks before. Amber and Justin were playing *Goldeneye*. Amber was beating Justin who was moaning as a result. Nicky and Felix were in the kitchen recording a new idea for a song on to Felix's four-track. I was with Frankie and Val, 'The Lovers Grimm' as Nicky had dubbed them, who were talking about whether Frankie should go to Milan for two weeks at the end of the month.

'But how could I leave you?' Frankie was asking in anguish.

'Well, I would have to come too. I'm not letting you near any greasy Italians geezers without me to protect you.' That was the advantage of having Carolyn's cash at your disposal, I thought.

'Sy's here,' came Justin's voice. 'Who wants a beer?'

We all sat in the kitchen, waiting to hear what Symon had to say.

'You're to play a showcase at some point in the next few weeks. A real industry thing. We've going to book somewhere next week so you'll need to get some rehearsing done before then.' Symon picked at the grapes that Amber had bought that morning. 'Mmm, seedless.' He sounded like Homer Simpson. He coughed. 'Everyone's so excited about it all.'

'I just want to write, for Christ's sake. We need new songs, we can't just rely on the same shit we've been playing for years to be reworked by some monkey in a producer's chair.' Felix flopped down next to Symon and buried his head in his hands.

'Oooohh!' said Amber. 'Touchy!'

'What the fuck would you know about it?' snarled Felix, turning on her. 'You just do what the hell we tell you to do. I doubt you even *mean* a word of what you sing.'

Amber simply did not put up with this kind of thing, especially from someone else in the band. She looked ready to cry, then changed her mind, took a large mouthful of orange juice and spat it over Felix. Despite her intention being to insult him, there was something disturbingly sexual about what she had done. Then I remembered that I had spat water over him on our first night together. The poor boy, I thought. Always getting second-hand liquids in his face. The orange juice soaked into Felix's T-shirt and dribbled down Amber's chin. He glared at her but didn't move. Symon stepped in.

'Guys, guys, what's going on? Listen, it's a weird time for all of you, I know, but it should be an amazing time, too. Felix, *mate*, you can take all the time you need to write. Jesus! That's all you need to do with your life at the moment. Why don't we get together tomorrow afternoon and run through some ideas?'

'I don't *need* to get together with anyone else,' said Felix. He hadn't meant it to sound rude, I knew, it was just the way that he worked. Then he stood up and looked at Amber. 'I'm going to change my clothes.'

I had never heard Felix like this before. What really concerned me was that Justin and Nicky looked completely relaxed, as if they had seen this happen a thousand times before. Even Amber, once she had cooled down, began discussing the first single with Symon as if what had taken place was so normal that she didn't want to waste any more time thinking about it. I followed Felix – well, of *course* I did, and found him upstairs, sitting on his bed, playing his guitar. I sat next to him and listened for a minute.

'*Not gonna sleep till I find the place, elusive thing, that personal space,*' he sang softly. I sighed uncertainly.

'I understand you, baby. You're under pressure, that's all.' Felix crushed my words with a hard kiss. I wanted him to take me, to obliterate his feelings through sex. But he didn't.

'You know, it's just like everyone always says. You wait and wait and wait for something to happen, and when it does, you're so shocked and nervous and confused that you don't know what to do with yourself. Then you start wondering whether it's what you always wanted in the first place.'

A frightening desolation had settled over him. I had never seen him like this. I only knew the boy who embraced the world as if it had been created for him alone. He pulled off his T-shirt, shook off his shoes and crawled under the duvet, pulling me close to him.

'Am I always going to be alone?' he asked, to no one really, certainly not to me. I just pressed myself closer and closer to him, until I couldn't see him, only feel him, burning hot and anxious. He smelled so strongly of Felix, of *him*. I wanted to get *inside* the smell of him, let it overwhelm me. I knew his eyes were wide open, his head on fire. I was bewildered and frustrated, but God damn it, I couldn't touch him. Somewhere between his head and mine there was just too much space, too much I just didn't *get*. I lay still. It seemed to get dark so fast. I could hear Amber laughing with Symon downstairs and James Brown blasting from the stereo. I felt a great heaviness come upon me.

'It's the Sunday night thing,' said Felix. 'I hate it so much. Going

238

back to school. Leaving Mum – not that she was ever there to leave – but leaving the thought of being with her. Getting on the train to arrive back in time for chapel and meaning nothing to anyone. Crying like a fucking baby and knowing that no one gave a shit. I hate it so much. I hate everything. I hate my life.' To my absolute horror and dismay, he burst into tears.

'You don't, you don't! How can you say that? You love the band, you love your music, you – you – you've made *me* happier than I've ever been. Christ, Felix, you're *everything*. Don't ever say you hate your life.'

But I could just as well have been speaking about the weather. The helplessness scared me so much. It was unbearable. I realised, with a sick feeling, that it wasn't that there was just a little bit of him that I didn't know, but only a little bit that I *did* know. Most of Felix was like an unexplored continent whose shores I hadn't even reached. And the thing that frightened me more than anything else was the terrifying sensation that there was no way that I could possibly get any further with him because there were huge chunks of *himself* that Felix was entirely confused by.

He cried for an hour – horrible, hot, appalling tears that soaked the pillow and mixed with his running nose. He clung to me like a little boy. My heart was so heavy I wondered whether I would ever be able to stand again. When I shifted my arm from under him when he eventually fell asleep, I glanced up at the photo of Carolyn Stewart.

'Bitch,' I whispered.

After that Sunday I carried with me the strange sensation of having lost and found something at the same time. In knowing that I knew so little about Felix I had experienced a revelation. A bubble had burst, but it wasn't *the* bubble, it was another bubble that I hadn't even known existed. He didn't mention the incident ever again. It was just as if it had never happened in the first place. When I awoke from the deep sleep that I always experienced after any sort of stress, Felix was already up and playing his guitar downstairs.

I shoved two slices of bread in the toaster and made a pot of tea. It was only nine o'clock. There was a note for Felix from Symon.

Felix,

Don't worry about anything. There is nothing that you have done that we can't undo. If it's any comfort, Laily was inconsolable just after signing her deal — she found the pressure too much. I'm always here to help you and talk to, so give me a call and we'll go out for beers.

Sy.

Then there was a PS in Amber's pretentious scrawl — all loopy Y's and random capitals: *Sorry Felix. We're both as bad as each other, but it wasn't your best T-shirt anyway. Love you, Amber.*

I was fairly certain that the 'Love You' had been inserted for my benefit. Felix was happy though, working on a new tune and scribbling lyrics on the back of his Vodafone bill.

When he played guitar the rest of the world ceased to exist — me included. Sometimes I felt almost as jealous of his Gibson as I did of Amber. It would always hold the key to something that I could never give him. And I wanted to be able to give him everything. I was starting to accept the fact that what I wanted was impossible. Maybe it was at that moment that I realised that I wanted to change Felix — a dangerous feeling.

'Amber said sorry,' said Felix, not looking up from retuning his guitar.

'Symon's note is adorable,' I replied. Why the hell was he mentioning Amber's rather irritating little PS when it was clearly Symon who was genuinely concerned for him?

'She always knows when she's gone too far.'

'Hmmm.'

'I'm going to meet Sy for lunch at Conspiracy. Go over a few things.'

'Hmmm.'

'What's wrong with you?' He looked at me in surprise.

'Just feeling a bit weird.'

'Why?'

'Just am.'

'Why?'

'Just am, OK? Like you were feeling a bit weird last night.'

'I see. So now you're making me feel bad for feeling shit on a Sunday night.'

'No! What are you talking about? Just forget it, I'll be fine.'

I had lost him again. He was flicking through yesterday's *Evening Standard*, totally absorbed. He read anything that he could lay his hands on. Sometimes I would arrive at Stanley Road with a new book to read and Felix would have devoured it within hours, before I had got past the first few pages. If there was nothing else for him to read he read the back of cereal packets or the TV guide. He also had a rather trashy habit of believing everything he read, which I was constantly surprised by. He bought practically every periodical in his local newsagents every month, including specialist magazines such as *Classic Car* and *Country Life*.

'Other people's hobbies are great,' he announced once without irony. 'There's nothing more absorbing than getting seriously *specific* about things.'

And of course he consumed the men's mags and *Vogue* and *Elle* and *Q* and *Melody Maker* and the *NME*. Looking back it's astonishing that he had any time for me at all, let alone the band. He adored popular culture, starlets and scandal, gossip and celebrities, and liked nothing more than discussing Posh Spice's new haircut or Ewan MacGregor's new film. In many ways he was very girlie. Then, in the same breath, he loathed the idea of his own inevitable fame, and confessed that he was quite unequipped to deal with any criticism. He was a star. He was difficult and confusing and magnetic and beautiful and full of contradiction. But above all of that, he was *my* baby. He rocked.

Chapter Eighteen

When you're young, don't belong
You gotta cushion the blows
When you're young, don't belong
Because tomorrow never knows.

User, 'Watercolour Serenade'

To prepare for the showcase, the band practised nearly every night. They rehearsed in a studio called the Blue Palace off Pentonville Road. I got into the habit of booking them a three-hour slot most evenings, and whatever else anyone was doing during the day, they would have to be there on time. We would be scheduled to arrive and set up by seven o'clock, and leave by ten. The Blue Palace had captured the dark, seasonless despair of a prison, but inside it was more like a haunted house, with the faint strains of some long-forgotten tune humming in melancholy rebuke round every corner. People came here to live out a little of the dream that so few ever realised. You only had to look at the diary of bands who used the studio to understand how few actually made it. Being in a band wasn't just the survival of the fittest (in every sense), but an endurance test for keeping friendships, money issues, administrative problems and musical differences in steady check. It was never, ever a case of merely arriving at the Blue Palace, tuning up and getting on with it.

Felix and I would arrive on the dot of seven to find Amber already there, sipping coffee and being chatted up by Damian, the gorgeous sixteen-year-old son of ex-drummer Greg, who ran the place. Amber never made any attempt to set up any of the instruments herself – she was very clear on the fact that she was a *girl* and girls didn't *do* that shit – but would issue loud instructions to Felix, who was pretty hopeless with leads and microphones. I would busy myself with lists; the band loved to see things written down – it created a false sense of achievement that was often the only compensation for a bad session. I would write down what songs needed work and any suggestions that Symon might have had.

Nicky was always ten minutes late but would arrive armed with chocolate and cigarettes so was quickly forgiven. Justin was never on time. He had decided a long time ago that everywhere in London took fifteen minutes to get to on the tube, a bafflingly inaccurate theory that was disproved by his consistent lateness. He had slipped into a comfortable role of arriving forty minutes after the start of the practice without excuse, and everyone was so used to it that they simply didn't bother getting angry any more. If Symon was present – which he frequently was – he would mutter a few words about 'needing to get on', but he never really got annoyed. The good thing about Justin was his unbelievable talent. He could pick up a new song or idea within minutes and was incredibly adept at dealing with Amber's tantrums and problems with the PA systems. So everyone had their place.

When, eventually, everyone was ready, it always started the same way. Maybe there was some comfort, some need for routine that meant that it had to be done like this. As soon as the drums were in position and the guitars plugged in they were off, often at such a pitch that there was absolutely no hope of any other individual being heard. Nicky played like he loathed his kit and needed to beat it to a pulp as some kind of punishment. Felix broke strings on his guitar every ten minutes and nearly set fire to his fingernails in his attempt to create more noise. Justin laughed a lot and encouraged as much general racket as possible by altering the levels on the bass so that it throbbed through his whole being like a plane about to take off in his soul. Then Amber would start to sing and realise that she might as well be miming. She would sing the first verse, face strained with shouting, then stop and glare at the boys who would ignore her for the bridge and the first chorus. Then Justin would agree to turn his amp down a little and as a result Nicky would shout, 'Can't hear you, mate!', so Justin would turn it up even louder than it had been before. Then Amber would stride over to me and Symon and throw her hands in the air and stamp her feet a bit. Sometimes she even stormed out of the room, but this never quite had the desired effect because once the boys were jamming, they wouldn't have cared if she had been abducted by aliens.

Justin was normally the first to break off and shout, 'All right, all right, let's turn everything down,' to which Nicky would suggest that Amber just 'sing a bit louder', which sent her spinning off into another fit of fury. I couldn't blame her, it was as if the band needed to get the volume out of their systems before they could think about doing anything else.

Amber hated the powerlessness that came when 'her band' had instruments in their hands, because she ceased to matter.

'You're just boys with toys!' she would shout. 'You're so selfish, all of you. You can just play as loud as you want, but I've only got my voice and I'm a *girl* – how can I compete with all your noise?'

Symon would step in at this point. The first time he came to a rehearsal he told everyone to unplug their instruments and play acoustically. He made Nicky use hot rods (softer drum sticks) and he encouraged everyone to listen to the words of the songs and concentrate on structure.

But whenever they first set up there was always that primal, urgent need to make noise. To drown out the world and themselves in a clamouring, physical blast of sound.

Felix, as the songwriter, was expected to come up with new material all the time. 'I've got a new song,' he would announce, and produce a crumpled piece of paper covered in illegible lyrics. He had a very limited knowledge of musical theory which meant that he got frustrated trying to explain to Justin and Nicky how the song was to be played. Justin had taken every grade on the piano – a fact which never ceased to astound me in view of the commitment required to achieve such greatness – and would wind Felix up by asking him about diminished sevenths and suspended fifths.

'It's a weird D,' was about as technical as Felix got.

I tried so hard not to read too much into Felix's lyrics, but it was impossible not to imagine that he was expressing some hidden

246

truth in everything he wrote. He wrote for Amber's voice – songs that girls would sigh over and adore. His words were clever and original and funny and so *very* Felix. Sitting cross-legged on the floor in the Blue Palace with Symon signing off invoices beside me, I would be completely overwhelmed by Felix's brilliance. He wrote so fast, never spending more than a few hours on any new song, and was constantly working on different ideas. He drew inspiration from everyone and everything – a phone call, a letter, an argument, a dusty punk album from 1978 or a techno recording that he taped off Radio One. The rest of the band seemed almost presumptuous about his talent – it was taken for granted that Felix wrote great melodies and knew how to express heartache and excitement and despair in three minutes. It annoyed me. After one rehearsal, when the others had been particularly relaxed about an amazing new song and Nicky had suggested that they leave early, Symon stood up and addressed Nicky, Justin and Amber in a way that he had never done before. Felix had gone outside to load up the car.

'Do you three have any idea how lucky you are to have Felix writing for you? I have never, ever come across anyone who produces the quantity and quality of work that he does. I'm not criticising you for not writing yourselves, but it's interesting what little encouragement he gets from you lot. I sit here and I hear hit after hit and I know how big this thing is going to be –' Symon's forehead crumpled in the anxiety of expressing himself – 'and I just want you to step back sometimes and realise that without the songs you are *nothing*. You're a pretty girl and a drummer and a bassist. The *songs* are the important things here. Don't forget it.' He smiled at them a little apologetically. It was a long speech for Symon to make, and out of keeping with his restoring-the-peace

247

character. But I felt tears shooting into my eyes with the relief of what he had said. The silence was interrupted by Felix re-entering the room on cue.

'Sorry, everyone, but I can't remember where I parked the car. Any suggestions?'

I hadn't forgotten the night at Pharmacy when Amber had suggested that Felix wanted Frankie. Something stopped me from saying anything to Nicky or to Amber about either issue; I didn't really know how to approach them about what they had implied, so their words just stayed in the back of my mind, never forgotten, just waiting there, loaded with insinuation and power.

One night after a rehearsal, Amber and I were on our own in Pizza Express. She was a little drunk, which was unusual as Amber was not a big drinker. After wolfing down their pizzas, Felix, Justin and Nicky had vanished back to Stanley Road to work out a new song that Symon wanted to hear the next day. Frankie and Val had gone off to meet some college friends of Val's in Clapham.

'Do you want to come too?' Val had asked Amber and me. We both answered 'No thanks' at exactly the same moment, then stared at each other, realising that one of us, at least, should have said yes to save us from being flung together. There was still half a jug of house white on the table.

'See you later then,' said Frankie. They left us. I opened my mouth to offer some lightweight chat, some irrelevant banter that could take us through our glass and a half each and home to the safety of the others, but Amber was too quick for me. My heart was beating faster than usual. No one made me edgy like Amber. She seized the moment without hesitation.

'It's a strange feeling, being in love,' she said.

'Why do you say that?'

'Just stating a fact. It's a difficult thing. It blinds and wounds—' She stopped. 'You see, I'm *so* in love. I have been for years. It never gets any less difficult. It's always there, every morning, burning inside me, never changing. Always there,' she repeated. She looked at me as if waiting for me to strike out and challenge her.

'I've never doubted the way that you feel about Justin,' I said.

Amber laughed a little to herself and offered me a cigarette. We both lit up from the same match. Sharing fire with her made me uneasy.

'But you see, you just don't get it, do you? I am in love with Moja. Not with any of them individually, but with . . .' She paused, searching for the word, then found it and clicked her fingers. 'I am in love with the *entity* that is Moja.' She pressed her hand to her chest to emphasise the point. 'I love Justin completely but it's almost like sleeping with him represents the way that I feel about the whole band.'

'Amber – here's the thing. I don't want to sit here and listen to you telling me how much you want to sleep with my boyfriend.'

'No, no! I don't want to sleep with Felix at all, it goes far beyond the idea of him *fucking* me – it's much more spiritual than that. It's all to do with what goes on in their heads. It's like we fuck each others' minds by being in this band together.'

'Oh, *please!*'

'But how do you feel about the fact that you will never be *in* the band? You can play along and pretend to be part of it all, but you'll never really *get* it. You'll never know what it feels to be

249

actually on the *inside*. The band is more powerful than all of us put together – it's bigger than all of us. It's out of our control. I just don't want to see you getting hurt by the fact that you can never touch that part of Felix. Because you can't. Moja is everything to Felix and to all of us, and sometimes I guess you must feel like there's no room for anyone else. Because, you see, everyone else is just . . . just geography.'

'That's not true. That's something that you've invented. And I never wanted you to hate me. You didn't *have* to hate me. You just chose to make it all difficult. I don't know why you're afraid of me. And even weirder than that –' something had struck me suddenly and I spoke it to Amber almost without thinking – 'I don't know why I *don't* hate you. You invited Frankie over to London because you wanted Felix to fall for her. I heard you talking to him at Pharmacy. You were encouraging him. Why? He doesn't even *like* Frankie. I'm sorry but your plan failed there.'

'You're getting too close to him. You're not right for him.'

'And you are, I suppose.'

'No. *No.* Felix never wanted me.'

'So you have to punish me as a result? This is getting scary.'

'Frankie would have been good for Felix. She would never have got close like you have. But you've got that novelty value thing.'

'What's that?'

'You're not beautiful. You're different. You're dangerous. You got him the record deal—'

'And *you* the record deal,' I corrected her

'OK – you got *us* the deal and you're clever and funny. Felix doesn't do clever and funny. I don't trust you. I don't like you and Felix, it bugs the hell out of me. They are *my* band. Felix is one of *my* boys. You may not understand it, but I have to look after them, and if I think they're with the wrong girl, I have to make that clear.' Then she picked up her glass, drained the rest of her wine and stood up. 'It's so much more difficult when you have three boys rather than one to worry about all the time. But I can't keep it in any longer. You're wrong for Felix, and if you don't get out now, he'll hurt you. You see, with Felix it's not really other girls coming between you that you have to worry about. It's an entire way of life, a whole mentality that you can never be a part of.' She was so lovely. I could see two of the waiters staring at her as she pulled on her jacket.

'You know what, Amber? I feel so sorry for you.'

'Thanks.' She shrugged and laughed. I smiled at her. I finished my cigarette and made my way home.

I lay awake thinking about what Amber had said. What confused me most was not her attitude, her ridiculousness and her arrogance, but the fact that I understood her. Somehow, through all of this, I knew where she was coming from and it was impossible for me to hate her. And deep down I don't think that she really hated me. At three in the morning, the phone rang.

'Lydia baby, can you hear me?' It was Felix.

'Yes – just.'

'I love you, I really do, and I'm sorry I'm a crap boyfriend sometimes.'

'You're never crap. You're just fucked up, but that's OK, I understand.'

Thank God he laughed. 'I'll see you tomorrow.'

'Yeah, see ya.'

'Well, don't you love me too?'

251

'So much.'

Amber wanted me to give him up. It was absurd, impossible. It was in that moment that I realised that Felix and I had become more than an extension of the band. We were our own thing, our own force.

Chapter Nineteen

Moja had a photo session the next day which Symon expected me to attend. It was due to start at mid-day in Battersea, but I told Justin to be there by eleven-thirty to ensure his arrival on time. I turned up at eleven, tired and edgy, hanging around with Symon and the photographer, Dina, who was a tiny, beautiful woman, which was some consolation as I knew it would irritate the hell out of Amber. Mimi had shouted at me in the morning because Felix's call had woken her up.

'What is the point in coming home to get some sleep then spending all night on the phone, Lydia?' she had asked. 'I knew that this sort of thing would happen once you left the museum.'

Dina floated around her studio in a pair of wide chocolate-brown DKNY trousers and a cropped top revealing a very tanned stomach, gulping black coffee.

'Africa last week, photographing a friend's new hotel,' she

explained in an accent that smacked of schooling at St Mary's Something. Symon, who as usual was showing no interest in the pretty girls, was sitting on the window ledge making relentless phone calls. He nearly jumped out of his skin when the buzzer rang and Jessie and Chloe, the hair and make-up girls, appeared, weighed down with products, mobile phones and vast bottles of water. Then, following them up the stairs, looking reasonably hungover, came Justin. Typical, I thought. The one time I tell him to get here early expecting him to be late, he arrives on time. Now I was stuck with him for half an hour before the others appeared.

'All right mate.' Justin shook Symon's hand. Symon was freaking out.

'Gaby, I've been to see them play and they are a *shit* band. I'm not going again, tell Douglas to send someone else. I want to go and see the Regular Fries tonight, and I'm not missing them for some crappy Corrs take-off act. Hello Justin.'

Justin turned to me. 'Where are the others?' he asked, his suspicious face darting around the room as if he expected them to leap out from behind the big screen that Will, Dina's assistant, was erecting. Will was gangly and awkward-looking with long wavy black hair and huge dark eyes.

'They're not here yet,' I said.

'Does this mean I'm the first?'

'Yes. Time for a public holiday, I think.' I meant to sound light-hearted but it came out sounding sarcastic and headmistressy.

'Oh, ha, ha. Please stop, my sides are hurting.' If Justin had meant to joke back it came out sounding just as cold as my comment.

'Do you want a coffee?' I asked, moving towards the kitchen.

254

'Yes. Bloody hell, I hate having my picture taken.' Justin was viewing Dina's large bag of film with distrust.

'You'll be fine. You look great today. You obviously got a bit of sleep last night.' I felt I should be generous.

'A bit. Felix and I talked for hours but I had run out of spliff and Rick wasn't around so I didn't smoke much.'

'Do you feel better for that?'

'No – a hundred times worse.'

'Do you think you'll ever give up?'

'Don't see any reason why I should. I'm not a singer, I don't need to protect my voice. And I definitely play bass better when I'm caned. Can I have one of these?' Will had been out to buy sandwiches and Diet Cokes. Justin took a cheese roll without waiting for the answer. 'They only really need to see Amber in the photos, don't they? I mean, it's not essential that me and Nicky are in the front,' he said through mouthfuls.

'I guess Amber will be the focus, but it's a band thing – you've all got to be seen.'

'I always look like such a prat in photos. Nicky's quite photogenic and a huge poser, and Felix is just a walking Calvin Klein ad, but I think I'm going to look stupid.'

'You'll have people around you making sure that you don't.'

'I suppose so,' he conceded.

I couldn't believe it. It was by far the most sympathetic conversation Justin and I had ever had. He had never, ever let his guard down to me like this and I wondered why he had decided to now.

'You never look stupid,' I found myself saying. 'You look scary and cool and arrogant and dangerous, but never stupid.' I went very red after saying this and Justin stared at me. I turned away.

'What one word would you use to describe yourself?' I asked him, to divert attention from myself. I had always wanted to ask Justin that question. 'Apart from unphotogenic, of course.' There was a pause while he considered.

'Salty,' he said. 'I'm very salty.'

'You're right. You're the saltiest person I've ever met.'

'Is that a good thing?' Justin was scrutinising the face of his mobile to avoid looking at me.

'You're very good at being salty. But I think you're sweet, too.'

'No!' He looked up and grinned at me and I almost wanted to reach out and touch his face to believe that he was actually smiling at *me*.

'Yes! You're adorable with Amber. You're the only person who can cope with her.' I wasn't being bitchy, I was merely stating a fact.

'I know *that*. That's not sweetness though, that's just, I don't know, habit or something. She's my *girlfriend*.' He used the word with startling reverence. 'I want to be sweet to her. It's not sweet, it's just the way that I am with her. She's different to everyone else, isn't she?' He sounded annoyed suddenly, as if he had come to this conclusion for the first time. 'Sometimes I think that she's the reason that I'm still doing all this stuff.'

'What do you mean?'

'I just can't stand the thought of her doing it without me. I'd go mental. At least when Amber and I argue we're in the same room. I'd rather be arguing with her in front of me than all nervous without her, wondering where she is, who she's flirting with.'

'You've er, really got your work cut out with her, haven't you?'

'Yup. What's that line? There's this Regular Fries lyric – *The feelings you never know are the ones you always want to show*. I can't always explain the way that I feel about her, so I get confused and we end up messing everything up. She can be a total nightmare – well, you of all people know that,' he went on. 'But she's just got that thing, that *Ahhh* factor that makes me just – well – I just really can't imagine not being with her.'

'Is the *Ahhh* factor just a sex thing?'

'No, no, it's like an addiction thing. She bugs me, but, look, I don't know why I'm coming out with all this now.' He looked suddenly nervous. 'They're all about to rock up here anyway.'

As if on cue, Jessie the make-up girl appeared.

'Are you Justin?' she asked.

'No, I am,' I snapped unexpectedly. I didn't want to be interrupted. Every time I got close to any kind of revelation with any of the band, someone or something came between us. Justin snorted.

'I've been told to make a start on you,' continued Jessie to Justin, ignoring my rudeness. 'You won't need much work but I do want you to come and sit down for a moment.'

I smiled at her. 'Sorry, I'm a bit tired this morning,' I said. I wasn't even capable of throwing my weight around. Justin grinned at me and sloped off with Jessie.

'I was exhausted this morning,' she was saying. 'I've been up at six and finishing work at eleven every night this week and I just didn't want to get up at all when my alarm went off.' Justin shuddered.

'Are you insane? How can you work that late?'

'I was doing a pop video.'

'Who were the band?' asked Justin.

'Oh, a new band, you won't have heard of them but they've just been signed to Element. A rock pop sort of band with a girl singer, really good, actually.'

'I hate them,' said Justin simply. 'Never heard of them, never want to hear them, crappy record company – forget it.'

Jessie looked over at me and raised her eyebrows questioningly.

'Oh, he means it,' I said.

'Right. Well, I'm just applying a mix of Mac and Clinique base to match your facial colouring,' she said to Justin, changing the subject to something less controversial.

'You'll be needing to mix a bit of green in with that then,' suggested Justin.

'Actually, I *am* going to use a little green powder which works as a calming agent to diminish any redness in the complexion,' explained Jessie patiently.

'Lydia's the only calming agent I want to have near my face,' came Nicky's voice from the door. Jessie giggled as he kissed me hello.

'Are you in the band too?' she inquired.

'I *am* the band.'

'Are you the singer then?'

'I'm the drummer. Without the drummer, there is no band.'

'You've got lovely freckles,' said Jessie admiringly, then stopped dead in her tracks as she spotted Felix and Amber crossing the room towards us. 'What a gorgeous couple,' she sighed. I was gratified that Felix came straight over to kiss me before introducing himself to anyone.

'You OK, baby?' he asked.

'Everything's cool,' I said.

'Hey – you're already here!' he exclaimed, seeing Justin being painted.

'Apparently,' said Justin, who was reading *Hello!* and making it impossible for poor Jessie to finish her work.

'I can't *believe* you're here,' said Nicky. 'Obviously couldn't wait to get your kit off.'

Amber was talking to Will. 'I worked at Chica for a year, but obviously with the band taking off I had to leave. I'd had enough of models, to be honest, and I just didn't want to spend my time dealing with them any more.'

'Did you say you worked at Chica?' asked Jessie. 'Are you *that* Amber? I've been booked for loads of jobs through you, testing new faces. Now you're in a band! Wow! That's so brave of you!'

'Far scarier to stay in your business,' said Amber with a shudder. 'Hi darlin'.' She squeezed Justin's shoulders.

Will was looking at Amber as if he would be delighted to spend his time dealing with her. He smiled at her. 'Dina's great to work for,' he said. 'So amazingly talented, I've just learned so much since I've been with her. I really want to exhibit my own work at the end of the year. I'm putting together a collection of portraits I've taken – mostly people who were total strangers when I met them.'

'As opposed to people you knew very well when you met them?' interjected Nicky sweetly. Amber glared at him.

'Go on, that sounds really interesting,' she said, peeling off her denim jacket and leaning forward in her tight pink T-shirt for Will's benefit. 'What kind of faces do you look for to photograph?'

'My style is very much mood-dependent,' Will revealed. 'I am captivated –' he pronounced it 'cuptivated' – 'by people with curious stories to tell. I think what I do best is to bring that out in the way that I catch them on camera.'

'What a very radical way of thinking!' cried Nicky, looking over to Will. 'I mean, no one has ever done anything like that before, have they?'

'Well, many of the greats have worked with the same philosophy,' confessed Will. 'It's just a theory that has stood the test of time, but I like to think that what I am doing will be different in approach.'

'In what way?' persisted Nicky. I kicked him.

'I just want to get away from the crowd, you know.' Will, encouraged by Amber's shedding of clothes, unzipped his Tommy Hilfiger jacket. 'And just be myself through my work.'

'I really admire that,' said Amber. 'That's what I want to portray through our songs.'

'Despite the fact that you don't actually *write* any of them?' said Nicky.

'Fuck off – it's all in the translation, the way you interpret things. Go and have your hair done or something,' Amber snapped at Nicky. 'Just leave me alone.'

'She really fancies him,' Nicky told me, picking up *Tatler* and making himself comfortable in the make-up chair recently vacated by Justin who had gone outside for a fag. 'I haven't seen her like this for ages. That thing where she walks into a room and sets her sights on someone, and before you know it there's trouble all round. My God, Liz Hurley's good-looking,' he added, scrutinising her photo. 'Don't let Justin see Amber with that little scamp or he'll go mental. Last time this happened there was a serious punch-up.'

Symon stuck his head round the door. 'Amber's trying on this silver mini-dress. She looks incredible but we need to have a discussion as to whether we think it's the right image for Moja.'

Amber was standing in front of a wall of mirrors that stretched down one side of the studio. She was half in, half falling out of the tiny silver dress and had shoved on a pair of pink plastic platform shoes that gave her legs that much-needed extension. She was pulling ineffectually at the front of the dress in an attempt to hide a little of her cleavage. She looked like an intergalactic fairy out clubbing. 'What do you think?' she asked Will, smirking a little apologetically.

'Don't ask Will, for God's sake, he's never even heard the music,' said Symon tersely.

'Well, my opinion, for what it's worth, is that she looks unbelievable. Huh, huh, huh.' Will had a terrible laugh.

At that moment, Justin reappeared and glared at him. 'Too right she looks unbelievable. Unbelievably fucking silly. She looks like a right slapper. It's completely over-the-top and camp and tarty. And actually it's too small, you need the bigger size anyway.' He turned round and stalked off.

Amber did the usual thing of looking like she was going to cry, then hardened fast like spat-out chewing gum. 'Felix,' she demanded. 'What do you think?'

'I don't like it much,' he admitted. 'You look beautiful but it's all wrong. Christ, can you see us being taken seriously with you dressed like that on the album cover?'

'Very Spice Girls,' offered Symon. 'Not sure it's right. Lydia?'

I never failed to find it sweet that Symon continually asked my opinion.

'I think it's cool,' I said slowly. 'I kind of like the idea of Amber's image being completely at odds with the music. I think it could work.' The words were barely out of my mouth before Amber was stepping out of the dress.

'No, no, no — I don't like it.' She stood there in her black knickers and bra, arms folded in defence. 'I've really gone off the whole thing. You're right. I want to keep everything much more simple.'

'I still think you looked great in it,' said Will, who was pretending not to stare at Amber's dinky little body. I smiled to myself. There was no way that Amber would have agreed to anything that I had suggested so the quickest way of getting her out of the dress was to tell her that I liked it. I was learning how to keep one step ahead with Amber. Most of the time it simply involved letting her think that she was winning.

She turned and smiled at Will. 'Thanks,' she said softly. Forty minutes later she sauntered back into the studio having had her hair and make-up perfected, and wearing the outfit that she had worn when I first saw her at the Lemon. She dazzled.

Dina was completely enraptured by Felix and could barely control her urge to take three reels of film simply of him, something about which Felix was encouragingly indifferent. Moja played in the background on the stereo. It never ceased to amaze me how I could separate the people in the band from the music that they produced. Whenever I heard their music I was uplifted and charged with excitement and longing. They were a pop band —

their mission was to fill the soul with that mind-blowing ecstatic thrill that only music can fire up. Independent of the love I felt for Felix was this quiet knowledge that they were the best band in the world. My feelings about Moja were so confusing because I loved being one of the only people in the world who 'got' them. There was that protective, possessive streak in me that wanted to keep them closely guarded forever. Yet at the same time I wanted to shout out loud that everyone should be listening to them, loving them.

Symon sang along to everything, drumming his fingers on his knees and talking about the gig next month.

'Wow, this is *great*,' exclaimed Dina after the first song finished. 'Who writes the songs?' Everyone asked that, I realised. It was vital that everyone knew that it was Felix, too, because his personal identity came from his songs. I often wondered how many people would assume that it was Amber, as the lead singer and focal point of the band, who was the songwriter.

'Felix,' said Amber quickly.

'Beautiful lyrics,' said Dina. 'Really genuinely heart-felt.'

'Thanks,' said Felix. 'I don't really aim to please anyone except the band, so it's always a bonus when someone else likes what I'm saying.'

'Can I run in for a second?' piped up Jessie, who was desperate to add more mascara to Felix's eyelashes.

'Quickly, then,' sighed Dina. 'Then we'll take another Polaroid, Will.' Will nodded sagely and made a great deal of fuss extracting the Polaroid film. Jessie entered the set of the photo and stretched the wand up to Felix's eye level.

'You have the longest eyelashes I've ever seen,' she exclaimed. 'Wow. Couldn't you give me a bit of that length?'

263

'What are you asking about Felix's length?' asked Nicky. 'I can tell you I've seen it and it's nothing to get remotely excited about. Now, if you want *real* length, look no further than myself.' Jessie seemed to think Nicky was hilarious and went puce trying to control a fit of giggles.

'Lydia could tell us more about Felix's length than anyone else in the room,' said Justin. I looked at him. He was smiling, not that usual mocking smile but a real smile, like he was making fun of me because I was his friend, and he could. I also felt that he was making it clear to me that nothing had ever happened between Felix and Amber. He just wanted to make me feel better, to let me know in the tiniest way that he had understood our conversation earlier. He knew that something had shifted between us. No one else noticed the change, of course, and I had no chance to respond because Will cut in with a remarkable lack of tact.

'I thought that Felix was going out with *you*,' he said to Amber, barely able to keep the delight out of his voice.

'No,' said Amber quickly, shooting him a wide-eyed look of surprise. 'Why did you think that?'

'You just looked like you should be together,' said Will. 'Without meaning to sound cringey, you're both so gorgeous-looking.'

'Polaroid, Will,' said Dina sharply. 'Lydia's gorgeous too,' she added, for the benefit of those who were unaware.

'Oh my God, I totally didn't mean that you weren't!' Will turned to me in a fluster of *faux pas*. 'I just thought that they were together, that's all.'

'Don't worry, it takes much more than that to offend me,' I lied. It was incredible, I thought, how the most random strangers could be so cruel without intention, merely through assumption.

'I could never put up with Felix in a million years,' teased Amber, staring at him in a way that challenged that remark.

'Not that you were ever given the opportunity,' cut in Nicky.

'Wow, I'm really vibing off the emotional issues going on in this band,' sighed Dina. 'Very inspirational for song-writing.'

'Not really,' said Felix coldly. 'I gave up writing about people's outsized egos last year.' He put his hand up to his forehead as if testing his temperature and sighed.

'Ooh! Hold that, Felix! That looks fabulous – Jesus, what a face. Amber, step back a bit and look at Felix. Will, we're shooting to film now. Nicky and Justin, stay right where you are.'

'Which is in the irrelevant bit of the photo,' muttered Nicky.

'And thank God for that,' said Justin.

'Justin, you look great,' I heard myself saying. Felix shot me a look of pure confusion.

Chapter Twenty

That night Felix and I lay in bed. I was wearing his Loser T-shirt and reading *GQ*. He was staring at the ceiling, the thundercloud look across his face again. I knew what he was going to say. Maybe this meant that I was starting to know him.

'You fancy Justin.'

'I do *not*! My God, how could you think that? Of all the people in the world, he is about the last person you should be worried about.'

'Bollocks!' Felix sat up suddenly. 'What was all that crap about how good-looking he was at the shoot? And you telling him to get there early just so you could spend a few precious moments with him on your own? How can you even begin to deny it?'

I tried not to, but I snorted with laughter.

'And how can you fucking laugh? How can you laugh at me!' Felix's face collapsed in agonised confusion. He began to cry. 'I just don't understand you! How can you laugh when I've been thinking about this all day? It's been driving me mad. How can you find this funny? I guess when you run off with Justin you can both have a really good laugh about me when I'm not around. Well, fuck you.'

I loathed him crying. I loathed that I had made him cry, however insane his reasoning.

'Oh Felix, angel, why are you crying? I was only laughing because it's so silly, you ever worrying about anyone else. I love you so much. I was only trying to make Justin feel better because he said he hated having his photo taken. That's just part of the manager's job. Felix!' He had turned away from me. I tried to pull him back into my arms.

'I know I'm paranoid. I know I'm a nightmare boyfriend. I know you can't even look at another boy without me freaking out, but I just—'

'I never, ever, want to look at another boy, don't you get that? How could anyone want anyone else when they have you? Felix, everyone loves you. Everyone thinks that you are beautiful. It's not up for general debate, it's a hard fact of life, like, I don't know, like me having a sister and you having a brother. You can't change it. You're the one people stare at when we walk down the street. You're the one who people fall in love with on stage. It's all you, baby. And it drives me mental. But the thing is, I don't care because I know that it's me that you love. I know that at the end of each day, it's going to be me and you in bed together. Not anyone else. Why should it matter what they think?'

'But you never even *talk* to Justin, then today it all changed, there was just something different in the way that he was speaking to you. He never speaks to you. Why was he being all matey today?'

'Well, I don't know, but would you prefer it if he was difficult and never talked to me? Don't you think that it's nice that he was making an effort for once?'

'No!' Felix was almost shouting. He turned round to face me again. 'I hate it! I just don't want you getting involved with him!'

'I'm not getting involved with him! What do you mean? Listen, Justin has been a real dickhead to me from the moment we first met, and today I felt that we had a real breakthrough and that he was accepting me at last, and I was really happy about it. But you've managed to make me feel like it's a bad thing, and that there's something fundamentally wrong with him talking to me and that it's all my fault!'

'I just can't help it, OK? I just hate the combination of you and Justin and I think that he fancies you or—'

'Oh please! Where the hell did that theory spring from? He's going out with Amber, remember?'

'Oh, and that is really going to stop him from liking you.'

'What are you talking about?'

'I don't know. I just think that maybe Justin might be after you to get back at Amber for when she flirts with other boys.'

'Thanks a lot!' I said. 'And you think that I might be stupid enough to fall for that?'

'You see!' Felix was triumphant. 'You're admitting that he's trying it on!'

'I am *not*! He loves Amber far too much, the poor bloke. Felix, do you realise what a waste of energy this conversation is?'

'I just feel that all this time, all this weird atmosphere between you and Justin is a sign of the fact that you want to get him into bed.'

'Felix, this is actually starting to piss me off. I take it as a massive insult. Does nothing that I say to you *ever* sink in?'

'I just don't know who to believe.'

'This is crazy, pointless talk!' I climbed out of bed. 'I'm going home.' I was surprised at myself, but relieved that I had the courage to do it. 'I just can't lie next to you and listen to this all night. Get yourself something real to worry about, for God's sake.'

'Oh, right, here we go. Now you're going to bugger off home and tell everyone how paranoid I am and how I have nothing better to worry about in life because I have this amazing house and all the rest of it, and what a spoilt brat I am and how I don't realise how much I have compared to the rest of the world. Well, go on then. Just walk out. Just leave me here.'

I pulled on my jeans and slipped my feet into my trainers. I kissed Felix on the cheek. He moved away. I wanted to cry. 'Felix, I love you. I always have and I always will.' I walked to the door. 'Go to sleep, you just need some sleep. You can't have a normal existence when you go to bed at four in the morning every night. You blow everything out of proportion. I'll call you when I wake up.'

'Lydia.'

'Yes?'

'I love you.'

'I love you too.'

'But wait—'

'What?'

'You don't, you don't—'

'*Don't* say it!'

'No, but I just have to check. You don't fancy Justin, do you?'

'No. I do not.'

I crept downstairs and out into the night. I walked nearly all the way home. I felt very much alone, but stronger.

Emma and I had a huge cooked breakfast together the next day.

'I hate to say this, but I had a feeling that he was going to be paranoid.' Emma slammed two pieces of bread into the toaster.

'What do you mean?' I asked irritably. 'How can you know something like that? Anyway, he's fine, he's just tired and stressed about the deal.'

'It's a scary thing, though,' said Emma. 'I can't handle boys like that. I just haven't got the patience to cope with it. You can deal with it because you love him, but it still sucks.'

'It only sucks because it makes him so unhappy. I just want to make him realise how much I love him and how I'll never want anyone else, but he doesn't get it.'

'I don't think that he's really worried about you running off with anyone else.' Emma spread a thick layer of Nutella on her toast. 'Wow, I haven't eaten this in years. Frankie got me back into it.'

'Explain,' I said.

'We always used to eat Nutella when we went to see Frankie in Spain.'

'No, you jerk, your theory on Felix!'

'He hates something else, someone else that's making him insecure and nervous and edgy. There has to be some reason for why he thinks that you don't want to stick around. I hate to get psychological on you,' she went on, 'but you have to admit it's a bit odd.'

'What should I do?'

'Listen, I don't know Felix like you do. But you have to find out what is making him freak out like this.'

'I've got a good idea about what it is,' I said, 'but he won't really speak about it. I don't think that it would help him to talk to me about it. He's very much a pupil of the school of thought that suggests that problems should simply be squashed to the bottom of your soul, from where they can never resurface.'

'We is in da nineties, girl,' said Emma in her best Ali G. voice. 'You can't expect to carry on like love's young dream with this stuff spooking you out. You is needin' to get real!'

'As if I could ever fancy Justin anyway.'

'Boys have no concept of who girls find attractive. I'm sure that Felix should be more worried about Nicky or even Symon – God, now *he's* gorgeous – rather than Justin.'

'But I genuinely have no interest in anyone else.'

'Well, maybe Felix can't understand that because he himself could never feel like that? Maybe he's the paranoid one because he knows what goes on in his own head?'

'Crap theory. I hate it. Look, can we talk about something else?'

'Sure. How are Frankie and Valentine?'

'Still obsessed.'

'Cringe.'

'What do you mean?'

'I don't know, there's just something very contrived about that combination. It's all a bit too perfect.'

'You've hardly seen them together.'

'I know, but you can just tell. It's the way Val is so delighted that she's a model, and older than him and all that.'

'My God, I wish that people thought Felix and I were a bit too perfect.'

'There's no way you ever would be.'

'Why not?' I didn't really want to know.

'Well, you just look like a strange couple, and there's all this weird possessive stuff flying around, and it's just a bit hard to get your head round.'

'No one *needs* to get their head round it,' I said.

'I know, I know. Don't get me wrong, I'm just talking about surface appearances.'

'Great. Now I have my own sister giving me the "Felix could have any girl in the world, why the hell has he chosen you?" line.'

'No, no. You know what? I actually think that you are really, really cool together.'

'Why?'

'It just works. And although I've been really negative about the paranoid thing, I really think that in many ways it's nice. I wish there was a bloke out there as good-looking as Felix who was stressing over me. It must make you feel quite powerful.'

'It used to,' I said sadly. 'But it doesn't any more.' Then the phone rang. It was Felix.

'Come over, Symon's on his way. We're all talking about the showcase.'

'I'm on my way.' I shoved the last triangle of toast and Nutella into my mouth. 'I'm outta here,' I said to Emma.

Chapter Twenty-one

Nicky was prancing around the room to the Bee Gees in a pair of multi-coloured patchwork flares. 'Aren't they just the grooviest?' he asked me. 'I got them yesterday in Portobello. When do we get to cover a Bee Gees song, Sy?' Symon was studying the artwork of an old Human League album.

'They've all been done before,' he said. 'If you want to cover something, make it ironic.'

'What, Alanis Morrisette?'

'No, I mean, if you cover a song, then make it a bizarre choice. Something tongue in cheek like "*Together In Electric Dreams*".'

'Amazing song,' said Felix, entering the room looking fresh-faced and just showered.

'You don't need to cover anything on your first album, anyway. You've got enough great stuff yourselves,' I said.

'I agree,' said Symon. 'Where are Justin and Amber?'

'Stuffing themselves with the food Carolyn sent over.'

'Food?' Symon looked interested.

'Carolyn sent Felix a hamper of food from New York to say good luck with everything,' said Nicky. I looked at Felix.

'I think she's well into the idea of us having a deal,' he said vaguely.

'There are Hershey Bars and M&Ms and Cheerios and everything,' went on Nicky.

'You can get all of those things over here now,' observed Felix.

'Yeah, but it's still cool that they came over from New York. I can't wait to do a gig over there.'

'I can,' said Felix quickly.

'Listen, we need to break in this country before we start thinking about America,' said Symon. 'We certainly can't afford to get you out there just yet.'

'I've got a travelcard zones one and two,' persisted Nicky. 'Does that cover the States?'

'Since when have you had your own travelcard?' asked Felix.

'OK, OK, it's borrowed. But Felix, these are the last few weeks of me having no money. Doesn't that fill you with excitement?'

'It would if I could believe it,' said Felix. 'I kind of figure that however successful you and Justin are, I'm always going to be bailing you out over something or other.'

'True. True,' conceded Nicky. 'Why break a habit?'

'Why indeed?' said Justin, coming into the room with a spliff hanging out of his mouth and nothing but a pair of Felix's jeans on. His hair was standing on end and his eyes were heavy and stoned. He was carrying his bass guitar. He sat down on the floor and played a very fast line from Moja's latest song. He looked unbelievably rock 'n' roll.

'Where are Val and Frankie?' he asked suddenly.

'Painting their room red,' said Felix. 'Or, according to Val, painting it "vermilion".'

'They get on very well together, don't they?' said Symon. It was strange hearing him speak about anything other than the band. I didn't really like it.

'Don't believe the hype,' said Felix dryly.

'OK, shall we get on with this?' Symon was blunderingly efficient again. 'I want to showcase you to the whole company in a good little venue – have you played the Camden Falcon before?' he asked.

'Yes,' said Nicky wryly. 'Nine times, in fact.'

'Good, so you're familiar with the place,' said Symon. 'You'll be less nervous.'

'No chance of me being anything other than terrified, I'm afraid,' said Nicky.

'You need to go into serious rehearsal and finish off all the new songs that you've started. The other thing is that I'm going to see the Regular Fries at the Scala tonight—'

'The Fries are playing tonight?' Justin's interest was clearly more focused on this fact than what Moja were lined up to do.

'Yes, come along with me if you want, I've got a couple of spare tickets.'

'Man, I am there,' said Justin. 'Amber, what are you doing tonight?'

'Going out,' she said. 'I'm going to a party with that guy, you know, Will.'

'Not Dina's imbecile assistant?' asked Felix incredulously.

'The very same,' said Amber sweetly.

'Why? What the hell are you encouraging him for?' asked Justin. 'I can't *believe* you!'

'You were invited too,' said Amber. 'Everyone was. I just didn't think you'd all be up for it.'

'Too right,' said Nicky.

'If you think I'm going to spend my evening with that jerk rather than the Fries at the Scala then you can think again,' said Justin.

'Frankie likes the Fries,' I said. 'Maybe you could take her?'

Amber looked livid. 'Fine by me,' she said to Justin. 'If she can tear herself away from Val for a few hours.'

'I don't care who else goes. I'm going,' said Justin.

'I'll come to the party with you, Amber,' I said suddenly. Well, what the hell? Amber looked amazed.

'All right.' She shrugged. 'Felix?'

'No thanks,' said Felix. 'Lydia, what the hell is with this boy?' He couldn't keep the panic out of his voice.

'Nothing, I just feel like going out.'

'Why?'

'I just do. Will you come too?'

'Fuck off!' Felix stood up. 'No way am I going to some dickhead's party who I hardly know. And I can't understand why you want to go.'

'OK, I probably won't go. It was just a thought,' I said.

When Symon left I caught up with Felix in the kitchen. He was munching through a box of peanut-butter-flavoured candies from Carolyn's delivery, on auto-pilot.

'I just want to go to the party so that I can spend some time with Amber,' I explained to him.

He had picked up his guitar and was strumming out chords and humming a melody over the top.

'What?' He looked at me as if my interruption was most unwelcome.

'I said, I'm going out with Amber so that I can talk to her and try and improve this crap relationship I have with her.'

'Do whatever you want,' said Felix, not looking up from his guitar. He started to play the chords again, this time adding words to them.

'*You have empires at your feet when you come up from the street,*' he sang softly.

'That's a great line,' I said.

'I didn't come up from the street though, did I?' said Felix.

I just didn't want to have this conversation now. 'So, I'm going to go with Amber. OK?' I asked.

'Whatever,' said Felix.

That was the crazy thing. When Felix was distracted by his music and by his own private problems, nothing really mattered. I could tell him I was about to board a flight to Mozambique and it would have been difficult to get a reaction. Yet he was as sensitive and as explosive as dynamite the rest of the time. He was so obviously deeply uncomfortable with both roles. The paranoid, possessive boyfriend was a part of him that he loathed; the insecure, self-obsessive was another part of him that he couldn't deal with. These negative traits, fused with his extraordinary charm and kindness, seemed to make him queasy with contradiction.

'You go to the party,' he went on. 'I'm staying here and going through some stuff with Sy and Nicky. We have actually got loads of work to do before this gig, believe it or not.'

279

'Nice of your mum to send over all that stuff.'

'Very useful. We had completely run out of food in this house. She's got great timing. Have a candy.' I took one.

'Delicious.'

'Of course. They're the best. Nothing less for Carolyn Stewart.'

'Have you decided what songs you're going to play at the gig?' I asked.

'Maybe. Sort of.'

I walked off. I was learning that there was no point in even trying to talk to Felix when he was in this mood.

I was to meet Amber at nine-thirty outside the party venue. I guess she didn't want to walk in on her own. I spent hours getting ready for the evening. Not that I had anyone to impress, but I wanted to make sure that I felt all right next to Amber for once. I wore my denim mini-dress and Frankie bought me some hilariously outsized silver glittery false eyelashes.

'It is kind of strange, you going to a party without Felix,' said Frankie, who was wearing a minute peach-coloured towel on her head and nothing else as she rooted around in her make-up bag for her mascara.

'Well, you're going out on the town with Justin and Symon!' was my response. 'And I can tell you, it has not gone down at all well with Amber.'

'I just like the Regular Fries. Why should she mind?'

'She's paranoid. Seems to be part of the job description for being in a band, if you ask me.'

'Good luck,' said Frankie. She had slipped on a long black satin dress with spaghetti straps and black sandals. 'What do you think?' she asked.

'You look amazing, but you're only going to a gig.'

I felt a tiny bit irritated. Keeping up with Frankie and Amber was virtually impossible from a fashion perspective. Neither girl minded turning up to anything in completely inappropriate clothing as long as they caused a stir. But while Amber's entire outlook was based on being the Most Beautiful, with Frankie it was more a matter of keeping up standards because her appearance was her career.

'You think I should change? I like this dress. It's Gucci.'

'I dare say. I'm just suggesting that maybe the nice designers in the House of Gucci don't make their clothes for people going to watch bands playing in dodgy venues in King's Cross.' Frankie laughed.

'OK, I'm changing.' Five minutes later she appeared wearing faded brown cords and a black tank top. She still looked phenomenally pretty.

'That's more like it,' I said. Frankie smirked a bit.

'Well, have a good night,' she said. Then she paused. I knew she wanted to say something. 'What?'

'I just – no, nothing, nothing.'

'What, come on!'

'I just, I am a bit worried about me and Val. You know, like I said before. He is so young, I just feel like maybe he needs to grow up a little before—'

'Frankie . . .'

'Yes?' She already looked guilty.

'I just want to say that however young Val is, you hold his heart in your hands. Just be careful, for God's sake.'

'I will, I will. Oh, you don't need to worry, I still adore him, I'm just—'

'Feeling bored?'

'No. *No!* How could I be bored of him? He is gorgeous and sweet and—'

'Seventeen.'

'Yes. He's seventeen.'

'Frankie – just be good.'

'And you too! No looking at other boys.'

'I can tell you,' I said, with absolute conviction, 'that I am far, far too in love to look at other boys. Whether that's a good thing or a bad thing.'

Amber was in high spirits when she met me.

'I find it very weird that you're here,' she said, 'but since you are, we might as well have a good time.'

'Nice to see you too,' I said.

She was wearing Nicky's patchwork flares with a black knitted top. She looked very low-key by her standards, but her face was so lovely that it never really mattered what she was wearing. We walked into the party and immediately Will was beside us, holding Amber in an embrace and kissing her hello like she was a precious doll that might break if he was not careful.

'Hi, Will. Thanks for the invite,' I said.

'Oh, hi, er, great you could come along. There's food and drink through there.' He waved vaguely towards a door.

'Great. I'm starving.'

I piled my plate high with chicken pieces and a big jacket potato and tomato salad. It was just what I felt like. There must have been about forty people hovering around in the room that I chose to settle down in. Pulp played on the stereo. With a jolt I realised that the last time I had heard them was at Ben's party where I had met Felix. How far I had come! Comparing myself on the two occasions was extraordinary. It was as if the old Lydia had died that night in Manchester, and my rebirth had been so frantic and so unexpected that I had not had a chance to contemplate it. But *had* the old me died? How much of myself had I taken into my strange new life with these peculiar new co-stars?

I had craved something new, something different and something to believe in. Felix had given me all of those things, through his love for me, through his style and his glamour and his band. Because I believed in Felix, I believed in everything about him. It was odd that despite the fact that I had been the one to get Symon along to see them play, I still felt on the outside. But I was closer to the inside than ever before. I had this confidence, this poise that I had only dreamed of possessing before I became involved with Moja. I was unafraid of the people in the room with me now. I had no idea about any of them, where they had come from or what any of them were doing, but I had my own conviction, my own credence. That was the most powerful thing I had ever possessed.

'I'm Leo. I'm talking to the prettiest girls here and asking what they do in life. Research for my dissertation.' A floppy-haired blond boy in a pale blue shirt sat on the floor beside me. I smiled.

'I manage a band.'

'Cool. Who? Anyone famous?'

'Not yet,' I said, echoing Felix's words to me, 'but they will be.'

'What are they called?'

'Moja.'

'Oh my God, you must manage Amber!'

'I try to.'

'Will is fucking nuts about her! She is going to be so famous! Wow! Have you got a copy of their CD on you?'

'No. I imagine Amber does.'

'Amber and Will are really serious about each other, aren't they?' Leo went on. 'He's been on the phone to her every night since they met and he's blown up a Polaroid of her and stuck it on his bedroom wall. He can't stop talking about her.'

Poor, innocent Will, I thought, and poor Justin. Or *was* it poor Justin? Nothing that Leo was saying was coming as any surprise. I decided to let him talk.

'I always thought that Will was a bit of a prick, actually.' He lowered his voice. 'Thinks he's God's gift to the female species—'

'Which he most certainly is not.'

'Correct.' Leo looked at me with respect. 'He is not. But he's got Amber now so I'm thinking that there must be something right about him. I mean, imagine what will happen when the band takes off and Amber is really famous. Will is going to become like a celebrity in his own right, isn't he? That's what I find so unfair. They'll be the new Posh and Becks.'

'Except he can't play football and presumably has only a fraction of David Beckham's money.'

'Well, you're right about the football,' conceded Leo. 'I was at school with the guy and he was a crap player, but I think he could give David a run for his money in a financial scenario, so to speak.' Leo was pleased with his word-play.

'What do you mean?'

'Will is loaded. Completely stacked. Rich. Loadsamoney. Very, er, affluent. Wealthy.'

'Is he?' I tried to hide my interest by prodding at my potato.

'His parents own a massive castle in Devon and they bought this house for Will for his birthday last year. Not a bad present, is it? They're always hanging out with the Royals and God knows who else in various incredible locations. Will was in the south of France last week on some yacht or other. But look, I don't want to sit next to you and go on about his money. God, I'm rude.'

'Think nothing of it,' I said. 'Listen, it's been nice to meet you but I need to find Amber.' I stood up.

'Nice to talk to you. See you later.' Leo grinned.

I found Amber talking to Will in the kitchen.

'I've just met your friend Leo,' I said.

'Oh, what was he saying?' Will looked concerned, as well he might.

'Nothing much. Amber, do you have a copy of the CD? I thought we could put it on and try it out.'

Amber looked at me coldly. 'It's upstairs in my bag.'

'Could you get it?'

'OK.' Amber was lured by the idea of her voice pumping around the house. I followed her up the stairs.

'Listen, what's going on between you and Will?'

'Nothing! Oh my God, what do you think?' Amber looked at me in disgust.

'That Leo boy I was talking to was implying that you and Will had been in serious communication since the photo shoot.'

'Well, I've spoken to him a few times,' she said testily.

'Look, Amber, I don't pretend to know what's going on between you and Justin and Will. All I know is that we can't rock the boat with the band at this stage. Justin would go mental if he thought there was anything going on between you and someone else.'

'Lydia, I just want a bit of space. I like Will. He makes me laugh.'

'He's not in any way remotely funny.'

'He is, you just haven't got to know him.'

'But why do you *want* to get to know him?'

It was lucky that Amber had drunk quite a bit already. She would never have talked to me so freely if she had been completely sober. 'I just need to feel loved, OK? I want to be adored. Will really likes me. It's attractive. It's something I can't help.'

'You will be loved!' How could anyone be so screwed up? I wondered. 'In a few months time you won't be able to walk down the street because you'll be so famous and so loved that you'll be recognised wherever you go. Can't you just wait for that?' It all seemed rather simple when I put it like that.

'I need it now, Lydia. Justin can't give me that feeling any longer.'

'Well, why are you still with him?'

'I love him.' She was about to cry again. 'I don't want to hurt him.'

'Well then don't,' I said. 'And just stay away from Will because I can see his angle and he's an idiot.'

Will strode up to us. 'Can I have the CD?' he asked. Amber handed it to him and he sped off to put it on.

'I just want to feel like I'm worth something to someone.' Amber shook her head. 'I feel so uncertain. First you come along and start distracting Felix, then we get this deal—'

'Because of me,' I had to remind her again.

'Yes, but you're missing the point.'

'What point – there is no point!'

'The point is that we had our own world which you suddenly invaded, you came into, you violated. You've opened us up, you've opened all these doors and it scares me. Sometimes I just want things to feel like they used to.'

'So you'd throw away the chance of fame and the record deal and everything just so that you felt like there was no one out there threatening you and your boys.'

Amber stared at me. 'Sometimes I think I would,' she said. 'I just don't know how strong I am, how much I can cope with this whole scenario. It's all happened so suddenly.'

Felix would never have said that, I thought. He had wanted this for so long. I recalled what Nicky had said to me on my first night in Stanley Road. Felix wanted it because he loves the music. Felix just wanted people to be able to hear his songs and to get the same buzz out of what he wrote that he got from 'I Don't Like Mondays'. The music was what he believed in. Amber had nothing to believe in. She was an excellent and compelling performer and a good singer, but she was essentially an actress. They weren't her words that she sang, and I couldn't imagine that she felt much of what she was singing about. She didn't believe in herself. Now it appeared that her faith in her band was slipping away. So she felt terrified.

'You know, Lydia, I have people like Will and Symon telling me how wonderful I am and how good my voice is and all that, but they're just empty words. The only people I care about, the only ones I want to love me are the band. Felix and Justin and Nicky. Especially Justin.' Her voice cracked. 'He's my *boyfriend*.'

She said it in exactly the same way that Justin had announced 'She's my *girlfriend*' to me on the day of the photo-shoot; with that peculiar reverence that eliminated any doubt I may have had about their relationship.

'They matter to me, not anyone else, not the punter in the street who can buy the album with the sexy photo on the front and wank over me at home. But I just don't get it from them, I don't feel any of that adoration from them any more. It's ever since you came along. You've changed everyone's lives and suddenly no one really thinks they need to comfort me any more. But if they don't love me then I can't go on.' She had that spooked look that people get when they have said too much.

'Amber. Listen to me. I don't like you because you've been a bitch to me. But I understand you. And there's something that you have to hear.'

'What?'

'You are the most beautiful girl I've ever seen, you're the most magnetic. You have such power and you're mezmerisingly talented and good at what you do. The only thing you need now is to believe in yourself, and in the band. Stop all this insecure bullshit. Be my friend. I can help you—'

My words were drowned out by track one of the Moja demo. The world could have been about to blow up and I still would have wanted to jump up and dance and shout about what a great song it was.

'And this —' I shook my head — 'is the most amazing pop music of our lifetime. We have this in common. Please, just let me be there when you make it. You can't deny the world this. Christ! It's like nothing else! You need to get over all this paranoia. Just rock 'n' roll, girl.'

Amber gave a laugh which turned into a sob. Then she hugged me . . . and wouldn't let go. I wanted to cry. We were interrupted by two strangers, both girls, tapping Amber on the back. She swung round.

'Yes? I'm having a very emotional moment here,' she said. She held fast to my hand.

'I just want to say that I think this music is so cool. I love it, and Will just told us you were the singer and we think you're going to be really famous. In fact, could we get your autograph now?'

'Of course!' said Amber, taking the pen from one of the girls. She smiled at them.

'You look famous already.'

'You better buy the album then,' said Amber, the pen flying across the page.

'We will.' They scampered off.

'You see. Everyone loves you. Your band love you. You have nothing to worry about.'

'Amber!' It was Will, signalling to her from the other side of the room.

'Except for him,' I said.

Amber squeezed my hand. 'Stuff him,' she said, her haughty self once more. 'Let's get drunk.'

Amber and I arrived back at two in the morning and Felix practically fell through the front door as Amber unlocked it.

'Where the hell have you been?'

'For God's sake, we've been at a party. What is your problem, Felix?' said Amber.

I had called Felix an hour ago and told him that we were on our way. It had taken us ages to find a cab when we left and I knew that he would be working himself up into a state of panic.

'Gotta have some water,' I said. Amber giggled.

'And why are you both laughing at me like a couple of school-girls? What gives you the right to get on and be friends all of a sudden?' Felix spoke absolutely without derision.

'Where's Justin?' demanded Amber. 'Is he back yet?'

'No,' said Felix. Amber looked amazed.

'He must be back!' she said.

'He's not.'

'Oh my God! He's with Frankie! He's not back!' she began to wail.

'Amber, get a grip please,' I hiccuped.

'And you're fucking plastered,' said Felix accusingly.

'I missed you,' I croaked. Felix's hair was greasy and he wore a sarong he had nicked from Val's room that belonged to Frankie. For once he wore no mascara so his eyes appeared paler and softer than usual. I kissed his hand and his fingertips – all hardened from constant strumming at the guitar. I noticed his lyric sheets spread out all over the floor. He had been writing.

'Have you got a new song?'

'Yes.' He still sounded like a sulky school-boy.

'Play it to me.'

'Why should I? You never want to be with me any more, you're always off with everyone else – Justin, Amber, and that Frankie—'

'Wait, wait! That's all such crap, and you know it. Please Felix, don't do this to me now.' He pulled me into his arms.

'Jesus, I'm behaving like such an idiot,' he whispered. 'I don't understand what's wrong with me, I've never done this before.'

'It's OK, it's OK, I just wish that you could realise how little you need to worry about me. The party was all right, Amber and I drank together and I protected her from that guy Will and we listened to Moja which sounded so fucking great. Oh, and Amber got asked for her autograph which was really cool, and Felix – I think everything could be all right between me and Amber now. I think we might be friends. It's hardly the end of the world.' I was afraid of saying it, in case it wasn't true.

'So why do I feel like it is?' Felix's luminous eyes searched my face for the answer.

'I don't know, but we can get through this.'

'But no one can ever stay with one person!' wailed Felix. 'Everyone's always looking out for someone new, someone prettier, someone funnier or taller or cleverer, or just someone different!'

'Speak for yourself, I'm not!' I said indignantly. 'I love *you* and I have this overwhelming faith in the way that I feel about you. It's the way that I felt when I first saw you in the bathroom playing the guitar, it's the way that I felt when I came to see you play for the first time—'

'Then you only love me because I'm a performer,' interrupted Felix.

'No!' I hiccuped. 'Don't be so silly. I love you when we're lying in bed—'

'Then you only love me for sex!'

'Don't flatter yourself,' I responded quickly. 'Look – I love you when I'm watching you sleep, or when you're munching crisps or drinking Coke, I love you when we're walking around London together – our magical London which becomes more (hiccup) magical when I'm with you. I love you when you're not even thinking about me, when you're writing or recording or talking to Justin, and it makes me nervous just to think that we might never have met.'

Felix crawled off the sofa to where I was sitting on the floor, pushing his guitar out of the way. He took my face in his hands and kissed me.

'*I feel scripted, everything is posed,*' he sang softly.

'Did you write that? That's a bit pessimistic for a Moja lyric,' I said.

'It's not mine,' said Felix quickly. 'You look so gorgeous tonight. I can't *bear* how beautiful you are.' He kissed me again and I pulled his hands under my dress.

'I want you now,' he said. We crawled behind the sofa where we were hidden from view of anyone entering the room. I pushed my hands up Felix's sarong and felt how turned on he was. I hiccuped as he slipped his fingers inside me.

'I think I can stop those,' he murmured.

'Condom?' I suggested hopefully.

'Fuck, I don't have one on me.'

'Do you want me to go and get one from upstairs?'

'No, I'll go, wait here.' Felix stood up, Pan-like in the familiar eerie moonlight. 'Keep yourself ready for me,' he whispered, and was gone.

I lay behind the sofa, listening to his feet thudding up the stairs. Then I heard the front door opening and realised that Justin and Frankie were back from the gig. I pulled my dress back down so that I was no longer half naked and decided I should follow Felix up to his room. But just as I was moving out from behind the sofa, the lights were switched off and Justin and Frankie were in the room with me, only they didn't know that I was there. I would have stood up at that point, but Frankie was talking and I felt that I should remain hidden.

'I just can't help the way that I feel,' she was saying. 'I think

292

that you're so gorgeous, I've been wanting to kiss you ever since we first met.' There was a silence in which I stuffed my hand over my mouth in case I hiccuped again, though I had a feeling that the shock technique of stopping them might actually have worked for once. Then Justin spoke up.

'Frankie, listen, I'm really stoned, I loved the gig, I loved tonight, it's great that you're into the Fries like me, but really, that's where it stops.'

'So you don't want me?' She was speaking very quietly now, almost whispering.

'Frankie, frankly, or rather frankly, Frankie, I don't want you at all. I've got Amber. Why would I want you?'

The eternal question, I thought. How could anyone resist Frankie when she was like this? I had seen her in action before. I imagined that she was standing very close to Justin, her eyes wide open, midriff exposed.

'I just really thought that there was something between us.'

'Forgive my stupidity, but I really thought that there was something between you and Valentine,' drawled Justin.

'I love Val, but I can't help the fact that I want you. Just one night. I could make it so wonderful. No one will ever know.'

Except they will, of course, so don't do it, Justin, for God's sake, I thought, barely breathing. It was like an episode of *Neighbours*. Any second now Felix was going to add to the charade by reappearing half naked.

'Frankie, you're a dangerous girl,' said Justin. I heard the sound of a brief kiss, 'but I'm going to bed. I won't mention this to anyone, but I think you should sort out the way that you feel about Val. I don't think he'd be too pleased if he was behind the sofa listening to this conversation.' I nearly exploded. 'Oh, and make sure you bring a warm jumper next time we go out. Amber'll lend you one. That little top is not warm enough for this time of year. We're not in Barcelona now, you know.' He walked out of the room and Frankie followed, but I heard one set of footsteps going upstairs and one clattering downstairs.

Felix didn't appear for another five minutes. I was still where he had left me. 'Where the hell have you been?' I hissed.

'Babe, sorry, but Val left a copy of the *NME* on my bed and they mentioned our possible deal with Conspiracy and talked about the gig. And they mentioned the fact that I'm Carolyn's son, so that's all out now, I don't know how. Did I hear the door? Are Justin and Frankie back?'

I hugged Felix close to me. He felt so right, so real, and so adorably safe next to me. I loved the fact that he had been reading the *NME* rather than being seduced by Frankie. But what if he already had been? What if she had tried with him and something had actually happened? Maybe that was why he claimed not to like her, not to trust her? I felt cold. I was thinking like Felix now. I just had to trust him. Anyway, I reminded myself, she didn't like Elvis. Felix could never be interested in her.

'They're back all right,' I said.

'Good. Amber's upstairs getting herself into a real state about those two going out together. I had to tell her to shut up. Anyway, if she hadn't gone off to see that Will bloke, this would never have happened.'

'What would never have happened?'

'Frankie and Justin going to see the Fries with Sy. I don't trust Frankie, so I kind of understand Amber being nervous.'

Blimey, I thought, so do I. 'Why don't you trust her?' I asked.

'Oh, don't start this again, I just don't really like her, and I don't think that she's any good for Val. Can we just leave it at that for once? This is one area in which we're going to have to agree to disagree. Time will tell who is right,' said Felix.

And sooner than you know, I wanted to say. But for the moment I was going to keep what I had heard to myself.

'Your hiccups have gone,' he said.

'So they have.'

'Shall we go upstairs?'

I noticed that he didn't even have the condom. If I hadn't been so distracted by Justin and Frankie, I might have been a bit annoyed.

Lives hang in the balance. Amber had invited Frankie over to London and now she was trying to steal her boyfriend. It seemed that all the time I had Amber down as the *femme fatale*, the one to be watched, it was Frankie who was the most dangerous. I had to work out what to do, and fast, before any real damage was done.

Chapter Twenty-two

It felt odd, everyone together as always, but me knowing about Frankie trying to seduce Justin. It was like knowing who the murderer was in a game of Cluedo but keeping your cards close to your chest and watching everyone else for signs that they knew something too. But of course, nobody did.

Frankie didn't appear until the following evening. We were drinking hot chocolate because Felix said it reminded him of Italy. He was lying on the floor wearing track-suit bottoms and a big grey jumper. Unlike Amber who moaned constantly about the cold and hated covering herself up, Felix suited summer and winter alike. Nicky had turned on MTV.

'How the fuck did they get a deal?' He was spitting at a new all-girl band.

'Look at the size of the lead singer's legs!' contributed Amber, who was always overjoyed to slag off any female competition.

'She'll be massive in ten years time,' said Justin with a shudder.

'Oh, she's already massive in the States. She's sold more—' began Felix.

'No, you jerk, I meant she'll be the size of a family car in a few years. You can just tell.'

'You can't deny she's done well.'

'Felix, just face it, she has no talent. I hate her. I hate everything to do with her, and more than that I hate the monkeys that signed her. Who's she signed to over here?' Justin turned to his guru for information.

'Actually, Element have just signed her to the UK,' Symon said. 'And we passed her up. I'm starting to regret that decision.'

'Why? Symon, mate, the one thing I always rely on is your artistic integrity,' wailed Justin.

'But she's shifting units,' sighed Symon. 'The kids are going for it.'

'Only because they're fed it and they have no choice!' cried Amber.

'But *we* can rock these cretins out of the country,' said Nicky. 'It makes me so mad, I just want to get on with it.'

'It's an amazing thing,' said Symon, gulping down his hot chocolate, 'knowing something that no one else knows, don't you think, Lydia?' I nearly jumped out of my skin.

'What do you mean?'

'Well, knowing that Moja are gonna be the biggest band in the country. No one else knows that yet. Those guys –' Symon gestured towards the window where three teenagers were lighting fags and laughing – 'they don't know it, but they're gonna be buying your records and coming to your gigs and plastering posters of you all over their walls.'

'Amber'll be on the front of *FHM* and *Loaded* pretty soon,' said Nicky.

'Great,' said Justin, 'Just what I've always dreamed of. My girlfriend's body on display for the benefit of the entire male population.'

'Don't be so pathetic, you should be proud of her,' said Felix, kicking Justin with a fluffy-socked foot. Nicky, Justin and Amber all yelled at once.

'Ooh! You little hypocrite! You'd be out there buying up every copy of the magazine if Lydia was on the front! You'd hate it! You'd blame *her* if anyone liked it!' This last observation was made by Amber who was plaiting her hair into bunches.

'Oh, fuck off. It's different if it's Lydia,' said Felix with a grin.

'I don't see why,' said Amber. 'Why should it be different for you and Lydia? Am I just the kind of girl you would expect to be taking off her clothes for any old grotty mag?' There was a silence.

'Well, no, but it kind of goes with the job,' said Symon.

'I will not be flashing my tits around for anyone,' said Amber huffily.

'Why change a habit?' asked Nicky in wholehearted surprise.

'Ha, ha, ha.'

'Do you two ever let up?' asked Symon.

'It's the way the band works,' said Nicky. 'I do the humour, I use Amber as my punch-bag and she loves it, Justin does the drugs and the, er, mysterious bassist thing. Felix does the beautiful, misunderstood songwriter thing—'

'And the paranoia thing,' added Amber.

'And Lydia,' concluded Nicky, 'does the keeping everyone together thing.'

'Symon and I do the looking in from the outside and knowing how massive this is going to be thing,' I said. It was what I had always felt, what Amber had spelt out to me. The outsider. But Justin spoke up.

'You and Symon are total *insiders*,' he said. 'It's Frankie who's the outsider.' I looked at him, trying to read his impassive features.

'Why are you saying that?' demanded Amber. 'I thought you all had a lovely cosy evening last night at the gig.'

'While you were out at that lousy party, getting smashed,' retorted Justin.

'Why the sudden dislike of Frankie?' Amber persisted.

'Not dislike,' said Justin, 'I just don't completely trust her.'

'Join the club,' said Felix. 'The sooner she dumps Val, the sooner he can get on with his life and not feel like he has to live up to her expectations.'

'What do you know about her expectations?' I asked. I couldn't help sticking up for Frankie, despite the fact that every second she was becoming more and more strange to me.

'She's just chasing rainbows,' said Felix. 'She likes Val because he's cute and arty and different, but she's dynamite and he's too young to handle it.' Dynamite, I thought. How gorgeous to be described as dynamite.

'I thought she was lovely last night,' said Symon unexpectedly.

'We know,' said Felix. 'I can't tell you *why* I don't like her, but I just don't.'

'So there *is* a reason why you don't like her?' I found myself asking the question that I dreaded being answered. It was easier to ask when everyone else was around, I don't know why. Felix stood up.

'Who wants some Jaffa Cakes?' he asked, and wandered out of the room. I followed him.

'Felix, I've never said this to you before, but I really need you to be honest with me,' I said. 'Just tell me why you don't like Frankie. I just don't believe any of this stuff about not trusting her. Give me a reason.'

Felix pulled a bottle of Evian out of the fridge and sighed.

'I didn't want to say this because she's your best friend and she's going out with Val, but, yes, I have got a fucking reason, as you put it.' I hoped that he wasn't going to go all defensive and make me feel like whatever he had to say was my fault. 'You've really pushed me into telling you this,' he warned.

'Jesus! What the hell happened between you two?' I was shaking and felt sick.

'Nothing!' he exploded. 'I wouldn't touch her with a barge pole.'

I felt completely out of control. 'You just feel uncomfortable having her around because all this time she's been seducing you and you've been *well* up for it. No wonder you want her to stop going out with Val – you want her yourself!'

'Lydia, do you have any idea what you're saying?' Felix yelled. 'Stop accusing me of all this shit I haven't done!'

'Yeah, well, now you know how I feel when you start telling me I fancy Justin and that I'm flirting with Nicky.' I collapsed heavily on the nearest kitchen chair. Unfortunately, the force of my landing shifted a plate of last night's unfinished pasta in tomato sauce into my lap. Once the remains of the meal had

301

been deposited over my boot-cut jeans, the plate crashed to the floor and smashed into a hundred pieces. Felix looked resigned.

'Leave it,' he said wearily.

'These trousers are new!' I protested, feeling that our roles seemed to have been reversed. Here was I, getting paranoid and losing control of my senses and spilling food all over myself. All of which were in Felix's job description, certainly not mine. I was completely unnerved. I stripped off my trousers and flounced over to the washing machine. 'Well, if you're going to put a wash on, do you mind if I run upstairs and get some darks?' asked Felix, on starter's orders to scamper off. I looked incredulous.

'Yes I do mind! What are you talking about? You're just trying to get out of telling me that you've been sleeping with my best friend!'

'But you're about to put a wash on with only one thing in it!' shouted Felix. 'It's a waste of energy!'

'Look! All I ever wanted from you was for you to be truthful with me, to make me feel a little bit different to all the other girls you've fucked in the past eighteen months, but you couldn't even manage that, could you? You had to go for Frankie because she's "beautiful" and "Spanish" and a "model".' I waved my hands around, frantically accentuating the quotation marks. 'So what that she hates Elvis if she's got a pretty face?'

'Right, that does it.' Felix slammed the water down on the table. I burst into tears. Felix evidently had a very low tolerance of the kind of jealousy that I had to put up with, I thought miserably. He stormed across the room to the door.

'Don't you start bringing Elvis into this,' he threatened in a low voice. 'He went through the kind of hell in his life that you can't even imagine.' Then he left the room.

Hearing Frankie and Justin last night had convinced me that I was being naive and stupid and that there was definitely something suspicious about Felix's seemingly irrational hatred of my best friend. I must have sat there for several minutes in my knickers and socks and my Blur T-shirt, the very same one that I had worn the night that Felix and I first met. Then Amber came downstairs looking for me.

'What's wrong, why are you half undressed?' she asked. She would never have said 'half dressed', because for Amber life was all about *un*dressing. So why was it that she was no longer the girl I feared?

'I spilt tomato sauce all over my trousers,' I said with a sniff.

'Don't worry, it'll come out,' she said kindly. 'I've done that loads of times when I'm wearing new clothes, but it's OK, you mustn't get too upset about it.'

'No, I'm not.' I allowed a snort of laughter at the fact that Amber thought that I was crying because my trousers were soiled. 'I just don't know what's come over me.' Amber tore off a piece of kitchen towel decorated with a *Rugrats* novelty design and handed it to me. I blew my nose. 'I've just lost my best friend and my boyfriend. You should be pleased.' I suddenly realised it was Amber I was talking to. 'It's what you always wanted to happen. You thought that Frankie and Felix were the ideal couple, well, maybe they are.'

'But there's nothing going on between those two,' said Amber. 'Anyway, you know that I feel differently about you now. I thought that we discussed this last night – or was I more drunk than I can remember?'

'It's all very convenient for you to like me now that you know

I'm not a threat to your precious band,' I said. 'What do you care about me and Felix? You hate us together.'

'I don't, I don't! I thought I did but I don't. You've kept everything together. My God, Lydia, I can't believe I'm saying this, but it's thanks to you that this whole show has kept going.'

'That's just crap. It would have gone on without me, I'm nothing, I'm just some girl that Felix picked up for a bit then got bored of.'

'Oh, spare me the self-pity,' snapped Amber. 'Pull yourself together. You're doing exactly what your idiot boyfriend is always doing. It must be catching.'

'Amber, he just told me that there was a real reason for him being edgy around Frankie, and I just don't want him to have to spell it out to me. I can't believe I could be so stupid as to have been floating around in this love bubble for so long. I should have listened to you in the beginning.'

'You're not making any sense.' Amber seemed livid that I was failing to grasp her point. 'Look, I know for a fact that Felix has never gone near Frankie. It's extremely annoying that I have to tell you like this, but you've clearly lost it and it's going to have to be me who lets you know.' She paused to allow me to appreciate the irony.

'Go on then,' I sniffed. Amber went over to the tap and poured herself a glass of water. She sat down next to me.

'I heard a conversation between Frankie and Felix the other day.'

'When?' I demanded.

'Oh, it must have been about two or three weeks ago.'

'Two or three weeks?' I shrieked. 'This has been going on for two or three weeks?'

'If you would just shut up and let me finish!' yelled Amber. She drained her water deliberately slowly. 'I came back here after the studio one day to change before I went out to meet a friend of mine from the agency. Have you got a cigarette?'

'No.'

'That pain in the arse Nicky nicked all of mine last night. He's always doing that. Anyway, I came back here and I ran upstairs and I heard shouting coming from Felix's bedroom.' I covered my eyes with my hands.

'Go on.'

'And I couldn't help overhearing, not that I *wanted* to or anything. Well, I heard Frankie saying to Felix that she wanted him to sleep with her. She came right out with it, just like that. I thought "Jesus!", and I crept outside the door so I could catch what he said.' I wasn't about to tell Amber that you shouldn't listen in to other people's conversations. She was so blatant and honest about it that it made it all right somehow. 'Well, Frankie said something like, "You know that you want to", and then she said she'd wanted him from the moment she first saw him or some such bollocks like that, and then, I remember this bit, Felix said, "Can you move, you're sitting on my lyric book", and I nearly laughed, so I moved away from the door and I missed the next bit.' She stood up and put the kettle on.

'Tea?'

'Yes please.'

'But I couldn't help hearing what happened then because Felix got furious and I heard him shouting at her, in a way that I've never heard him shout before. He said, "You're going out with my brother, you little slut", and she said, "But I can't help the way I feel about you", and he said, "What about Lydia, or is she completely irrelevant", and Frankie said, "She's not right for you, she's not as beautiful as you".' (At this point Amber had the good will to check and see how this remark had affected me.) 'And Felix shouted "She's five hundred" – or it might have been a thousand, I can't remember – "times prettier than you and she's the most beautiful girl I've ever seen". Then he said, "I'm not going to tell Val about this because it would break his heart, but I suggest you end things with him pretty fast, and the second that you do I want you out of my house—"' Amber threw herself into the part by slamming her hand down on the table, '"And I never want to see you again". Then I moved out of the way and I heard Felix say, "And I want my Elvis CD back". Then I think Frankie was crying because I heard her leaving the room and slamming the bathroom door behind her. Well, I decided to tell Felix that I had overheard—'

'What!'

'Yes, because I thought that he should tell you, so I marched into his room and he was sitting on his bed looking completely fired up and ready for a fight, and I said, "Felix, I heard all that", and he said, "Well unhear it then", and I said, "Are you going to tell Lydia and Val?", and he said, "No, I'm going to give her a chance to go", and we ended up having a huge fight about it and it ended up with me agreeing to shut up about it all and just wait until Frankie had gone. He had this idea that you and Val would be more hurt by the truth, so he decided that he would just go on trying to put you off her without actually telling you that she had made a massive move on him. I just had to tell you, now that you're sitting here getting all panicked, that there is nothing and never could be anything going on between them.' Amber poured out two mugs of tea. It was deliciously comforting. 'Felix is mental about you,' she said.

'Amber, there's something that I need to tell you.'

'What?' she asked sharply.

'It's going to sound ridiculous in the light of what you just told me, but I overheard Frankie making a pass at Justin.'

'When?' asked Amber quietly.

'Last night.'

'Were you going to tell me?' she asked.

'No, well, yes – I didn't know. I just couldn't figure it out. I was lying behind the sofa after the party—'

'On your own?'

'Yes. Well, Felix had gone upstairs but he was going to come back down again.'

'What were you doing behind the sofa?'

'Just kissing and stuff. Anyway, I heard Frankie and Justin coming in and I didn't move because I heard Frankie saying the same shit that she said to Felix, that you just told me, to him.'

'And how did Justin react?' asked Amber bitterly. 'OK, babe, take me now?' She threw her arms into the air, a gesture that curiously aped Frankie when she was distressed.

'Oh my God, he was so rude. He said he was caned and drunk and then he said, "Frankie frankly, or frankly Frankie", and told her he wasn't interested. He just wanted her to go.'

'You're not making this up?' asked Amber.

'No. I wish I was. It's way too strange for me to understand. I knew that Frankie and I had grown apart but I trusted her. She's my best friend, for God's sake!' I sobbed. 'I didn't want to listen to everyone saying that they didn't like her, I didn't understand it.'

Amber had burst into tears as well and was ripping up more and more kitchen roll in her excitement.

'The bitch from hell!' she wailed. 'What do we do?'

Felix loves me, he loves me, he loves me. So I had lost Frankie. But I had got the boy. I was dizzy with relief.

I went home that night. I needed to think. I phoned Felix to apologise and he told me that Amber had confessed to him that she had told me what she had heard. He sounded worried sick.

'Baby, I am so sorry—' he began.

'Why, you didn't do anything.'

'No, I'm just sorry that she's your friend. What a horrible thing to have to hear.'

'You could have told me,' I said, 'instead of trying to convince me that I shouldn't like her. I feel like such an idiot, sticking up for her all this time.'

'I thought that she was going to go,' said Felix. 'And she never tried it again. I was just waiting for her to end it with Val. You and Val are the only ones that I care about in this equation, not anyone else. Christ, this is going to smash his heart into a thousand pieces.'

'Where are they now?' I asked.

'Out, as usual,' said Felix. 'Frankie has no clue that you and Amber know about what she's been trying, and anyway, why the hell didn't you tell me about her trying to seduce Justin?'

'It only happened last night!' I protested. 'I was in shock. I just didn't know what was going on. But that's why I got so nervous, thinking that she must have seduced you. You've never been faithful to anyone, you told me that, and Frankie's so beautiful, I just convinced myself that you had been taken in by her and were covering it up by saying you didn't like her.'

'She is so *not* beautiful,' said Felix icily. 'So far from pretty. She's a little witch.'

'I thought she was my best friend,' I said dumbly. 'I thought she loved me.'

'I'll be your best friend now,' said Felix. 'I knew there was something odd about her because she didn't like Elvis.'

'Oh Felix!' I was half laughing, half crying. 'What do we do?'

'Amber's going to contact Chica. Get Frankie booked on a plane to New York as soon as possible. I'll tell her that if she breaks it off with Val and goes quietly then he need never know about what a fool she's made of herself. That's the strange thing,' went on Felix, 'she seems to have this weird pride thing. I think it'll work.'

'Jesus, I hope so. I don't think I could face her again.'

'Oh, and by the way –' Felix's tone was ultra-casual so I knew it was something exciting – 'Sy rang to say that the Falcon gig is all booked out. Sold right out, apparently.'

'Standing room only,' I said.

'Well, there's only ever standing room at the Falcon,' conceded Felix. 'But, yeah.'

I felt a shiver of excitement.

Frankie left by the end of the week. She had told Val that there was no way that they could continue to be together when she was working all over the world and had no real base. She called me before she left.

'I never meant to hurt anyone,' she sobbed. 'I just wanted to be a part of everything. I felt so outside it all. And you didn't care!' She spat out this last accusation with all the venom of a captured criminal.

'How can you say that!' I wailed. 'Frankie, I wanted nothing more than for us to be friends forever. Val loved you, he still loves you, you just needed more than him. But you can't step in and take whoever you feel like, for God's sake!'

Frankie was silent on the other end of the phone.

I knew then that I would definitely take Felix with me on my desert island. But I still cried.

Chapter Twenty-three

Moja played the Falcon on a cold Thursday a week later. The morning of the gig I woke up next to Felix and padded downstairs in my pyjamas. I opened the front door and breathed in the October dawn. The house was silent. I shivered and stepped back inside, into that strange place that I had grown so accustomed to. It no longer scared me, like Amber no longer scared me. I clicked on the stereo and turned up the volume. The house needed a constant soundtrack, just like I did. I sang along to the Rolling Stones, 'Let It Bleed', all the way down to the kitchen. I drank tea and waited for the next person to appear.

It was Nicky, still yawning but fully dressed.

'Jesus Lydia!' I made him jump. 'What the hell are you doing up so early?'

'I might well ask you the same question.'

'*Tonight — we dance*,' said Nicky theatrically, peering out of the window at the grey dawn.

'Are you nervous?'

'No, it's just another gig, innit?' Nicky pulled a face. 'You know what I'm like. I couldn't sleep. I'm so nervous now I'll literally be a wreck later. I mean, *literally* a wreck.'

'Symon says it's going to be packed out,' I said.

'Really? Did you have to tell me that? Look, I need to go through some stuff with your boy, can't you get him up?' Nicky poured a generous helping of Carolyn's Cheerios into a bowl.

'I'll go and wake him for you,' I sighed.

'Get everyone else up while you're at it,' said Nicky. 'You're the manager, aren't you?' He grinned at me. 'Thank God.'

I ran upstairs and crawled back into bed with Felix. He kissed me without opening his eyes.

We got to the Falcon at five o'clock for the soundcheck. I had arranged for all the equipment and the band to be collected from Stanley Road at four, much to Justin's delight.

'Wow, if we have this arrangement every time we play I would be quite happy to do it every night,' he kept saying.

Amber and I sat together, discussing what she should wear.

'I'm really nervous tonight,' she said. 'And I never get nervous. I don't want to wear anything too mad, I just want to go quite laidback.'

'No way! Laidback is so *not* how you should be looking tonight,' shouted Nicky from the front seat.

'Shut up. Amber's the most important person in this car, it's up to her what she wears!' yelped Justin.

312

'Set list, set list!' said Felix. 'Shall we just stick to the original plan and open with "I Win"?'

'No, I feel really uncomfortable doing that song to start with,' said Amber. 'I just don't think my voice is up to it as an opening song.' She was shaking with nerves.

'Yes it is, you'll be fine,' said Felix breezily.

'Do you have any vague *clue* how it feels to be the person who everyone is staring at the entire way through the set?' demanded Amber. Her voice had risen a key and several decibels.

'Don't flatter yourself,' said Felix, squeezing her knee.

'No one's forcing you to do it – you *want* to do it,' pointed out Nicky.

'I don't *want* to, I *have* to,' said Amber. 'There is a difference. It's my calling. It's just something that has to happen.'

'Like Justin's calling to support QPR?' asked Felix.

'Exactly,' said Amber. 'It's something that you don't question – you just go with it.'

Camden throbbed with its peculiar atmosphere of threatened peace. Symon was waiting for us all, organising the guest list and looking stressed.

'Go and speak to Andrew, the sound bloke, and see what you think of the general set-up,' he said to Justin and Nicky. 'It's gonna be packed out.' He rummaged in his bag and pulled out a Crunchie. 'You better not let me down.'

The venue was about the same size as the Lemon. There were big posters of the band everywhere that we had selected from the shoot with Dina. I felt that heart-thumping nervousness that I knew was only going to get more and more intense until the band had finished playing. Amber was chatting with the girl behind the bar who was a model at Select.

'Wow, you're a booker for Chica *and* you're the lead singer!' the girl was saying. 'That's so cool, I can't wait to hear you tonight. What kind of stuff do you do? Who do you sound like?'

'We don't sound like anyone else,' said Amber haughtily.

Nicky was setting up his kit at the back of the stage and looking edgy.

'I hate the picture of me in those bloody posters,' he said. 'I told you time and time again, Lydia, not the one where I'm wearing the hat.'

For the last reel of film Dina had thrown a leopard print top hat on to Nicky's head. When the photos were developed it was obvious that they were the best shots. I had also noticed, with a pang, how Amber had managed to look breathtaking in every single picture. Felix, rather to my surprise, was less photogenic, but then much of his allure was in his physical presence and the sexy fluidity of his movements.

Justin gave a whoop of delight at the sight of Rick the dealer, who had made his way into the building and was composing a spliff, hands shaking.

'I was up all night at this cross-dressing theme party,' he explained to no one in particular. 'I got off my head on tequila and then wasted valuable drinking time chucking it all up. I'd totally forgotten that alcohol is just the worst drug for the morning after.'

Justin jumped down off the stage and took the spliff.

'Jeez, man, thank God you're here,' he said.

'Justin!' came Amber's voice from the microphone. 'We need to soundcheck the bass in two minutes.' Her voice was drowned out by the thud, thud, thud of Nicky's foot on the bass drum pedal, gradually becoming louder as Andrew the sound bloke fiddled with microphones and levels.

'So how long have this lot been together?' he asked me as Justin prepared to launch into his usual run of bass lines.

'Three years,' I said.

'You manage them, right?'

'Yeah.'

'Who else do you look after?'

'No one at the moment,' I said. 'God, I couldn't deal with anyone else.'

'Symon's such a nice guy,' said Andrew, lighting a fag. 'You really went to the right record company there, but then I guess that was a deliberate move, I mean, where else is there that you would like to go?'

'Conspiracy were the only ones that we were interested in from the start,' I said, amazing myself with every informed word that was coming out of my mouth. 'Symon has such an incredible reputation and he really knows how to look after his artists, which is so rare at the moment.' Andrew nodded.

'Symon thinks that this band are the best thing he's seen in ages,' he revealed. 'I'm really looking forward to tonight. Lead singer's fucking beautiful. I usually fancy blondes but I think I'd make an exception for her.' He looked at me for confirmation that he had said what every other boy in the world thought.

'She's amazing,' I agreed. 'It's sometimes difficult to deal with the fact that my boyfriend works with her.'

'Oh? Which one?'

'Felix – the guitarist.'

'Of course.'

'Why, of course? Most people seem to find us the strangest combination.'

'No way, you just look right together. I knew from the moment you walked in.'

'Yeah, because he had his arm around me.'

'No, because you just looked right.' We were interrupted by Nicky's voice booming into the microphone, laced with feedback.

'Joss North, *come on down!*' And sure enough, there was Joss at the back of the room.

'Amber, my darling!' He enveloped her in the folds of his dark blue hooded Laily Winter *Run To Be Free Tour 1997* macintosh.

'Jossy!' she wailed in delight.

'How is everyone, then? How are the songs sounding? Are we all ready? You are all going to be *fabulous*.' Wherever Joss was he seemed to fill the room with his categorical optimism.

'Good to see you, mate,' said Justin, passing the spliff back to Rick to shake Joss's hand.

'Can I have some guitar please,' came Andrew's voice. Felix plugged in and strummed out the first few chords of 'Make it All Right'. He immediately broke a string. There was a screech of feedback.

'Shit,' said Felix.

'My God, you hear a band soundchecking and you really ask yourself how they can ever hope to get signed,' whispered Rick to Joss.

'But we love this lot,' said Joss quickly. 'Nicky, you look wonderful in the posters, love the hat!' he shouted.

'Fuck off,' grinned Nicky.

'It'll become your trademark, like Jay Kay,' went on Joss. 'I can see you using it for your logos, sleeve designs—'

'OK, OK, put your ideas down on paper and get them to Lydia,' said Felix, who was anxious to rehearse for as long as possible.

'Did you hear about the dyslexic pop star?' persisted Joss.

'No?'

'He sold his soul to Santa.'

Felix gave a bark of laughter and Amber, quite uncharacteristically, lost control completely and couldn't talk into her microphone for ten minutes. Symon lumbered up to the stage just as they finished running through the first song in the set.

'Hey, Symon!' shouted Amber. 'Did you hear about the dyslexic rock star?'

'Probably,' said Symon in a resigned voice. 'Bound to be signed to our label.'

'No, it's a joke, stupid.'

'Go on then.'

'Did you hear about the dyslexic rock star?' repeated Amber.

'What happened?'

'He sold his soul to Santa.' Symon's big face looked confused for a second, then seemed to break into pieces as he laughed.

'Yeah, then he DO'd on his own Vimto,' he added.

There were two other bands playing before Moja, who also had to soundcheck. I went out into the bar area and saw them arriving.

'The other bands are here,' I said to Amber. 'You'd better hurry up – you've already overrun your allocated time.'

'We'll take as long as we need,' retorted Amber. 'Who are these other bands anyway?'

I consulted their flyers. 'There's one called Urban Fox and another called Rio,' I said.

'They sound awful. Are there any girls in the bands?' she demanded.

'There's a girl over there,' I said, 'talking to that guy with green hair.'

Amber's flashing eyes were like searchlights.

'You call that a *girl*?' she said. '*Please!*'

I giggled. 'Don't be such a bitch.'

Nicky appeared looking mutinous.

'Some guy in the band supporting us – Urban Box or something – wants to borrow my drum kit to save time. I said, listen mate, with all due respect, do you have—'

Amber and I both joined in at this point. '—*Any idea how much this kit is worth?*' we chorused.

'Anyway, he's going to borrow the other band's equipment. I mean, really, the *nerve* of these people.'

Justin and Felix loped up.

'The girl from the other band's asked me if she can borrow my bass amp to save change-over time,' he said.

'Well I hope you told her where to go,' squeaked Amber.

'No, don't be stupid,' said Justin in surprise, 'I said she could use it.'

'Great!' screamed Amber. 'Why couldn't you just do what any normal person would do and tell her she can't borrow it?'

'Stop getting so worked up,' said Justin.

The green-haired boy sauntered up to the bar and smiled at Amber.

'You the singer in Moja?' he asked her. Amber regained her composure.

'Yes,' she said sweetly.

'I just wanted to ask if I could dump my bag in the green room. Apparently it's reserved for the headline band, but I don't want to get it nicked when we're on stage.' There was a pause.

'Of course,' said Amber. 'Whatever you want.' She shot him her most alluring smile and flipped her hair back.

'Thanks,' said Green Hair Boy, blushing like a tomato. 'Well, good luck tonight,' he added, walking off.

'Yeah, thanks. You too,' said Amber.

There was a silence. Then Justin exploded with his contagious laughter.

'I love you Amber!' he said.

Nicky was without doubt the most nervous an hour before the band were due on stage. Amber was applying make-up, her mobile clamped to her ear.

'Shit! Lydia, I've got eight girls from Chica who want to come down tonight. Can I bung them on the guest list?'

'Amber, there's no more room on the guest list, just tell them to come down and queue.'

'Queuing!' whimpered Nicky. 'What the hell is going on?'

'Everyone's talking about you,' said Symon.

'What, me personally?'

'No, the band, of course.'

'It's fucking scary. Fucking scary.' Nicky looked white.

'Nick, come and have a drink,' came Justin's soothing advice. He had his arm round Amber who was wearing a pair of skin-tight pink trousers and a top that she had been working on constructed with safety-pins and lace.

319

'God, no. If I drink in the mood I'm in now it'll be game over by the time we're on.'

'I don't look like one of the Corrs, do I?' Amber fretted.

'You look more like Bob Geldof in 1979,' observed Symon.

'Bob Monkhouse, more like,' said Felix.

'Oh please, you're just too hilarious,' said Amber sarcastically. But nothing could dent her excitement and her glamour.

'I've just been out there, looking into the crowd, and I'm thinking to myself, why the hell am I doing this?' It was the first time that I had heard Justin express any kind of doubt over his musical ability. He frowned at me, expecting an answer. An unlit cigarette dangled from his mouth. He wore a tight black T-shirt and faded blue Levis.

'Only you can answer that question, Justin,' I said, 'but I imagine you'd be pretty annoyed if you were just watching.'

'And there is the issue of my phenomenal talent,' he added. 'I'm shit hot on the bass.'

'And so say most of us,' said Nicky.

Felix was dressed and ready to go. Glitter and eyeliner had smudged under his eyes.

'Lyds, come outside with me for a second,' he said. I followed him on to the street. We crossed the road to where the Jaguar was parked and he lounged against the bonnet, hair up in the usual pineapple, sludgy eyes smiling. He took my hand.

'Breathe in,' he instructed, 'and close your eyes. Pretend that it's the middle of August again.'

I looked at him, seeing that heavy glow of nostalgia radiating from his face. It was a nostalgia that I was a part of now. People were flooding past us and into the venue – expectant, hopeful. But for a moment they ceased to exist, and Moja ceased to exist, and everything that had happened since that crazy night at Ben's house ceased to exist. Felix and I were the only reality, and I realised that no matter what else was happening, we always would be.

'Can't you just *feel* the summer?' said Felix.

STANDING ROOM ONLY the single, performed by **MOJA**
will be released in summer 2000 by V2 Music.

For further information please contact **www.v2music.com**